HOUSE CALLS

CALLAGHAN BROTHERS
BOOK 3

ABBIE ZANDERS

Created with Vellum

CHAPTER ONE

"Come on, Mags. It'll be fun," Sherri pleaded, her big blue eyes wide and beseeching. She sat at the massive walnut table, sipping Irish coffee and munching on the thin, delectable, buttery sugar cookies. "And you have to teach me the secret of making these. I can never get mine this thin. Makes all the difference in the world."

Maggie Flynn paused with the coffee mug halfway to her lips. The last time Maggie had tried to teach her how to make something from scratch, she'd spent the next week cleaning batter out of the most unlikely spaces. Sherri's skills definitely lay outside the kitchen.

"You cannot be serious."

"About the cookies? Of course not. I'll stick to the Pillsbury tubes. You know, premade and presliced."

Maggie wrinkled her nose in distaste.

"But about the dancing? Absolutely. You do all that

Zumba and belly dancing and crap. You'll be awesome."

Maggie looked at her as if she were insane. "I do all that *crap* in the privacy of my own home for exercise," she said, trying to remain calm. "Not in front of a bunch of horny men for profit."

"These guys aren't like that," Sherri confided. "I've danced for them before. Complete gentlemen, I'm telling you, although the way they look, I wish they weren't." Sherri got that dreamy look in her eyes, the one she always got whenever she regaled Maggie with stories of the men at the Irish pub.

Maggie herself had never actually been to the place, but from Sherri's graphic, detailed descriptions, she had a clear picture of exactly what it was that drew Sherri's repeated interest.

"No." Maggie stood up and carried her mug to the sink, rinsing it out and placing it in the rack to the side. She would reuse it later. There was no point in dirtying another or wasting hot water and soap when a simple rinse would do. Maggie was very practical that way.

"Maggie"—Sherri's tone softened—"don't you ever want to, you know, get out there and live a little?"

"I live just fine," Maggie said defensively, wiping her hands on her apron. It was a vintage, full-frontal-coverage style, hand-stitched from a faded pink-and-white gingham print that her great-grandmother had once worn in the same kitchen more than half a century ago.

"You live *alone*," Sherri pointed out. "And you rarely go anywhere anymore."

"I get out," Maggie countered.

Three times in the past week alone, to be exact. She'd delivered herbal teas and wraps to some of the older folks around Pine Ridge, who could no longer make the trip up to her farm—the same ones her grandmother had taken care of for years before she passed.

"And I am not alone. I have George." Maggie glanced fondly at the aging basset hound sleeping peacefully next to the cast iron radiator, no doubt a result of a major sugar crash caused by the cookies Sherri had slipped him under the table. "I am perfectly content."

"Remember when we used to go out? God, we had so much fun."

"*You* had fun," Maggie corrected. "You always left with the hot guy, and I got left behind with the wing-man." Which wasn't always a bad thing, she had to admit.

She'd met some very interesting people that way. Men who were like her—guilted into going out with their hot-looking friends, so they wouldn't have to go out alone. In general, wingmen tended to be more down-to-earth and more interesting than the "gods and goddesses," as Maggie secretly called them.

While she was quite fond of Sherri, going out with her was a true exercise in humility. Sherri was classi-

cally pretty with light-blonde hair and flirty blue eyes
that sparkled with promises of fun. Around five-seven
—with at least half of that belonging to her long,
shapely legs—Sherri was the female equivalent of
magnetic north for men. Their dicks always pointed
right to her. Of course, it didn't hurt that she moon-
lighted as an exotic dancer at Angels, Pine Ridge's local
gentlemen's club. The woman was a walking, talking
fantasy for most functioning, postpubescent, hetero-
sexual males.

"Can I help it if I'm approachable?" Sherri asked
with no trace of vanity whatsoever.

"No," Maggie sighed.

Sherri had been born beautiful, lithe, and innately
friendly. How could Maggie hold that against her? It
would be akin to hating a spectacular sunset or a soft
summer breeze. She *could* do it, but she'd feel even
worse about it.

"Please, Mags. I'm really out on a limb here."

Now, there was a visual Maggie didn't need—
Sherri dangling gracefully from a tree with a dozen hot
firemen from the community charity calendar
reaching up to save her. In fact, she believed that had
been one of the pictures in there two years ago.

Maggie shook her head to clear the image. "Maybe
Crystal will come through."

"Mags, she broke her leg. I don't think that's going
to heal by tomorrow night."

"Don't they make walking casts?"

"Not for pole dancing, no."

"Good point. But there's got to be someone else you can ask. Someone from the club maybe, wanting to make a couple extra bucks."

"No one who's as pretty as you."

Maggie turned around, expecting to see the mischievous, playful smile on her friend's face—the one Sherri always wore when she was blatantly blowing sunshine up someone's ass to get what she wanted. What she saw instead was a look of total seriousness.

"And the guys are very particular."

Maggie wondered exactly what it was they were particular about, followed immediately by what she had that they might be interested in. She came up with nothing. Last she'd heard, most guys weren't dreaming of Suzy Homemaker introverts dancing at their bachelor parties. Maggie had no false perceptions of what she was. Too short, too curvy, too plain. Especially next to someone like Sherri, who oozed feminine sexuality.

"Yank someone else's chain, Sher," Maggie said, recovering. "I'm not biting." She slipped off the apron and hung it on the hook beside the back door.

"Mags, have you looked at yourself lately?"

"Not if I can help it." *After all, why add insult to injury?*

"Spencer was an idiot," Sherri said softly from right behind Maggie, her arm going around Maggie's shoulders. "Losing him was the best thing that could have happened to you."

Spencer Dumas *was* an idiot—that much was true

—but he was a good-looking, wealthy, successful idiot. Maggie had him trumped, easily surpassing him on the moron scale though. She had actually believed all of his lies, had believed that someone like him could love someone like her. At least until Maggie decided to surprise him one night while he was working late and discovered his secretary taking *dick*-tation while bent over his imported desk.

An added bonus: Maggie got to hear firsthand Spencer's own account of his "prudish, chubby fiancé," the one he was only marrying to get her land.

It had hurt.

But Maggie was made of some strong stuff. After calmly revealing her presence, she'd left quietly, canceled the engagement, and removed herself completely from the social scene to lick her wounds in private. How many of her supposed friends had known all along? How many had laughed behind her back or shaken their heads in silent pity at her total ignorance?

Apparently, quite a lot. She hadn't been able to face many since. Sherri was the one exception, but that was mainly because the woman was as tenacious as she was gorgeous. Sherri didn't have a mean, catty bone in her body, the bitch.

"You *are* beautiful," Sherri told her, reaching up to pull out the clip that held Maggie's hair. The result was voluminous waves of ruby-red hair that cascaded halfway down her back. "God, I wish I had your hair."

Maggie reached back and snatched the clip. She

resecured her hair, turning crystalline green eyes on her friend, staring pointedly at the curtain of silken platinum that framed Sherri's perfect features.

"Yeah, I've heard that men hate natural blondes. It's a real turn-off. Must be hard on you. My heart bleeds. Really."

Sherri ignored her, raking her gaze up and down the oversize man's flannel shirt that practically reached to Maggie's knees. "You're hiding your best assets."

Maggie snorted. "Hardly." Not that it mattered. That was the beauty of living and working out of her own home.

She lived in soft, comfortable flannel and baggy jeans that hid what her grandmother used to refer to in hushed tones as a "full figure." She could sweat to as many oldies as she wanted, but she would never have Sherri's lithe, slim body. No, she would always carry a little more on her hips, and the only way her breasts would get smaller was if she had a reduction. The best she could hope for was to tone what lay underneath. *Way* underneath.

"Please, Mags. Just help me out this one time, and I swear I'll never ask you again for anything as long as I live."

Maggie shook her head. "No way, sister. I love you —I really do—but no."

Sherri sighed heavily and then pulled out the big guns. "Thirty minutes of dancing pays around five hundred bucks, and that's not including tips."

"Five hundred dollars?" Maggie hated the interest the flash of a little cash could spark in her.

But, hey, it would pay a couple of bills—a definite plus since she hadn't been successful in finding work outside of her sporadic contract jobs from home. Her savings were down to nothing. Most of the people she made homeopathic herbs and wraps for were barely making ends meet themselves, and Maggie didn't have the heart to take what little they had, so that certainly wasn't pulling in any income. She was already living from one paycheck to the next, budgeting out every penny, stretching her meager income so thin that it was almost translucent.

"Uh-huh." Sherri went in for the kill. "*And* you can wear a costume and a mask. No one will know who you are."

Maggie bit her bottom lip. "No one?"

"No one."

It *was* tempting. Something the old Maggie might have jumped at in a heartbeat—back when she had been naïve and optimistic and *fun*. Before she became "chubby" and "prudish" and "boring."

"All I have to do is dance?"

"I swear it, no funny business. These guys are first-class."

Five hundred bucks, plus tips. Total anonymity. Dancing.

An illicit thrill went through her at the thought of doing something so brazen, so naughty, so un-Maggie-like. "All right. I'll do it. Just this once."

"Yes?"

"Yes."

Sherri bounced up and down and almost knocked Maggie over with her fierce embrace. "You're not going to regret this, Mags."

Maggie wished she could be as certain.

CHAPTER TWO

J ake's Irish Pub was closed to the public. The event was invitation only, in honor of Ian Callaghan's upcoming wedding. Those in attendance consisted of family and close friends.

"Oh. My. God." Sherri stared, slack-jawed, at Maggie in full regalia.

Maggie was dressed in layers upon layers of thin veils and silk, bedecked with rings and bracelets, her unique green eyes outlined in black kohl beneath the mask, her dark ruby hair cascading freely.

"Honey, it's a good thing Crystal's not here because if she saw the way you filled out her costume, she'd hang up her veils for good."

"I feel ridiculous."

"You look amazing," Sherri said, shaking her head in disbelief. "I can't believe you are the same woman who spent half the morning horking cookies! How can you eat that much and have a body like that? I don't think I like you anymore."

Maggie rolled her eyes but refrained from replying when there was a soft knock on the door. Sherri opened it, allowing one of the largest men Maggie had ever seen to slip into the room with them. She swallowed audibly as her gaze lifted up ... and up.

"Hey, Sherri. You look stunning, as always. We're ready when you are," the man said with a smile that could have powered half the state for a month. Then, he swung that gaze over to Maggie, who had instinctively taken a step backward toward the corner. His smile faltered for a moment. "You're not Crystal."

Maggie couldn't have spoken if she wanted to. Clearly, this was one of the infamous Callaghans. Sherri hadn't been exaggerating when she described them as forces of nature. If anything, she hadn't done them justice.

Thankfully, Sherri was not quite as stricken and was able to respond coherently. "Crystal broke her leg. This is my friend Maggie. She's filling in tonight."

The man's eyes were hypnotic as they regarded her. Maggie had never seen that color blue before. His devastating smile returned slowly. The wider his grin grew, the faster her heart beat. *What the hell was I thinking, believing I had the courage to go through with something like this?*

"Nice to meet you, Maggie," he said smoothly. "My name is Jake, and this is my place. You need anything, you let one of us know, okay?"

Maggie somehow managed a nod. His grin widened.

"I like her," he said to Sherri with a wink. "She's less verbally abusive than Crystal."

Sherri laughed. "That she is. But this is her first time, so go easy on her, okay?"

"Mmm. A sacrificial virgin. Been a while since we had one of those." His blue eyes glittered like finely cut sapphires. Or aquamarines. Or both.

"Play nice, Jake. I promised her you'd behave."

He chuckled. "Sorry, Maggie. Couldn't resist." He winked again and turned back to Sherri. "We'll be good, Sher. Taryn will kick my ass otherwise."

Maggie had a hard time imagining anyone kicking his ass. Beneath the blue button-down and jeans, he looked like he might have been carved from solid marble.

"I'll be out in just a sec, Jake," Sherri said, handing him a CD. "Get this loaded, will you?"

"You got it."

Then, he was gone, and Maggie released the breath she hadn't realized she'd been holding.

"Relax, girlfriend." Sherri laughed. "Jake's married and a daddy. Insanely in love with his wife, too. Lucky bitch."

"Are they all like that?"

"The Callaghans? Yep, pretty much."

"Shit."

Sherri laughed. "Yeah. Come on. Sit at the bar and have a drink. It'll loosen you up. I'll go on first."

Minutes later, Maggie found herself in the shadows of the bar as the lights dimmed and the music began. Sherri appeared on the small, raised platform, looking dazzling. Maggie fidgeted nervously, fighting the sudden urge to throw up or pass out—or both.

"Nervous?" the bartender asked, startling her enough that her rear end left the barstool for a moment or two.

He was huge, just like the other guy, but leaner. And gorgeous. Chiseled, masculine features. Strong, clean-shaven jaw. Sinfully long, dark lashes that had no business on a face that stunningly male. Glossy black hair that captured the lights and made them dance. Blue eyes deeper than the ocean.

Maggie could only nod, afraid that anything that came out of her mouth would be utter nonsense.

"Don't worry; we don't bite. Sherri thought you might like one of these." He placed a drink in front of her.

Maggie eyed the glass uncertainly. She'd already had a few shots from what remained of her grandfather's Irish whiskey before she left the house, just to get herself out the door and into Sherri's car. Not being much of a drinker, she was not particularly adept at holding her liquor, but she figured her supercharged case of the jitters would burn off the alcohol before it could fully absorb into her bloodstream. She glanced back to the stage, where Sherri was seductively removing her ankle-length trench coat, and decided that more alcohol was required if she was going to pull this off.

With trembling fingers, she lifted the glass and tipped it into her mouth like she'd seen her grandfather do. Whatever it was, it burned like crazy but went down smooth. Much more so than the cheap stuff she had at home. She coughed as her eyes started watering.

"Thanks," she rasped out in a choked voice.

The bartender laughed. It was a rich, deep sound that made her feel warm inside. Or maybe that was the alcohol. She curved her index and middle fingers toward her, indicating that she wanted another. He smiled, and she couldn't help thinking how beautiful that smile was.

Clearly, the alcohol *was* having an effect, because she'd never been quite so stricken simply by looking at a man before. Now, it had happened twice in one night.

"I take it, this isn't your day job?" he said as he poured her another drink.

"It's that obvious?"

"It's very subtle, really. I doubt anyone else would notice."

He was being kind, but she appreciated it all the same. Men typically weren't all that kind to her, if they noticed her at all. And why was he talking to her when he could be watching Sherri dance?

Then she remembered that, tonight, she wasn't her usual, boring self. She was a temptress. A seductress concealed beneath veils and a mask. A man like him wouldn't be talking to a woman like her otherwise.

The bartender folded his arms on the bar between them and leaned in close, as if to share a confidence. He smelled heavenly. Feeling bold, Maggie took a deeper sniff. She had the sudden, strange desire to bury her face in his neck and take a nibble, see if he tasted as good as he smelled.

"You don't have to dance if it makes you uncomfortable," he said quietly. "I'll tell them you aren't feeling well. They'll understand."

He was giving her an easy out. The question was, should she take it? Maggie looked back to the stage where Sherri was casting her magic. Sherri sure looked like she was having a good time.

What would it be like to feel that free? Maggie wondered. *To let go and move like that, like some wicked fantasy?*

The men were hooting appreciatively, but not one of them tried to touch Sherri. Even when Sherri grew bold and slid into their laps, they were careful to keep their hands to themselves. No wonder Sherri liked dancing for these guys.

Also, there was the allure of five hundred dollars cash in her pocket.

"Thanks," she said, lowering her voice in an attempt to make it sound sexier. At least, she hoped it had. She really had no experience with this sort of thing, but that was what the women did in the movies. "But I promised my friend ..."

He smiled again, and she couldn't help but notice that one side of his mouth curved a little more than the other. He had nice, full lips. Maggie fixated on them as she felt the warmth of the alcohol coursing through her limbs, wondering what it would be like to be kissed by lips like that. No doubt she'd find out when she drifted off to sleep that night because she was pretty sure the hot bartender would have the starring role in her dreams.

"Taking one for the team, huh?"

She giggled, surprising herself. This guy made her feel at ease, which was strange because people—especially men of godlike beauty—tended to have the opposite effect. But, she supposed, that was one of the things that distinguished a mediocre bartender from a great one—the ability to put people at ease. And this guy was definitely *good*.

"Yeah, something like that."

"Then I think you'd best get ready," he said, glancing up to where Sherri's performance was coming to an end. "Because it looks like you're up."

A brief moment of panic rushed through her. She took the glass he'd offered, brushing his fingertips in the process, and tossed it back. His eyes glinted with amusement; his deep chuckle lent her courage.

"That I am." She winked at him, feeling kind of wicked as she let the hard, pounding bass reverberate through her body.

Touching the mask around her eyes to make sure it was in place, she walked carefully toward the back, loosening her hips so they swayed, and said a silent prayer that she would not trip over her own feet.

As it turned out, dancing in front of an audience wasn't nearly as hard as she'd thought it would be. With the aid of liquid courage and the anonymity of the mask, she let her body respond to the music. The cheers and catcalls died away as the men watched, transfixed, while she moved before them. Her muscle control and isolation were excellent—the result of more than a dozen years of dance and yoga. She spun around them, teasing them with veils, jingling the trinkets that dangled from her hips and encircled her ankles and upper arms. Her natural ruby-colored hair hung loose, moving with her body; her emerald eyes, outlined in a smoky black, sparkled through the openings of the mask. Tonight, she wasn't Maggie, jilted, antisocial recluse; she was Magdalena, exotic male fantasy.

She lost herself in the music, in the lights, in their blatant appreciation. For those thirty minutes, she allowed herself to become someone else—someone sexy and desirable, someone without worry or fear. Before she knew it, she was on her last song. With a deep-seated feeling of satisfaction, Maggie worked her way back up to the stage for her grand finale, her movements serpentine and hypnotic.

Her heart pounded in excitement, her mind and heart freer than it had been in a long time. She felt wonderful as she gave her final bow to their applause, her steps light as she walked out of sight. Sherri was already taking her place back onstage, the music transitioning into something hard and sexy.

She'd done it!

Maggie felt as if her body were filled with light. Dancing in front of those men had been one of the most exhilarating—and terrifying—things she'd ever done. She had let herself go—mind, body, and spirit—and they had been enraptured. It was a feeling she would remember for a long time. If Sherri asked her to do this again, she realized, she probably would.

At least until her mask shifted and she stepped off the back of the stage. The trance was jarringly broken, and she tumbled down, all grace forgotten as she landed face-first against one of the small bar tables pushed back there in storage.

Lights exploded behind her eyes with the impact. Her body followed, crumpling as she rolled off the corner and hit the floor with a resounding thud. As if from far away, she heard deep, rumbling sound, like thunder.

Thunder was good, she decided, her head swimming deliriously as she tried to remember where she was and what she'd been doing. Maybe it would bring with it cool rain to ease some of the white-hot pain across her face.

She cried out when someone tried to turn her over. Instinctively, she curled herself into a ball to make a smaller target, though for the life of her, she couldn't fathom why someone was trying to hurt her.

The music was still playing, the vibrations of the

bass hammering into her head like a sledgehammer. Someone was talking, but it sounded muffled, wrong. A bright light shone in her eyes, and she tried to bat it away. Then, she had the feeling of movement, right before the blackness claimed her.

CHAPTER THREE

Michael was enthralled, unable to take his eyes off the woman. He was quite sure they hadn't met before; he definitely would have remembered the exotic-looking redhead.

She hadn't noticed him behind the bar at first, which gave him a chance to study her. Not old, but she was no kid. Beautiful, intelligent green eyes. A full, lush figure. And completely out of her element. She looked scared stiff.

Then, she'd spoken, and he knew he had been right. The uncertainty he'd heard in her soft, quiet voice was at odds with the lusty harem-girl costume she wore.

All traces of uncertainty vanished when she took the floor, however. There was no hesitation in her movements, just sensual, hypnotic beauty. He remained transfixed during her entire performance, unwilling to turn away, even for a moment.

"Her name is Maggie," Sherri said when she joined him at the bar. Apparently, his rapt attention hadn't escaped her. "Maggie Flynn."

"She's incredible."

"Yeah, she is, isn't she?" Sherri said thoughtfully as Maggie worked her way around the room. "This will be good for her."

"Yeah? Why's that?"

Sherri fingered the glass Michael had placed before her. "She has no self-confidence."

Michael watched the beautiful woman dancing with total abandon, weaving a spell over the room. He tore his eyes away to cast Sherri a doubtful look.

"I'm serious. She's become a total recluse ever since ..." She stopped mid-sentence, clamping her lips together.

"Since?" he coaxed.

Sherri shook her head. "Forget I said anything. Mags would be mortified if she knew I'd said even that much."

Michael pinned her with hypnotic blue eyes, leaned in closer, and spoke the words softly, as if they would be sharing an intimate secret, "I won't tell." It was beneath him, he knew, to manipulate her like this. He usually left that kind of thing to his brothers, but something about the redhead intrigued him. He wanted to know more.

Sherri stared into his eyes, and then shook herself free. "Oh no, you don't," she chided. "If you want to know, you can find out for yourself."

"Come on, Sher. Help a guy out here, will you?"

She laughed and slid off the stool. "No way. Maggie's a good friend, and I'm not vapid enough to jeopardize that, not even for the likes of you, Michael Callaghan."

Sherri left to prepare for her next number. Michael continued to watch Maggie as she took her bow and left the tiny stage. She was out of sight of everyone else, but from his position behind the bar, he could see her perfectly. The look of pure joy on her face was something to behold, and he found himself smiling right along with her.

She didn't seem to notice that the back edge of the stage ended abruptly. He knew what was going to happen an instant before it did. He vaulted over the far end of the bar, even as her foot stepped off the stage and into nothing. She clawed at the air, instinctively twisting her body in an attempt to protect herself as gravity did its thing.

Michael reached out, but he was a step too late. The side of her head slammed against one of the tables; the rest of her body followed milliseconds later, bouncing with the force of contact. Her big eyes, wide with fear, looked up into his face as he bent over her, but she didn't acknowledge him before they closed, and her body went limp.

A quick check assured him she had no broken bones, but she did have one hell of a contusion on the side of her face. Lifting her carefully, he took her back to the kitchen and gently placed her on the padded bench seat there, then turned on the lights to take a better look.

Her mask had dislodged in the fall. Blood, matching the shade of her dark ruby hair, trickled along the side of her face where she'd hit, creating a Goth-like image against her pale, creamy skin and dark kohl liner. Satisfied that none of her injuries were immediately life-threatening, Michael covered her with a warm blanket and knelt beside her to begin the task of cleaning away the makeup she had so artfully applied to expose and properly treat the wound.

When he was finished, Michael sat back on his heels and took a deep breath. In costume, she'd been striking and exotic. Without the makeup, with her eyes closed and her face relaxed, she was the picture of innocence. From her long lashes to the smattering of freckles across her nose, she barely looked old enough to legally enter a bar, let alone dance in one.

She let out a soft moan as she began to come around. Michael finished applying an antibiotic ointment and bandage to her wound, then secured a soothing ice pack on top to stem the swelling.

"Maggie." The low voice was very pleasant, though it held a trace of worry.

No voice that rich and deep should sound worried, she decided. She tried to get her bearings as her senses began to return. The music was much fainter now, and she felt something soft beneath her.

"Maggie, can you hear me?"

She tried to pry her eyes open, but only one would cooperate. The other seemed to be stuck, weighted down with something cold and heavy. She lifted her hand, but another bigger, stronger hand covered hers and gently pushed it away.

"Leave it," the nice voice said. "The ice will help with the swelling. Do you know where you are?"

Maggie tried to focus, the image before her large and blurry. The voice was familiar, as was the scent. *The bartender? The gorgeous guy with the heart-stopping smile and bedroom eyes?* She'd been dancing, feeling free and buoyant, and then ...

She winced as she remembered her fall.

"Hang on. I'm going to turn off some of these lights." Seconds later, the level of brightness—and thus the sensation of knives shooting through her skull —was substantially reduced. "Better?"

She nodded gingerly. The right side of her face felt like it had been slammed against a two-by-four. Or a table edge. Her cheeks flamed.

"Maggie, I'm going to take you to the ER. We'll get some X-rays, maybe an MRI."

"No," she protested, then winced. Her voice sounded distant and far away while echoing painfully throughout her skull.

ERs were expensive and X-rays even more so. No

steady employment meant no health insurance, and she didn't have an overabundance of funds. After this little tiptoe through the tulips, she was quite certain she wouldn't be getting paid. If she was lucky, the cost of any damages she'd caused wouldn't be more than what she had in the petty-cash fund she kept for emergencies.

Not to mention that the only way she would go to the hospital was if someone was carrying her unconscious body there without her knowledge or consent. She would never go willingly—and definitely not for a little bump on the head.

"I just need to get home." She hissed in pain as she tried to sit up, but strong hands kept her down.

"I don't think so. You might have a concussion."

"No concussion," she insisted, trying for a wan smile. "I'm naturally obtuse."

The corner of his mouth tilted up in that lovely, crooked grin. "And inherently clumsy?"

There was a twinge of amusement to his voice. At least, she hoped it was that, as opposed to him making fun of her outright. He'd seemed so nice earlier. It would be a shame if he turned out to be a jerk. Not surprising, based on her track record with men, but disappointing all the same.

"Now, you know." Her cheeks flamed again.

"Seriously," he said, "what happened out there?"

Maggie looked down at her hands. "I wasn't watching where I was going. I probably should have eaten before I came. And I shouldn't have had those shots to calm my nerves."

"How many fingers am I holding up?"

He held up two—no, four—no, two, *definitely* two—long, tapered fingers. *The man even had sexy fingers!* Given the sharp, stabbing pain through her temple, she shouldn't be imagining what else he could do with those fingers.

She pushed his hand away, annoyed with herself and uncertain of the answer. "What are you, a doctor or something?"

"Yes, actually," he said, shining a light in her eye. "Michael Callaghan, at your service."

The combination of the pain and the humiliation made her snappish. She snorted, wishing immediately that she hadn't because it *hurt*.

"Yeah, right. Why would a doctor play bartender?" The idea was almost as insane as a mild-mannered farm girl doing the Dance of the Seven Veils at a bachelor party.

As if he had read her mind, he answered, "Probably for the same reason a nice girl like you would play exotic dancer."

His fingers—warm, gentle, and feeling way too good—wrapped around her wrist to take her pulse.

Maggie groaned. "Touché."

"That aside," he continued, "my family owns the pub. I enjoy tending sometimes."

Oh.

He *did* bear a striking resemblance to the other

men she'd seen. It was just her luck. As if he hadn't been unattainable enough as a gorgeous bartender, he had to be a Callaghan *and* a doctor, too. Totally out of her league. She felt even more foolish.

"Look, uh, Dr. Callaghan," she began, searching for words that might minimize further embarrassment.

"Michael," he corrected.

Why did his voice have to be so low and smooth, wrapping around her like a favorite down comforter? It would be so easy to close her eyes and listen to that wonderful voice as she drifted away again, away from the pain and humiliation. Unfortunately, she couldn't allow herself to do that.

"I should go before I make an even bigger fool of myself," she said. *If that was even possible.*

"You have nothing to be embarrassed about, Maggie. Accidents happen. But you do need medical attention."

"And you gave it to me. Thank you, by the way. I'm feeling much better." She forced a smile and sat up— he allowed it this time—holding the smile in place while she fought the urge to heave.

Wouldn't that just be the perfect end to a perfect day? Fall on her face, insult the sexy doctor, and then vomit in his lap. Best to cut her losses and get out while she could.

"Do I owe you anything?"

He didn't answer. When she glanced back up to his face with her one good eye, he looked annoyed. Well, that was too bad. He wasn't the one nearly dying of mortification.

He lifted the ice pack to examine her right eye. "You shouldn't be alone until we know you're okay. Concussions aren't something to mess around with. Is there someone who can stay with you tonight?"

Are you offering? The crazy thought zinged through her head, proving just how hard she must have hit it. The chance of someone like him spending the night with someone like her was about as likely as her winning the lottery, which was pretty much impossible since she didn't have the money to waste on foolish things like Pick-6 tickets or scratch-offs.

Still, he seemed genuinely concerned. She wondered if he treated all his patients like this. That thought was immediately followed with one that suggested there would be a long line of broken hearts if he did.

Maggie didn't want to join their ranks. Michael seemed like a nice guy, trying to do a nice thing. Nothing more, no matter how her heart skipped a beat when he looked at her like that. She wondered if he'd felt the irregular pattern when he took her pulse, flushing again at the thought.

Let him off the hook so he can get back to the party without feeling guilty, her woozy mind urged. That would be the responsible thing to do.

"I don't live alone," she said, choosing her words carefully. It was kind of true—as long as they weren't limiting the household to actual *people.*

Michael looked at her with those amazing blue eyes, so clear and probing that she cast her own downward in guilt.

"Really," she said quietly, "I just want to go home now. Please." She hated the feel of the hot tears that burned in her eyes. She wasn't an overly emotional person by nature, but this day had pushed her beyond normal limits. She just wanted it to end.

"Hey," he said softly, laying his hand on her upper arm. "It's all right, Maggie."

The shock of warmth sent shivers through her but not as much as the concern in his eyes. Eyes that looked deeper than they should have. Eyes that were too genuine, too caring. Once again, she found herself turning away rather than face him.

"I don't think you're in any shape to drive," he told her. No matter how much she wished otherwise, he was right.

"No, I'm not," she agreed, "but I came with Sherri anyway."

She sighed, glancing toward the room where the music still played. Sherri had been looking forward to this night for weeks. She would be devastated if she had to leave early. Maggie couldn't do that to her, even if it meant spending next week's food budget on a ride home.

"Would you call me an Uber?"

"If you won't let me take you to the hospital, at least let me drive you home," Michael suggested.

"Oh, I really couldn't ask you to do that. I've already ruined enough of your evening."

He smiled again, that sexy, lopsided smile that made her breath hitch. "Technically, you're not asking; I'm offering. And I don't mind. Really," he added when he saw her look of disbelief. "I'm not all that into bachelor parties," he said. "They won't even know I'm gone."

She raised an eyebrow, wincing as she did. Such a small gesture shouldn't hurt so much. Maggie made a mental note not to do that again for a while.

"Consider it my fee, if you'd like," he added, a twinkle in his eye.

"You would consider driving me home as payment for scraping me off the floor and providing first aid?"

"My fees are steep, I admit, but I'm just good enough to be worth it."

Despite herself, she smiled. Resisting such charm was difficult when he laid it on so thickly.

What would it hurt? He'd see her safely home and know that he did his good deed for the day, Sherri would get to stay and enjoy herself, and Maggie would get home all that much sooner. It would be a win for everyone.

"Here," he said, handing her a flannel shirt and a pair of sweats. "You'll swim in them, but they should be easy to get into. I'll just grab your things and pull the car around. Wait right here."

By the time she blinked, Michael was already gone.

Maggie looked at the clothing he'd thrust into her

lap. Definitely men's, definitely huge, and—she lifted them up to her face and inhaled—definitely his. Slipping them on over what remained of her costume was easier than trying to wiggle her way into the clothes she had worn earlier. Most of her right side was uncooperative or too painful to move much, and every time she looked down, her head pounded like the devil was performing a hearty rendition of *Riverdance* on it.

None of that, however, diminished the prevented her from appreciating the feel of Michael's clothes against her skin. She would have to be careful, her fluttering heart warned. It would be too easy to misconstrue his kindness for something more than it was.

Michael returned as she was trying unsuccessfully to button the shirt. Double vision continued to plague her, and her fingers didn't seem to be working the way they should.

"Here," he said, kneeling before her once again. "Let me."

The sexy bartender/doctor brushed her hands aside and fastened each of the buttons as she gazed on, certain that she was hallucinating.

Maggie placed a hand on his shoulder for support when she felt herself leaning sideways and sucked in a breath. Beneath his cotton shirt was warm, solid marble, bunching and flexing as he worked his way upward on the flannel's buttons. She couldn't help but wonder what it would be like to touch him without the thin cloth in the way, then decided that such thoughts were not helpful.

The room spun nauseatingly when she tried to stand. Before she could get her bearings, Michael wrapped the blanket around her. He placed one arm behind her knees and another under her arms and gently lifted. Maggie thought briefly of protesting, but with Michael's arms cradling her so nicely and her face tucked against his collarbone, she couldn't for the life of her remember why she should.

CHAPTER FOUR

I t was a moonless, cloudy night, heavy with the threat of yet another snowstorm. Maggie gave Michael her address, and then she sat back and drifted in and out of consciousness for the half-hour drive. The sleek black sedan rode smoothly; the seats were plush and oh-so comfortable, the interior warm and filled with Michael's rich, sensual scent. Even feeling as miserable as she was, there was pleasure to be had in the experience.

When he finally pulled into the long drive, the single porch light she'd left on was enough to spear through her optic nerves, forcing her to shield her eyes with her hands.

Michael positioned the black Jag as close to the house as possible. His low voice held the comfort of soft down when he said, "Here we are."

Maggie was glad for the darkness; it made the current state of disrepair less obvious. She had planned on restoring the place after her grandparents passed away, but those plans, like so many others, had been necessarily placed on the back burner when she walked away from a decent, steady paycheck. Still, she wouldn't trade the old house, outbuildings, and secluded acreage for anything.

Infinitely glad she hadn't thrown up in his beautiful car, she placed her hand on the door handle and turned to thank him, but he wasn't there. He was already outside and opening the door for her.

Had he moved that fast? Or was she just processing everything in slow motion?

"Thanks for the ride." Maggie accepted the hand he held out to her, discreetly enjoying the warmth and strength of it. "I'll be fine from here."

"Humor me."

Perhaps he suspected that his gentle but firm hold was the only thing keeping her from crumpling to the ground.

"Ah, you're the chivalrous type," she said, leaning into him as he slid one of those massive arms behind her and around her waist. "You think just because a woman nosedives off a stage and knocks herself senseless, she needs a man's help."

She stumbled across the gravel; Michael caught her before she hit the ground.

"Yes. Apparently, it's one of my more irritating qualities."

He helped her up the couple of extra-wide steps to her large wraparound porch. She fumbled with her house key for several minutes—she kept seeing two or three and couldn't decide which one was the right one—before he took the keys from her and opened the door himself.

She paused at the threshold and tilted her face up to his, trying desperately to focus while her body swayed backward. "I suppose you feel the need to see me safely inside?"

His mouth quirked at the corners, even as his arm kept her upright. "The thought did occur to me, yes."

She gave a resigned sigh and stepped through the doorway. Michael followed dutifully with his hand on her lower back, closing the door behind them. They were met by an odd thumping sound from below. With obvious effort, a huge basset pulled himself to his feet. His ears were so long that he tripped on them in his excitement, head-butting Maggie around the knees and pushing her against the wall.

Michael chuckled. "At least I know where you got that last dance move from."

Maggie shot him a reproachful glance, but her ire faded when she caught the playful smile tugging at his lips. "Yep. Now, you know."

The hound turned soulful eyes up toward Michael.

"Michael, meet George. George, Michael." She chuckled. "Ha. George Michael. Like Wham."

George immediately laid himself across Michael's shoes and rolled over to offer his belly. Maggie's eyes widened as much as possible through the swelling. George didn't like strangers and was more likely to slink off and hide than angle for a belly rub. It had taken the pooch forever to warm up to Sherri, and she had given him *cookies*.

"Would you mind petting him?" Maggie asked, pledging silently to abstain from saying anything else ridiculous. "He's a real hands-on type of guy, and I just don't think I can bend over right now."

Michael crouched down and gave George a good and thorough rub across the chest. George gave a little doggy moan of pleasure. The foyer began to spin, and Maggie placed her hand on his shoulder for balance.

"Watch him," Maggie warned Michael. "He's vicious."

"Yes, I can see that."

MAGGIE SWAYED, a timely reminder of why he'd felt compelled to see her home safely in the first place.

"Sorry, big guy," Michael said to George, standing slowly. "I think she needs me more than you do at the moment."

Maggie snorted softly. As if to prove him wrong, she let go of his shoulder and stood on her own. With much focus, she unsteadily made her way down the narrow hallway, keeping one hand on the wall for support. Michael followed, wondering at her stubbornness. He remained ready to catch her again if necessary, which looked increasingly probable with each step she took.

With his attention focused on Maggie, he only managed brief glimpses of her home as she led him down the hall. The place was old. Immaculately clean but decidedly lived in. The colors were warm and welcoming; the polished hardwood floor glowed on either side of the multicolored runner that ran down the center. The stair banister looked handmade, carved a century or more ago, and smoothed from years of use. This wasn't a house. This was a *home* with lots of history.

She pushed through a swinging door and into a kitchen big enough to rival the one at the pub. It spanned the entire width of the house. A single, low-wattage light burned over the sink at the far end, illuminating the large space with a warm glow.

Michael inhaled deeply, taking in the mouthwatering aromas of freshly baked bread, butter, cinnamon, and chocolate. Images immediately flooded his mind. Maggie, bustling around, pulling a fresh loaf of bread out of the oven. Maggie, washing dishes at the sink while wearing a pretty pink apron. Maggie, her face lighting up as she turned and saw him coming through the back door. They were so clear, more like memories than stray thoughts.

"Ah," she said, misinterpreting the momentary longing on his face, "a man after my own heart. Here." Maggie hobbled over to the counter and grabbed a covered platter piled high with cookies.

Michael, shaken by the clarity of the images and the intensity of their effect, accepted the plate with one hand and steadied her with the other. "Maggie," he commanded, his voice slightly less professional than it had been earlier. "Please sit."

Her face was growing paler by the minute, and he hadn't missed the way the plate trembled in her hands.

She sat without argument, which confirmed his suspicions that she was winding down in a big way. Thus far, she had resisted his every attempt to help her, so her easy acquiescence was telling.

"I made them today," she said slowly, as if it was an effort to get the words out. "I was so nervous ..." She tried to conceal a yawn with her hand. "I tend to bake when I'm nervous."

Michael took a cookie, mainly because she seemed to expect him to. "They're delicious."

"Glad you like them. George likes them too."

"I can see that." Michael kept his expression neutral, though the weakness in her voice had him concerned. It wouldn't be long now. Her eyes were losing focus, her lids growing droopier by the second. Still, she resisted.

She absently took a cookie from the plate and offered it to George, who had conveniently placed himself on the floor between them and was looking at her with pure adoration.

"Thanks for bringing me home, Michael. I wish I could be a better hostess, but I'm afraid I'm feeling very sleepy."

"It's okay, Maggie," he said in his soothing voice,

the one he used to lull his niece and nephew to sleep. "I understand."

"You're a kind man. And you smell wonderful. I bet your patients love ..." Her voice faded as her head fell forward.

Thankfully, he was prepared for it and managed to get his arm between her already-bruised face and the scarred wooden tabletop before she hit.

Gathering her into his arms, Michael cradled her against his chest. George whimpered and regarded him curiously.

"Don't worry," Michael told him. "I've got this." If he didn't know better, he could have sworn the hound smiled.

Michael carried Maggie back to the living area and laid her on the couch. He slid his finger along the front of her wrist. Her skin was warm and silky; her pulse, steady and strong.

He gently lifted her lids and checked her eyes, pleased to find the pupils responsive. He pushed the hair away from the side of her face, frowning at the swelling and the dark purple bruising that had already begun to show. They *should* be at the hospital, getting an X-ray, but Maggie had made her wishes abundantly clear—no hospital. Since she didn't seem to be in any immediate danger, he would have to respect her wishes.

Michael sighed and lightly ran his knuckles over her cheeks, feeling a tug behind his breastbone. She was so stubborn. So proud. And so beautiful.

Given the fall she'd taken, he didn't feel comfortable just tucking a blanket around her and leaving. He settled into the chair adjacent to her, rationalizing his decision to stay. It was merely a result of the same desire that had steered him toward the medical profession in the first place—namely, the desire to care for others.

An inner voice called bullshit and suggested a different reason—one that had more to do with the way his chest tightened when he looked at her than fealty to the Hippocratic Oath he'd taken.

George, who was quite possibly the biggest basset hound he'd ever seen, nudged his leg and interrupted his musings. Expressive, big eyes looked up at him.

Michael reached down and scratched the dog behind his ears. "Is she always so stubborn?"

The dog thumped his tail, which Michael took as a yes.

"Well then, I guess it's up to us to take care of her tonight."

CHAPTER FIVE

The shrill chime rang out from an ancient ringer box mounted on the wall, cutting through the peaceful silence. Maggie groaned and pulled the covers up over her head. Michael remembered seeing a landline phone in the kitchen. He rose to intercept the call before it woke Maggie but didn't get there before the answering machine picked up.

"Maggie! Where are you? Why did you leave? Pick up the damn phone!" a feminine voice demanded through the speaker.

Michael crossed the kitchen floor on quiet feet and lifted the receiver. "Sherri, right?"

There was a brief pause. Then, with much more caution, she said, "Yeah. Who is this?"

"Michael Callaghan," he said.

"Where is Maggie? Is she okay?"

"Maggie is fine. She's sleeping."

Another pause.

"Alone?"

"Yes," Michael assured her with amusement. "Her virtue remains intact."

"Only Maggie ..." she mumbled, sounding almost disappointed. "So then, why are you there?" Equal parts curiosity and suspicion colored her voice.

Michael hesitated, unsure of just how much he should say. "It's a long story."

"Try me."

Michael grinned. *Everyone should have such protective friends.*

"Maggie can tell you herself when she's had some rest. She has your number?" As dismissals went, it was smooth and polite, but it was still a dismissal.

After Sherri ensured him somewhat huffily that Maggie did in fact have her number, Michael wished her a pleasant night and hung up the phone.

WHEN MAGGIE WOKE HOURS LATER, she exhaled with great care, letting the breath escape slowly to lessen the pain in her bruised ribs.

The sound of fierce, howling winds rattled against the panes, competing with the crackling of the fire in the sturdy, old farmhouse. It took Maggie several minutes to get her bearings. She was on the sofa in her living room, tucked beneath a warm down comforter, with a fluffy pillow beneath her head.

That's weird. I don't even remember going to bed. Or making a fire.

That last thing she *did* remember was the hot bartender-slash-doctor driving her home after...

Oh God.

Maggie sat up quickly, immediately wishing she hadn't. The pain in her head was fierce, and unlike the previous night, she didn't have the benefit of finely aged bourbon or the natural adrenaline from dancing to temper it. The entire right side of her body felt stiff and bruised.

She looked down. She was still wearing the shirt and sweats Michael had given her. Lifting the soft flannel to her face, she inhaled the scent that'd had such a devastating effect on her, hoping it was the post-crash delirium that had made it so appealing. It wasn't. In fact, the scent was even more enticing now, because it was mixed with hers.

She gave herself a mental shake to free herself from those unhelpful thoughts. As soon as her head stopped spinning, she looked around for her canine shadow. It was unusual that George hadn't woken her to go out or to remind her about getting his breakfast. For as lazy as he was, the dog never missed a meal.

Then again, maybe he had tried, she thought guiltily. She'd been pretty out of it.

The poor guy is probably crossing his stubby little legs in front of the back door.

Bracing herself, she eased her way off the cushions, remembering how George had placed himself at

Michael's feet the night before. He'd really taken to Michael. They said that dogs were excellent judges of character, and in this instance, she had to agree. How many men would have gone out of their way to help as he had?

Maggie snorted quietly. Not many. None that she knew, not without expecting something in return.

She made up her mind then and there to make some fresh cookies and send them over to the pub with her thanks. She vaguely remembered Sherri telling her that some of the brothers lived on the upper floors; she was fairly certain Michael was among them.

Her eyes were mostly open now, except for the right one, which she could only open halfway. Her hearing seemed to be working fine. But something wasn't right with her nose. Amid the light scent of wood smoke from the fire and the delicious scent of Michael on her clothes, she thought she also smelled … bacon?

It took longer than usual to travel the short distance from the living room to the kitchen. Her balance was off, and her ankle and hip were stiff and achy. Each step was a blaring reminder of her unfortunate misstep off the back of the stage. She wasn't the most graceful woman on earth, but neither was she typically clumsy.

A fresh wave of embarrassment rolled over her. What must they think of her? Michael had said no one else had witnessed her fall from grace, but surely, they all knew of it now. Would they laugh and snicker if they saw her again? Probably. Maybe someday, she would look back and find it funny, too, but it wouldn't be today.

When Sherri called later—and Maggie was sure that she would—Maggie would ask her to deliver the cookies on her behalf. That way, she could avoid the humiliation, and Sherri would have a valid reason to place herself in the presence of the Callaghan men again. Sherri would like that. It would go a long way in making up for any hurt feelings caused by Maggie's abrupt departure.

At least now Maggie had a better understanding of Sherri's obsession with them. They had been polite and friendly—not to mention, romance-novel-cover gorgeous.

One Callaghan in particular seemed to be commanding her thoughts this morning. Despite the knowledge that he was way out of her league, she liked him. He was kind and caring with an easygoing manner and just a hint of something darker beneath the surface.

Not that she'd felt any fear. On the contrary, she'd never felt safer than she had in his presence. Michael Callaghan had an aura about him that exuded confidence and capability, but without the massive ego that usually accompanied those things. He was the type of man who would always take care of what was his.

An unbidden sigh came to her lips. *Talk about the perfect fodder for a romance novel!*

Maggie couldn't help but wonder what Michael

thought of her, if he gave her any thought at all beyond providing first aid. He hadn't seen the real Maggie; he'd seen her wild alter ego. The real Maggie didn't toss back shots of bourbon or dance the Dance of the Seven Veils in a room full of men at a bachelor party. The real Maggie didn't wear makeup or sexy clothes. She farmed, she cooked, she baked. She used her skills to work freelance consulting jobs from the comfort and safety of her own home so she could scrape together just enough to keep the bills and taxes paid.

The more she thought about it, the more she was glad that Michael had seen *Magdalena*. If he'd met plain old *Maggie*, he wouldn't have given her a second glance.

She sighed again, shuffling along the hardwood floor, one hand on the wall for support. Despite the unfortunate accident and the aches and pains surfacing with a vengeance, Maggie didn't regret the decision to help Sherri. It *had* been fun. For a little while, she had been allowed to be someone else— someone free and passionate, wild and sensual. Someone so unlike the hardworking, quiet, do-the-right-thing girl she was. More importantly, she'd met Michael. Even if nothing could come of it, she could tuck away the memory of his dazzling smile, brilliant blue eyes, and soft, soothing voice for when she needed it.

Maggie pushed open the swinging door and stopped abruptly. She had to blink several times, certain her eyes were playing tricks on her. George didn't even notice her. His attention was focused solely on the huge man positioned in front of the stove.

Michael.

He hadn't left. He'd stayed the night. He was still here.

Maggie swallowed hard. He looked good, even better than her concussed, bourbon-soaked mind remembered. He wore a heavy flannel shirt, untucked and unbuttoned, over the white t-shirt, and a pair of well-worn Levi's hugging a perfect backside. The shadow of a beard graced his strong, masculine jaw. His blue-black hair was slightly messy, as if he'd recently run his hands through it. It was just long enough to give him a touch of that bad-boy look, especially with the way he left it longer in the front, teasingly hanging down to his brows when he inclined his head a certain way.

And he was barefoot.

In her kitchen.

Making breakfast.

Dear sweet Virgin Mary.

She stood there, rooted to the spot, convinced she was dreaming. Perhaps she had a concussion after all. That might not be such a bad thing, if it brought on visions like this.

George finally noticed her and began wagging his tail. The thumping caught Michael's attention, causing him to follow the dog's gaze to where she stood in the doorway.

His eyes raked her from head to toe before a

dazzling smile lit his face, making her blush furiously. She could only imagine what she looked like. Why hadn't she thought to splash some cold water on her face or try to finger-comb the tangled mess of hair that probably bore a striking resemblance to Medusa's?

"Good morning," he said. His voice was even deeper than she remembered, sending shivers up and down her entire body. "How are you feeling?"

"I think I'm hallucinating," she said weakly, leaning against the frame for support.

In two long strides, he crossed the floor and towered next to her.

Concern etched his perfect features when he cupped her face and tilted it up to his, looking intently into her eyes. His hands were so big and warm, commanding yet gentle. Maggie fought the urge to lean into him—it would be so easy. Instead, she concentrated on keeping her trembling legs beneath her.

"Why do you say that?" he asked, staring first into one eye and then switching to the other.

Because the hottest, sexiest man I've ever seen is in my kitchen, making breakfast.

She'd read about something like this in a romance novel once. In the story, the man ended up lifting the woman onto the table and having *her* for breakfast. She shook her head slightly, trying to dispel that lovely image, and answered him.

"Because you're here."

CHAPTER SIX

Michael couldn't completely conceal his grin as she allowed him to lead her over to the table. Did she have any idea how absolutely adorable she looked, standing there in an oversize man's shirt—*his* shirt—only the tips of her fingers visible, with her tousled curls and her flushed cheeks? Not even the blossoming dark purple bruise extending from her right temple to her jaw could detract from her beauty. It did, however, evoke a powerful and protective instinct within him.

Michael gently pressed down on her shoulders, guiding her into the chair. Her eyes were clearer than they'd been the night before, as sharp and multifaceted as finely cut crystal. One was partially open, the other wide and regarding him with genuine puzzlement and a touch of suspicion.

"Seriously, why are you here?" she asked.

That was an excellent question—one for which he

didn't have an acceptable answer. *I didn't want to leave*, while true enough, seemed neither appropriate nor adequate at this stage. So, he used one of his younger brother Ian's tricks and opted for a little misdirection instead.

"You weren't exactly honest with me," he chided. "You led me to believe there was someone here who would take care of you last night."

"I said I didn't live alone," she corrected as he pulled a chair up close to hers, nudging his large body against the inside of her knees. Then he leaned in and looked deeply into her eyes.

ALL THAT MAN, all that heat between her thighs, made her heart race faster.

He's a doctor, she told herself repeatedly. *He's looking at you as nothing more than a patient. Get a grip.*

Yet no part of her rational mind could explain the scorching chills his closeness seemed to generate.

She *really* had to lay off those Salienne Dulcette novels.

"Hmm," he hummed, making her feel like a naughty child who'd just been caught telling a fib.

The tips of his fingers skillfully examined the side of her head and face as she clamped her lips shut, determined not to let the sigh escape. His touch was gentle, sending thousands of tiny electrical impulses down her neck, searing through to the tips of her breasts and down into the juncture between her legs. It took a lot of effort to keep her breathing controlled and even, especially when her heart was pounding so fiercely against the inner walls of her chest. As close as he was, he must have heard it.

Why did he have to be so freaking good-looking? Weren't doctors supposed to be old and pudgy with glasses and the personality of a dishrag? Weren't they supposed to smell like antiseptic and latex, not peppermint and coffee and warm spice and male musk?

Hell. This man didn't conform to any of the typical doctor stereotypes. And he was far too handsome and aromatic to be in her kitchen, sitting on her chair, examining *her.*

She caught her breath when his index and middle fingers paused at the pulse point just under the side of her jaw. His expression stilled for a moment as his eyes questioningly sought out hers, and then he looked away, the hint of a knowing smile pulling at those delicious-looking lips.

Damn it. He knew exactly what he was doing to her!

What was it about him that made her lose control? Maggie Flynn was an intelligent, capable woman. She shouldn't be responding to him like a starstruck teenager. The fact that she was, irritated her. And it still didn't explain his presence.

Does he feel sorry for me? Is that it?

She rejected that idea almost immediately. Michael wasn't the pitying type. How she knew that with such certainty, she wasn't sure, but she did. He was caring and kind and would be the first one to help but never out of pity.

Maggie couldn't fault him for that. No, if she was perturbed with anyone, it was herself for being the one to put him in this situation. Worse, she hated that there was some small part of her that secretly hoped Michael had stayed out of something more than a sense of professional duty. That small part was currently being bludgeoned by her much stronger, practical, rational side—the realist within her that said she was a fool for even considering such a thing.

And, it logically pointed out, even if he had stayed out of something more than a professional interest, it was Magdalena he was attracted to, not Maggie.

"You still didn't answer my question," she prodded. "Why are you here?"

SATISFIED that she exhibited no obvious signs of a concussion and was in no immediate danger, Michael pushed the chair back, stood, and returned to the counter. He poured her a cup of coffee and placed a plate of eggs, toast, and bacon in front of her. She stared at it as if she'd never seen such a thing before.

The truth was, Michael was stalling because he didn't know how to answer her question. He'd been asking himself the same one all night. He could ratio-nalize as much as he wanted, but each time he'd checked on her through the night, she was resting comfortably. He continued to stay anyway. It was the strangest thing; even though he'd known he *should* head back to the pub, he couldn't bring himself to do so. Maggie brought out his protective instincts.

"I didn't feel comfortable, leaving you alone in the state you were in," he answered finally, gesturing for her to eat.

"I see." She kept her expression neutral, but emotions swirled in her eyes. Such pretty green eyes. "Well, Dr. Callaghan," she said carefully, "caring for others is obviously more than just a profession for you. I can't say I've encountered anyone quite as dedicated. I'm sorry I caused you so much trouble."

Michael's eyes narrowed. Perceptive as he was, he wasn't sure how to take her words. Her tone hadn't been cold, but neither had it held the natural warmth he'd come to expect from her. Instead, it had been shielded, cautious, and ... confused?

He studied her from beneath his lashes as he leaned back against the counter and sipped his coffee, trying to formulate an appropriate reply. Surely, he hadn't imagined her physical response to him just moments ago. She found him attractive. All the signs were there. The lovely flush that made her skin glow; the shallow, hitched breaths; the rapid, forceful pulse hammering just below the delicate curve of her jaw.

She had a profound effect on him as well, enough that he'd felt the need to cross the room and put some distance between them before he did something even more unprofessional than spending the night. Michael had never had a problem with examining a patient before, but with Maggie, those usually clear, solid lines separating business and pleasure blurred.

How could he look into those eyes and not start to lose himself? How could he touch the heated silk of her skin and not feel his own heart rev in response?

Granted, she was a beautiful woman, but the odd, unfamiliar sensation in his chest couldn't be attributed to physical attraction alone. It wasn't unpleasant. On the contrary, he liked it. What he objected to was the emotional distance she seemed to be putting between them. Until now, she'd been relatively at ease, if not entirely comfortable, with his presence. She'd trusted him enough to allow him to drive her home, to enter her home, and to let him examine her. He refused to accept that she had done so solely due to the influence of alcohol or blunt force trauma.

When she'd walked into the kitchen and found him earlier, there had been no fear, no anger, no disappointment. Just surprise—and he could have sworn, delighted surprise at that. So, where was this polite, unaffected response coming from?

Two things he knew for sure: one, this wasn't the real Maggie, and two, he didn't like it.

The answer dawned on him as she sat there, arms drawn in tightly and resting on her lap, looking up at him with genuine bafflement. She wanted to know why he'd remained—a valid question. He'd fallen back on his profession as an excuse when the truth was far simpler than that. He'd stayed because he wanted to. Because he liked being there with her in her cozy, warm kitchen. Because liked taking care of her. Hell, he even liked her dog.

And she hadn't picked up on any of that.

"She has no self-confidence." Sherri's words came back to him, making more sense now than they had the night before.

Surely, a woman like Maggie was used to male attention, wasn't she? And how was he going to rectify the situation, convince her that he was here for more than just a professional obligation without coming across as a psycho?

It would take time. And patience. And effort.

He quickly decided she was worth it. No other woman had struck such a chord within him in so short a time, and that had to mean something. After witnessing what had happened to two of his brothers over the past two years, he had to at least consider the possibility that lightning had struck the Callaghan clan for the third time.

For now, he offered what he hoped she would accept at face value. He moved back to the table and sat down with his coffee.

"Call me Michael, please. And it was no trouble."

"I don't mean to sound ungrateful. You've been more than kind."

Her eyes were doing that flashing thing again, momentarily losing focus and then slamming back with astounding clarity. It fascinated him. He'd noticed the same thing the night before when she sat at the bar, waiting for her turn to dance. He'd give anything to know what was going through her mind right then. Maybe with a bit of luck and a lot of persistence, she'd learn to trust him with her thoughts. He had a feeling he would be on a very short list if she did.

"It's easy to be kind to you," Michael said before he could stop himself.

Worried that he'd said too much, he watched her reaction carefully. Her eyes widened just a bit, and then her facial expression softened, giving him another glimpse of the woman he'd sensed behind the facade. That was the woman he was interested in. In addition to hanging around to make sure she was okay, he'd also wanted to know if he'd imagined the inexplicable effect she had on him.

He hadn't. It was there in spades, stronger than ever.

"You know, Michael, I think that's one of the nicest things anyone has ever said to me. Thank you." The natural warmth was back in her voice, and it spread through him like liquid sunshine. That, he could work with.

"It's the truth." He shrugged, but he was pleased. He pushed the plate closer. "And you should eat."

EAT? As if she could. Her stomach had so many butterflies that swallowing even a single bite was unlikely. Keeping it down, even more so. She did manage to take a sip of coffee though, and damn if it wasn't some of the best she'd ever had. Her eyes closed momentarily as she savored the rich, full flavor. He'd already added sugar and cream, exactly the way she liked it. *How did he know?*

"This came out of my coffeepot?" she asked incredulously.

He nodded, a heart-stopping grin curving those sensual male lips yet again. He really needed to stop doing that if he expected her to hold a rational conversation.

"It's wonderful," she said truthfully, but even that small sip made her stomach clench in warning. She put the mug back onto the table.

He glanced expectantly at her plate. She nibbled her bottom lip. She didn't want to offend him, but she didn't want to embarrass herself either.

"Are you feeling nauseous?" he asked.

Am I? No, she thought, *this is different*. Her stomach was doing that funny flipping thing because of *him*, not because of her unfortunate tumble.

"No, I don't think so."

Michael raised an eyebrow in question, which shouldn't have sent those butterflies fluttering again but it did. He stood and pulled a pen light out of his pocket, then leaned over her in what was becoming a familiar move. Part of her was annoyed, but another part longed for the closeness it brought with it. At this range, she could clearly see the dark shadow along his jaw and feel the heat radiating from his body. Also rather disorienting was the familiar peppermint scent of his breath, now infused with coffee and, if she wasn't mistaken, a few of her cookies as well.

She shuddered. As gorgeous and intense as he was, it wasn't fair that he smelled like cookies too. How could any woman resist that?

Hopes that he hadn't noticed her body's reaction to his nearness were quickly dashed. "Are you cold? Do you have chills?"

He stepped back, putting her at eye-level with his hips. She was completely unprepared for that.

And that was unaroused. Oh my.

"No. Not cold. No chills." She shivered again, her cheeks heating as she averted her eyes.

He moved in close again and lightly pressed his hand to her forehead, as if to check for a fever.

"Maybe we should get you back to bed."

Was it her imagination, or was his voice lower than it had been before?

The words *we* and *bed* should not be coming out of his mouth as part of the same sentence, she decided. It made the butterflies in her stomach flutter even faster —not to mention, it sent yet another rush of heat toward the center of her body. She squirmed uncomfortably.

"Um, no, not a good idea."

Michael folded his arms in front of his chest. It struck her as odd, how such a small gesture could command so much authority. Even odder was the fact that she felt the need to explain herself. As a general rule, she didn't explain herself to anyone.

"I mean, there's no reason I should lie around in bed all day."

"Oh, I don't know," he said slowly. Seductively. "I could think of a few."

One side of his mouth lifted, and she felt her face burn.

"A concussion, for one," he finished slyly.

She finally saw the glint of amusement in his eyes. The sexy bastard was having fun with her! Maggie couldn't be too irritated with him. She'd brought it upon herself with her wicked imagination. She'd left the door wide open in blatant invitation. It was no wonder he had stepped right in.

"I don't have a concussion," she said firmly.

"Is that your professional opinion, Doctor?" He grinned, no longer hiding his amusement.

"As a matter of fact, it is." She sniffed, but even she was having trouble containing her own smile. "Besides, I have George to think of."

They both looked over at the beefy hound, dozing on a big doggy pillow in the far corner, next to the old-fashioned radiator as it clanged and hissed. A *good* dog would have had the decency to back her up by looking pathetic and hungry or dancing at the back door to go out.

As if reading her mind, Michael said, "I fed him this morning and took him outside. We played ball."

She blinked in disbelief. "He brought you his

favorite ball? The squeaky green one with the yellow star?"

She couldn't remember the last time George had wanted to play with anyone besides her. Painfully shy, the dog usually made himself scarce when anyone else was around. Michael Callaghan, apparently, was proving to be an exception, in more ways than one.

"Yes." George opened his eyes and yawned, and then he laid his head back down. "He's a great dog."

Well, well, well. The fact that Michael had taken care of George spoke volumes about the type of man he was. As a doctor, he might have felt compelled to take care of her after her injury, but there was no reason to care for her dog. And the most amazing thing? George actually *liked* him. Twelve years of Catholic school lessons nagged at the back of her head, insisting it had to be a *sign*.

"Thank you."

"My pleasure." He looked pointedly back at the plate again. "Now, eat, please. I'm starting to doubt my culinary skills."

"Well, we certainly can't have you doubting yourself." Maggie picked up a piece of toast and took a small bite. Thankfully, her stomach didn't revolt, and she took another. With each one, she began to feel a little better. The toast was followed closely by the scrambled eggs (done perfectly, fluffy but not runny) and the bacon (thoroughly cooked and slightly chewy). She was tempted to ask how he knew her preferences but then decided not to look a gift horse in the mouth. Besides, she wasn't sure she really wanted to know.

It took a while, but she managed to eat nearly everything on her plate in between sips of that liquid nectar he modestly referred to as coffee.

"I'm impressed," she said around the last bite of toast. "You're a doctor, a bartender, and a great cook. Is there anything you can't do?"

"I'll let you in on a little secret," he said, winking. "This is the only meal I can make. If you're craving anything else, you're on your own."

"Good thing I like bacon and eggs then," she said and then caught herself. She had no business suggesting this would happen again.

CHAPTER SEVEN

"Is there anything else I can get for you?"

Maggie laughed softly from deep within the nest he'd created for her on the sofa out of a multitude of pillows and a down comforter. Remotes for the television and DVD player sat within reach along with a selection of movies and books. A glass of water and a tray of fresh fruit, crackers, and cheese were there, too, as well as her cordless house and cell phones.

Michael had insisted on sticking around until she emerged from a shower, unscathed, donning fresh, comfortable clothes and fuzzy socks. George was snuggled up on the far end of the couch, snoring loudly. The fire was blazing, and he'd already brought in enough wood to last for several days.

The sound of her laugh was like music to his heart. It made the pain of seeing her bruising flesh and stiff movements slightly more bearable.

"No, Michael," she said, grinning. "I'm good."

At first, she had resisted just about every attempt he made to do something for her, but eventually, she'd come to realize that he was not easily dissuaded and that it was simpler to just go along with him on some things. She was a smart woman.

"I think you've thought of everything."

Not everything. He couldn't think of a good enough excuse to stick around. He *should* leave, but once again, he simply didn't want to.

"You're sure?" He looked around, stalling, searching for more to do.

"I'm sure. You're spoiling me rotten," she teased. "I'm not used to this kind of attention."

"Now, see, that's just not right. Every beautiful woman should have a man to dote on her."

"Not all women need men to take care of them," she countered.

Was it his imagination, or did her voice have a breathy quality it hadn't had earlier?

"No," he said slowly, drawing the word out. "I suppose that is true."

Maybe Maggie counted herself among those women. If so, he would have to convince her otherwise.

"Although," she said with a twinkle in her eye, "I have yet to meet a man who can say the same."

"Ouch." Michael widened his eyes in mock umbrage, placing his hand over his heart, making Maggie laugh again. "I'm wounded."

"Yeah, I can see that." When Maggie smiled, his whole body felt lighter.

"But you do make a good point," he agreed. "A man is always better with the right woman beside him."

He let his gaze hold hers just long enough to see the lovely flush darkening her cheeks. Her eyes lowered shyly. Something strong and powerful coursed through his veins, made his dick as hard as stone.

As much as he would like to continue expressing his ideas on the matter, he heeded the inner warning telling him not to overdo it. He'd given her enough to reflect on. Now that he'd planted the seed of suggestion, he had to let it take root.

"So ..." he said, firming his tone into what Maggie had dubbed his "doctor voice." He hadn't realized he had one, but if it gave her another excuse to tease him, he would use it more often. "I've left you something for the pain. Two tablets every eight hours—with food, if you can manage. They'll make you sleepy, so no operating heavy equipment or driving."

Her lips twitched. "Got it. Keep the tractor in the barn."

He grinned back. "Exactly. And for today at least, consider yourself on bed rest with bathroom privileges."

"Don't you think that's overkill?"

"Not at all. Concussions don't always present themselves right away; you need to be very careful for the first twenty-four to forty-eight hours. Or ... you could let me take you down to the hospital for a quick, pain-less scan and know for sure."

Maggie shook her head—slowly and with great care. "Not happening. I already told you, I'm fine, just a little sore—that's all."

Damn, but the woman is stubborn. Worse, she wasn't being completely honest with him. He could see the pain in her eyes, see the trouble she had with focusing or following anything on her right side. Not to mention, the stillness with which she held herself, as if the slightest movement was difficult. Yet she continued to resist any and all suggestions to get checked out. He'd even offered to do the tests himself if that would make her more comfortable, but she'd refused to consider it.

"Right. Then, you won't mind if I stop back by this evening to check in on you? Say, around six?"

Something sparked in her eyes and then disap-peared as quickly as it had come. She looked down at her hands. "Michael ... just so you know, I don't hold you or your brothers responsible for what happened last night. It was my own fault. It was stupid and care-less and clumsy, but it was an accident."

Michael bristled as her meaning sank in. "Is that why you think I'm here, Maggie? Out of fear of litigation?"

"No, not really," she admitted, her shoulders lifting in the slightest of shrugs. "But perhaps you do have a bit of chivalrous knight in you."

When it came to Maggie, he wanted to be exactly

that. It defied rational explanation, but he refused to analyze it too thoroughly just yet. The bottom line was, Maggie needed someone whether she admitted it or not, and for whatever reason, he wanted to be that person. She might think he felt that way about *all* women, but that couldn't be further from the truth. Would he provide medical care for another injured woman in the same situation? Absolutely. Would he stay the night, make her breakfast, and try to anticipate her every need? Hell no.

"Perhaps. Does that bother you?"

She studied him carefully before answering, "No. I rather like it actually. It suits you."

In the span of a heartbeat, the heaviness lifted, and he felt light again. "Then, my lady, I am satisfied." He bowed deeply, making her giggle. "Now that we've gotten that out of the way, I've programmed my private number into your house and cell phones. I want you to call me immediately if you feel any dizziness or nausea or if you begin to experience blurry vision." He continued on, listing a myriad of other symptoms and warning signs.

When he reached the end of his lengthy instructions, Maggie lifted up a hand and saluted him, though the little smirk she wore as she did so let him know exactly how much she intended to follow them.

Michael exhaled. Maggie was going to be a handful and a half.

He tingled with anticipation.

Maggie remained on the couch for a good several minutes after the sound of Michael's car faded away. Then, she pulled back the comforter and tucked it around George with a kiss to the hound's head.

"He's going to come back!" she told him. "Of course, maybe he was just saying that. Maybe something will conveniently come up, and he won't be able to make it."

George opened his sad, big eyes and gave her a look of reproach.

"No, you're right. If he said he's going to come back, he probably will. I just can't read too much into it—that's all."

George nudged her hand.

"Still, if he's going to make the effort, there should be a hot meal waiting for him. And a fresh batch of cookies, I think. Or even better, a pie. Everyone likes pie, right?"

George wagged his tail.

"Exactly. It's the least I can do."

Leaving George to nap in solitude, Maggie pulled herself to standing, a woman on a mission. Ignoring the ache in her head, she made her way into the kitchen to assemble what she needed. If she moved slowly and with care, the pain was tolerable. If she wanted to have everything ready by dinnertime, there was no time to waste.

FIVE MINUTES into his drive back to the pub, Michael was tempted to turn the car around. Ten to one, Maggie was already off the sofa, doing something she shouldn't. He never should have told her he would be back. If he were smart, he would have simply left and called later to say he was swinging by to check in on her. Or better yet, called her once he was already on his way. That way, she could have spent the day resting, believing that there was no reason to do otherwise.

He forced himself to keep going. Turning back now would only have negative consequences, and that was unacceptable. No, he had to trust that she would take care of herself. She was a grown woman after all. She'd managed most of her life without him. Surely, she'd be fine for a few hours.

Michael jacked the heat up in the Jag, appreciating the heated leather seats. The temperature outside was dropping quickly, no doubt a result of the front that was rolling in. From the moment he'd stepped outside of Maggie's cozy farmhouse, the icy-cold wind had blasted into him, but he suspected the sudden chill he'd felt had less to do with the weather than it did with the separation from the unusual woman who had captured his instant and complete attention.

Maggie. Even her name strummed a chord inside of him. It *fit*, just like everything else about her. Her humility, her sense of humor, her willful stubbornness.

Michael reached out, allowing his fingers to skim

over the plastic Rubbermaid container filled with the chocolate chip cookies she'd insisted he take with him. Warmth radiated outward from the center of his chest, and it wasn't because of the heater.

The slightest hint of Maggie's scent remained in the car. He took a deep breath, letting it fill his lungs while trying to identify it. It was unique—soft yet potent with undertones of warmth and freshness. It conjured images of sunshine and heated embraces, homemade cinnamon rolls, and hot chocolate with a touch of mint. Scents that didn't seem to belong together yet formed a perfect harmony, as complex as the woman herself.

And she was complex—he was certain of that. Last night, she had been a sexy harem girl; this morning, a fresh-faced farm girl. She'd played it cool and wary, but her racing pulse and dilating pupils had belied her interest. She was obviously intelligent but incredibly obstinate whenever he suggested professional medical care.

Michael was more than interested. He was intrigued.

When he pulled into the lot behind the pub nearly a half an hour later, he hadn't managed to come up with any answers, but he would. He glanced at his watch. Ten a.m. He'd told her he'd stop by around six. *Only eight hours to go.*

"Where have you been?" Shane asked when Michael entered through the private entrance into the large kitchen.

Shane gripped a mug of coffee like a lifeline. He was unshaven, and his eyes were bloodshot, but otherwise, he didn't look too worse for wear. The fact that he was alone in the kitchen at that hour spoke volumes. If Callaghan tradition held, the rest of them probably wouldn't make an appearance until noon at least.

Without going into too much detail, Michael explained about Maggie's accident.

"Shit. Is she okay?"

"Yeah, I think so." Michael pictured Maggie as he'd left her—snuggled into the oversize couch with her cheeks pink and her green eyes sparkling. He absently rubbed the center of his chest when that same warming sensation he'd felt in the car earlier started up again.

"*Jesus.*"

"What?"

Shane looked horrified, backing toward the stairs that led up to their living quarters. "You're *smiling.* Fuck, Mick. Not you too."

"I don't know what you're talking about."

Shane groaned, mumbling something about another one biting the dust as he made his way up the stairs. Michael grinned and then began to pull ingredients from the fridge and cupboards.

CHAPTER EIGHT

"**W**hat the hell do you think you're doing?" Ian's voice was hoarse, his eyes red, as he emerged from the room he shared with his fiancée and saw Michael sitting in front of the large hi-def screen.

Michael wasn't surprised. Ian did not take kindly to anyone touching the bank of high-grade computer equipment that took up the length of the entire wall. As the resident genius when it came to anything digital, Ian was very protective of his toys and took it personally if anyone messed with them. For that reason, Ian kept the rest of the family well-stocked with the latest and greatest tech. *His* things were strictly off-limits.

"Drink that," Michael said, indicating a thermos he'd placed beside the monitor.

Ian looked at it skeptically, and then he twisted off the lid and took a sniff.

"The Cure?" Ian blinked in disbelief.

"The Cure," Michael confirmed.

No one knew exactly what was in Michael's Cure, but it was known to end the effects of even the worst bender almost instantly. He rarely mixed it up for anyone, a firm believer in making his brothers reap what they sowed. On those occasions when he did offer it up, it wasn't for free.

"What's the price, bro?"

Michael scanned the room. "Where's Lex?"

"Sleeping," Ian said smugly. "I don't think she'll be getting up anytime soon."

Judging by the arrogant smile on his face, Michael had a pretty good idea how Ian had spent his night. That was one of the benefits of having his wife-to-be nearby after an evening of drinking and watching beautiful women dance seductively around him.

"I need you to run a profile."

"That's all?" Ian asked with suspicion.

"And we keep it between us—for now."

Michael would have preferred to keep Maggie to himself for a while longer, but he believed in being prepared. Ian could provide useful background information and save him time. Besides, they all had their secrets, didn't they?

Ian narrowed his eyes, no doubt suspecting a catch. Michael simply smiled in return. Ian's hangover must have been bad enough to take the risk.

"Done." He snatched up the thermos and downed

the brew before Michael had a chance to change his mind.

Ian stumbled toward the bathroom. Michael made a fresh pot of coffee in the kitchenette and then contented himself with munching on the cookies Maggie had given him while doing a few basic searches. Half the tub was gone by the time Ian emerged fifteen minutes later, showered, shaved, and looking like a new man.

"I'm telling you, Mick, you could make a fortune on that. You're a chemical genius, you know that?"

"Yeah, so you say." But Michael was pleased with his brother's praise.

"You give this to anyone else?"

"No. Only you."

"Awesome." Ian grinned. He grabbed some coffee and sat down, flexing his fingers. "So, who are we stalking today?"

"I want anything and everything you can tell me about Maggie Flynn."

Ian narrowed his eyes. "Personal or business?"

Michael didn't answer. He didn't have to—the look on his face said it all.

Ian smiled knowingly. "Right. Personal then."

With skill, speed, and the knowledge of how to bypass the security on just about any system, Ian quickly assembled a baseline bio. "Magdalena Aislinn Flynn. Age thirty. Only daughter of Rowan and Amelia Flynn, who emigrated back to Ireland when their daughter was just five, leaving her to be raised by her grandparents, both now deceased."

Michael's brows drew together. *Why would a mother and father leave their only child?* "Any idea why?"

Ian shook his head. "No, but I can probably find out, given more time."

Michael considered it. He sensed a story there, but he was already pushing acceptable limits by using Ian's skills to violate Maggie's privacy. He wanted to keep the fact-finding to semi-publicly available general knowledge as much as possible for now. Anything that personal, he would prefer to hear from Maggie herself.

"No, that's fine. Go on."

"She graduated near the top of her class at Pius Catholic High School. Double-majored in business administration and logistics at the state university, where she got her bachelor's. Worked in the city for a while in the IT department of Dumas Industries. Resigned suddenly a little more than a year ago. Never been in trouble with the law, not even so much as a parking ticket. Hey, are those cookies?"

Michael smoothly moved the tub out of Ian's reach without looking up. "What about medical records? Travel info? Phone records?"

Ian's fingers flew across the keyboard. "Last recorded exam was about thirteen years ago. Looks like the mandatory one required for college admission. Nothing remarkable. Guess she has something against doctors." Ian laughed. "Sucks for you, huh?"

Michael shot him a withering glance.

Ian cleared his throat and continued, "No passport. Looks like she was born here. No online reservations in the last five years—unless she used an alias, of course. Has a mobile"—Ian whistled softly—"that she's amassed a total of twenty-seven minutes on. *In the last two years.*"

So, Maggie was quiet and shy, tended to stick close to home, and kept to herself. Had he not seen her house and spent some time with her that morning, it would have been difficult to reconcile those facts with the harem-girl seductress he'd met the night before. Such a huge deviation from what appeared to be her normal, everyday life. It begged him to ask the question, *Why?*

"Ah, here's something. One credit card. Personal, non-business, with accounts at Amazon and Barnes & Noble." Ian chuckled. "Judging by her order history, she's a big fan of Salienne Dulcette. You could arrange an intro, bro. Get in her good graces. Maybe that would help her overlook the whole doctor thing."

Salienne Dulcette, best-selling author of erotic romance nearly ten years running, was well-known to the Callaghans as Stacey Connelly, the wife of one of their cousins in the next town.

"Oh," Ian continued, "and she's purchased at least a dozen exotic dance DVDs—everything from belly dancing to Zumba." Ian sat back, taking a long pull from his coffee mug and eyeing the cookies longingly. "So, what put this woman on your radar, anyway?"

"She's the redhead who danced at your bachelor

party last night. Ended up doing a header off the stage right afterward, giving herself a nice little concussion in the process."

"I'll be damned. Let me guess—you played the role of the concerned physician." Ian's eyes glittered.

"Something like that."

"Did she give you those cookies?"

"Maybe."

Ian's eyes grew almost lusty with longing. "They smell awesome. You're going to share, right?"

Michael pointed to the empty thermos. "I already paid."

"For this," Ian said, waving his hand in front of the computer screen. "Public info—and pretty vanilla stuff at that. You could have discovered that yourself through Google. But for a couple of those"—he pointed at the cookies—"I can tell you what you won't find online."

Michael considered it. Ian would probably offer up the information anyway, but far be it from him to forego such an opportunity when it presented itself— that was just Ian. There was no better source of personal, local information than his roguish brother. Ian was plugged into the local news and gossip. As a general rule, people tended to bare their souls to bartenders, but Ian had turned it into an art form. If there was anything worthwhile to be learned, it would most likely come from his younger sibling.

"Six cookies. If it's worth it, I'll give you six more."

"Mick, it's worth it, trust me." Ian stuffed one of the

cookies into his mouth and chewed; his eyes rolled back in pleasure. "Holy shit, these are good. What is that ... coconut mixed in the dark chocolate? I should take some to Lex."

Ian's bride-to-be, Alexis Kattapoulos, was currently the head chef at one of the hottest restaurants along the East Coast. She coveted traditional, passed-down-through-the-ages type of recipes. Maggie's cookies would be right up her alley.

Michael waited patiently while Ian wolfed down a few more and took another gulp of coffee.

"Okay, so you saw that Maggie worked for Dumas Industries, right?"

Michael nodded. Half the town had worked for Dumas at one point or another; it was easily the largest employer in the county.

"Well, Maggie caught the interest of the golden boy himself, Spencer Dumas."

Michael scowled. He knew Spencer Dumas. The man was the epitome of the wealthy playboy. Never did an honest day's work in his life and had to be pulled out of more than one scrape by his rich father. He made a point to be at every newsworthy event with at least one glamorous female on his arm.

"Maggie doesn't seem to fit his usual type."

"No," Ian agreed. "But rumor has it that Maggie's land *does*."

"Son of a bitch."

"Couldn't have said it better myself. Dumas wined and dined her for months until she finally said yes.

Shortly afterward, she caught him doing the nasty with his personal assistant and overheard him bragging about how slick he was in seducing her. How once they were married, the land would become part of Dumas Industries' assets. Apparently, he wasn't too complimentary in the process either."

No wonder Maggie had been skeptical of his intentions. That must have been what Sherri had been alluding to. It certainly explained a lot. Michael had a sudden, fierce urge to make Spencer Dumas pay for making Maggie doubt herself.

"Maggie broke off the engagement and quit on the spot, leaving Dumas to explain to daddy how he fucked up royally. The company had been depending heavily on acquiring her land. Immediately after she showed Dumas her backside on the way out, the shit hit the fan. Several partner companies backed out of key projects, and DI stock took a decent hit."

"That had to hurt."

Ian laughed. "Yeah, a little. Spencer's been trying to cozy back up to her, saying he's seen the error of his ways, he's a changed man, blah, blah, blah, but she's having no part of it. Actually threatened to slap a restraining order on him if he didn't leave her in peace, though it doesn't look like she followed through."

Michael's chest swelled with pride while a possessive fury burned in his blood. He barely kept his lip from curling back in a snarl. There was no way in hell Spencer Dumas—or any other man for that matter—would be cozying up to Maggie again.

The unfamiliar surge gave him pause. He'd met Maggie less than twenty-four hours earlier, and he knew next to nothing about her. Michael was neither impulsive nor prone to such strong, visceral emotions.

"So, what is she doing now?" he asked, trying to inject some note of rationality into his voice.

Ian swiveled back to the computer. "Looks like she picks up some consulting jobs on the side. She's building up a good reputation, but that takes time, especially if you don't have a lot of connections. Ten to one, Dumas isn't stoked about singing her praises, though I doubt she'd use him as a reference anyway. If her last tax return is accurate, she's barely making ends meet. The property's hers, but the taxes alone on that much acreage are substantial."

"How much are we talking about?"

Ian's fingers danced over the keys. "Two hundred acres at least, all prime agricultural land on the south-facing side of the mountain," he reported. "Maggie's family quietly acquired the land in parcels over the better part of the last century."

Ian paused, looking thoughtful. "Hey, I know that place. Mom used to take us there when we were little to pick our own apples and shit. Had the biggest goddamn pumpkins for Halloween carving too."

Happy, vague memories surfaced. "Older couple? We used to go on hayrides there every fall."

"Yeah! Man, that property has got to be worth a fortune. Southern exposure, overlooks the lake. No wonder Dumas wants it."

Another piece of the Maggie puzzle fell into place. Michael now understood why Maggie had agreed to dance at the bachelor party—because she needed the money. It was the one thing that he hadn't been able to reconcile.

"Thanks, man," he said, pushing the last of the cookies toward Ian.

Michael looked up to find his brother watching him intently.

Ian whistled softly. "So, it's like that, huh?"

"Like what?"

Ian grinned. "Right. The denial stage. I remember it well."

"Fuck off."

Michael returned to his own room, thinking over all he'd learned. It had certainly given him valuable insight into the woman consuming his thoughts and would definitely influence what he did next. He already knew he would be seeing her again—and often.

The snow started falling around noon. Michael showered and dressed, then went down to the bar to hang out with Jake and Ian. The crowd was small, consisting mostly of locals, grabbing a few drinks, shooting pool, and talking about the impending storm. What was originally supposed to be a few inches from a quickly moving clipper was now forecast as an all-out blizzard. Eyes were drawn toward the mounted flat screens as each subsequent weather update seemed worse than the last.

By four o'clock, Michael couldn't sit still any longer. He still had two hours before he was expected at Maggie's, but simply waiting, biding his time, wasn't working for him. He felt anxious, and news of the powerful nor'easter bearing down on them was doing nothing to ease that. Everything Ian had told him weighed heavily on his mind as well. All he could think about was Maggie in that big house, alone, injured.

"I'm heading out," Michael announced, convinced there was no good reason to delay any longer.

He threw an overnight bag in the back of the truck, temporarily exchanging his Jag for one of the many vehicles they kept at his brother Sean's garage. If things went the way he intended, he wouldn't be back this evening.

He was glad he'd left when he did. The usual thirty-minute drive quickly surpassed an hour before he'd even gone halfway. Clearly, the reporters urging people to get their errands done before the bulk of the storm hit weren't broadcasting from the mountain, where the roads were fast becoming treacherous, the visibility measured in mere feet instead of yards.

Michael breathed a sigh of relief when he brought the truck to a stop in front of Maggie's house. The snow was already piling up in drifts along the porch. The weather didn't bother him as much as the thought of breaking his promise to Maggie. At least he was only a few minutes later than he'd said he'd be.

He barely stepped one foot on the porch when the

front door flew open. Maggie stood there, her red hair fanning around her like some kind of ruby halo, her green eyes wide and filled with worry. Michael felt that odd tingling in his chest again.

He offered an apologetic smile as she ushered him inside. "Sorry I'm late."

CHAPTER NINE

Maggie had been watching the news reports on and off all day, waiting for the call from Michael, informing her that he wouldn't be coming. But he hadn't called, and she vacillated between worry and hope that he might try to make it and anticipatory disappointment that he wouldn't.

As the clock drew closer to six, Maggie cleaned up the kitchen and went to the living room to wait. The large window looked out onto the driveway, which was already covered with several inches of heavy, wet snow. It was dark as pitch beyond the meager reach of the porch light; Maggie could see the wicked whirls of white whipping around the porch railings.

Minutes ticked by, the howl of the wind and the rattle of the windows doing nothing to ease her anxiety. As weather and road conditions rapidly worsened, the certainty that Michael wouldn't show grew. Even

George was anxious. He didn't like storms and stuck close by Maggie.

For the hundredth time, Maggie picked up the receiver to make sure she still had a dial tone. Maybe she should call the pub and tell Michael not to bother. She would feel awful if something happened to him because he was worried about her.

Assuming he still planned on coming, that was.

It seemed like an eternity later when she finally saw the slash of powerful headlights cutting through the darkness. With a wave of profound relief, Maggie limped her way to the front door as fast as her aching body would allow.

"You came," she said in a sudden rush of breath as she helped him take off his coat.

Michael had come, just like he'd said he would, despite the weather, and he was safe. Maggie didn't know whether to hug him or beat him over the head with a log from the fireplace for risking the treacherous roads.

"You doubted me?" he asked, half of his mouth tilted upward in that crooked smile.

HER RETURNING smile lit a fire in the center of his chest. And the look in her eyes, the one that told him how genuinely happy she was to see him when she had clearly expected not to, made him glad he'd left early. Any later, and the roads might have been closed.

That wouldn't have stopped him from keeping his promise, but it would have slowed him down considerably.

"I guess I shouldn't have, huh?"

"Never doubt me, Maggie," he said, his blue eyes intense as he gazed down at her.

Her lips parted slightly in response, and Michael fought a strong urge to kiss her right there in the foyer.

"I'll try to remember that," she replied softly.

She took his hand and led him toward the kitchen. Warmth spread through him from the point of contact.

"Are you hungry?"

"I am." It would have been rude, he thought, to say that his mouth was watering from the heavenly aromas that had hit him as soon as she opened the door. "But first things first. Sit down and let me take a look at you."

Maggie flashed her green eyes at him, the hint of defiance on her face, but she did as he'd asked, and Michael silently acknowledged the small victory. Sitting dutifully at the kitchen table, she allowed him to examine her. Her eyes never left his, making it difficult for him to concentrate. Something told him she knew this. But when she leaned slightly forward and he realized she was inhaling discreetly, he almost lost his train of thought completely.

"Do I pass?" she asked when he finished.

He hesitated to answer. On the surface, everything appeared all right, but something nagged at him. It was more of a gut feeling than anything he could put his finger on, and Callaghan men put a hell of a lot of trust in their instincts.

"How's the headache?"

"Not too bad."

The way she averted her eyes led him to believe she wasn't being entirely truthful.

"You're about due for another dose of meds."

"I'm fine," she said with a dismissive wave of her hand.

The feeling in his gut intensified. His eyes narrowed. "Maggie, you *did* take the pain pills I'd left for you this morning, didn't you?"

She stood and walked over to the stove, where a huge Dutch oven sat, her limp no less pronounced than it had been that morning. Had she stayed off of it as he'd advised, there should have been some improvement.

"I made some stew. Would you like some?"

"Maggie, you were supposed to take the pills and stay off your feet today."

"I don't like pills." She pulled two ceramic bowls from a nearby cupboard and began ladling the stew into them. She placed one bowl in front of him and one adjacent to him, avoiding his eyes. "And I get bored easily."

"Maggie."

She hobbled back to the brick chimney and removed a fresh loaf of crusty bread from the oven, placing it on a cutting board with a bowl of whipped butter, and then she brought that over as well.

"*Maggie.*"

Turning on her heel, she grabbed a pitcher of iced tea from the refrigerator and two glasses before she finally sat down.

With anyone else, he would have been annoyed with their blatant refusal to acknowledge him, but with her, he wasn't. Especially when he noticed her trying to hide the tiny quirk at the corner of her mouth. She was teasing him with her defiance. He liked that show of spirit. What he didn't like, however, was that she obviously wasn't taking care of herself the way she should.

With substantial effort, Michael fixed her with his best stern look. "As wonderful as this looks and smells, you were supposed to be resting, not cooking all day."

"I did rest"—she insisted, unfazed by the use of his authoritative physician's tone—"for a while. But I need to eat, don't I?"

"Most people would pop a frozen dinner in the microwave or open up a can of soup, not make a home-made stew and bake their own bread."

She lifted her shoulders in a subtle shrug and looked down into her bowl. Once again, the truth struck him like a bolt of lightning. She hadn't done this for herself. She'd done it for *him*. Because he had told her he would be coming back. Suddenly, he felt like the world's biggest ass.

"It smells wonderful, Maggie."

She lifted her head and offered him a small smile that made his heart clench. She'd prepared this for him despite the fact that she was hurting, and he'd chastised her for it.

Michael tried a spoonful of the stew. He closed his eyes, savoring the taste. A perfect blend of vegetables —carrots, potatoes, a tiny bit of corn, onions, tomatoes —tasted as fresh as if they'd just been picked from the garden. The beef was so tender that it practically melted against his tongue. *Damn, but the woman knew how to cook.*

"This is amazing," he said truthfully and was rewarded with a full-fledged smile. "Do you cook like this all the time?"

"It's no big deal," she said, but he could see that she was pleased.

"So, tell me, Maggie, what do you do? Besides dance and cook, that is." He bit into the crusty bread, stifling a groan as it, too, melted in his mouth.

"My dancing skills are definitely lacking," she said, lightly tapping her bruised face.

"For the record, I think you are a wonderful dancer. It's walking you seem to have a problem with."

Maggie gave a soft feminine snort and continued as if he hadn't spoken, "And I cook out of a combination of necessity and boredom. But officially, I suppose I'm what you would call a logistical analyst."

"A logistical analyst? What exactly is that?"

"Well, I look at a business, see what its needs are, and then draw up and execute a plan to make that happen." She sighed. "Call it a professional organizer, if you will. You'd be surprised how inefficiently most offices are run."

Michael nodded, thinking of some of the red tape he'd had to deal with at the hospital, and encouraged her to continue.

"I got my BA, worked for a couple of small businesses in town, and then applied for a position at Dumas Industries."

"Big place," he said carefully, wondering how much she would share with him.

"Yeah. They kept me busy." She frowned. "I don't work there anymore though."

"Why not?"

She looked away, slicing another piece of bread for herself. She had yet to touch the first one, he noticed. "I guess I just wasn't cut out for the corporate life."

It was interesting how she hadn't really answered his question but hadn't lied to him either. Was she embarrassed by what had happened with Dumas? Given the little bit he knew about her, probably.

"Not everyone is."

"What about you?" she asked in a blatant change of subject. "Do you practice independently, or are you involved in a partnership?"

"Independently."

Maggie looked down at her hands, breaking the slice of bread into smaller pieces with her fingers, absently feeding them to George. Her eyes were doing that swirling, flashing thing again; he could practically see the wheels turning in her head.

"Do you have an office downtown?"

"No, I keep an office at the hospital."

He was a doctor, but most of his "practice" did not involve the general population. He and his brothers—all former Navy SEALs—now ran a covert team, completely off the books. He couldn't explain that to Maggie, however. Not yet.

"That's a bit unusual, isn't it?" She kept her tone light, but he could sense her curiosity.

She'd probably been doing some investigating of her own. She wouldn't have found much—Ian was a master at covering their tracks. On the plus side, the fact that she'd been following up indicated interest, didn't it? After all, he'd spent the afternoon doing the same thing, although he'd had the benefit of Ian's mad skills.

"Perhaps," he admitted.

How much dare he tell her?

That depends, he answered himself. *How much do you want her to know?*

Everything, came the immediate response.

"I do a lot of pro bono for the hospital," he said slowly, watching her reaction closely. "In return, they provide me with an office and use of the facilities."

"Oh." She considered that for a moment. "Doesn't sound very lucrative."

"It's not. There are some things more important than money."

She nodded. "Yes, that's true enough. Although it sure does make life easier when you have enough to get by." She added that second part so softly that he guessed she hadn't meant for him to hear it.

Three bowls of stew later, Michael finally forced himself back from the table. "That was fantastic, Maggie. I can't remember when I've eaten so much in one sitting."

"You have a good appetite." She smiled. "A fine mon's appetite," she added, coloring her words with a distinctive Irish accent.

Michael raised an eyebrow. She seemed to have a knack for doing little things that surprised him.

"That's what my grandmother would say," she explained, slipping into the familiar brogue once again. " 'Ah, Maggie darlin', 'tis a man with a good appetite you'll be wantin'. A good appetite an' a fine arse te hold on te when he's givin' you a good tuppin'.' "

She laughed at Michael's slightly shocked but definitely amused expression. Her eyes twinkled mischievously. "She would have *loved* you."

Is she talking about my appetite or my ass?

"This place seems so much bigger without her," she said wistfully. "My grandmother was a tiny woman, but she was filled with so much life and love."

There was a sadness in her eyes he hadn't seen before, and he knew instinctively that he was seeing a side of her not many got to see.

"You miss her."

"Terribly," Maggie admitted with a heavy sigh. "Have you ever known someone who understood you?

I mean, *really* understood you? Who knew what you were feeling without words, without doing anything more than just looking at you? Gram was like that. With me anyway. Gramps used to say we were cut from the same cloth."

"Then, I'm sure she was a remarkable woman."

Maggie studied his face, as if trying to gauge his sincerity. Her eyes softened, just enough to make him believe he'd passed the test.

She stood, gathering their bowls and silverware.

Maggie hadn't eaten much. Throughout the meal, she'd spent more time playing with her food than eating it. George benefited by having the remains scraped into his dish. Her lack of appetite, combined with her slow, deliberate movements, suggested she was still hurting. The fact that she'd gone to all this trouble for him—despite what she'd said—tugged at his heart.

Michael took the dishes out of her hands. "You've done more than enough, Maggie. Sit down for a while and let me take care of these, okay?"

"Doctor's orders?" She smiled.

"Absolutely."

"Then, I guess I'd better listen." She eased herself back into the chair and let him take over.

It pleased him greatly that she'd heeded his advice. George was curled up at her feet; she lazily stroked his side with her good foot while she propped the other on another chair.

"So, tell me, Dr. Callaghan," she said a few minutes

later, "do you take this much of a personal interest in all of your patients?"

"No," he answered honestly.

The only sounds in the kitchen were the howl of the wind outside, the soft clink of dishes as he washed them and placed them in the drainer, and George's rumbling snores. He finished with the dishes, carefully folding the towel and draping it over the edge of the sink.

He turned and caught Maggie watching him with an odd expression on her face. It was unguarded, almost longing. She covered it quickly.

"Would you like some pie?" she asked, getting up stiffly.

"You made a pie too?" he asked incredulously. He couldn't decide if he was impressed or exasperated with her seeming inability to sit still for more than five minutes.

"Apples from the orchard." She shrugged. "Might as well use them. A slice of pie would go great with some of that heavenly stuff you managed to brew this morning, if you're willing."

"It's a deal."

While the coffee brewed, Maggie stuck the pie in the oven to warm it up.

Michael tried—and failed—not to stare at her backside as she bent over. "So, you get a lot of apples?"

"Apples, peaches, cherries, pears, apricots. Bushels and bushels of them."

"What do you do with them all?"

"A substantial amount goes to waste. I'd venture to say I've got the fattest deer this side of the Appalachians," she said with a smile. " I preserve what I can, dehydrate a bunch, make lots of jams and whatnot. Give a lot away, too. I have more in my basement than I could use in a lifetime."

"You're kidding."

"Nope. Wanna see?"

Maggie asked him to precede her, keeping one hand on his shoulder as they made their way down the steep, narrow stairway to the cellar. An old bar had been riveted against the stone foundation wall that could be used as a handrail, but there was no railing to grasp on to on the other side. When they reached the bottom, Michael looked in wonder at the massive ancient timbers that shored up the house, the dirt floor, and the walls of rough-hewn granite stone. Along with the smell of earth, he was hit with a heady mixture of spices.

He blinked once and then twice. It looked like an old-fashioned farmers market. A multitude of layered, hand-knotted baskets hung from the timbers, holding onions, garlic, potatoes, and yams. Huge bunches of aromatic, dried herbs were suspended as well, neatly tagged with handwritten cards: rosemary, basil, parsley, oregano—not to mention, several varieties of mints and herbs Michael knew was used to brew homeopathic teas.

But none of that compared to the walls of shelving containing hundreds of jars of canned peaches, pears, apples, applesauce, jams, butters, tomatoes, sauces, pickles, carrots, corn ...

"You did all this?"

"Uh-huh," she said modestly. "I have a big garden."

Well, he'd been right about one thing. The woman obviously couldn't sit still for a moment.

CHAPTER TEN

Though he wouldn't have believed himself capable of swallowing another bite, Michael polished off a large piece of Maggie's home-made apple pie while she sipped coffee.

"Maggie, I don't know what to say," he said finally, wiping his mouth. "Everything was delicious."

Maggie's eyes shone. "Thanks. It's nice to have someone to cook for."

George chose that moment to let out a soulful woof, prompting Michael to give him the last bite of the pie.

"Excluding you, of course, George," she added lightly.

"One thing is certain," Michael told her. "My brothers aren't coming here. You'll never get rid of them."

Maggie laughed. "An entire kitchen filled with

Callaghans. Now, that's an image." She sipped at her coffee. "I get the sense that you are all close."

"Very," Michael agreed. "Do you have any brothers or sisters?"

"No," she said softly. "Just me."

There was a hint of sadness to her voice, and he sensed there was a story there, but she didn't elaborate. Hopefully, Maggie would eventually feel comfortable enough to share some of those personal thoughts with him.

Maggie put her hand up to her mouth, stifling a yawn.

"You're tired."

"Just a little," she replied with an embarrassed smile.

Her lashes fluttered. Once again, he felt that strange energy coursing through his chest.

"Maybe I should be going, so you can get some rest."

The change was instantaneous. Her eyes widened, and she sat up suddenly, eliciting a protest from George when she inadvertently poked him with her toes. "You want to leave? Now? In the middle of a blizzard?"

Hell no, I don't want to leave. His desire to stay had nothing to do with the weather and everything to do with the woman regarding him with those pretty green eyes. The one who'd fed him homemade stew and bread and eased a loneliness inside him he hadn't known he had. The one who'd, only moments before, had eyes filled with such longing that his heart ached.

But as much as he wanted to stay, he had to think of her and what she wanted.

He hesitated, then decided to be honest with her. "I really enjoy being with you, Maggie, and I don't want to do anything that might jeopardize seeing you again. That includes overstaying my welcome."

Her lips parted slightly, as if she was caught off guard by his words. "You had no problem staying last night."

"You were semiconscious. I didn't think leaving you alone was a viable option." *Not that I wanted to*, he added silently.

"I see." She bit her bottom lip, and he noticed her eyes swirling again. When she spoke, it was slowly and deliberately, as if she was working through a particularly complex problem. "So, as a doctor, that would have gone against your sense of duty and responsibility."

He searched her face for some clue as to what she was thinking but found nothing, except the subtle glimmer in her eyes. "I guess you could say that."

"Well then, you should probably know that I'm not feeling that great right now."

The glimmer brightened as she looked up at him from beneath slightly hooded eyes, and a tendril of hope began to bloom.

"No?"

"No. I'm feeling a bit light-headed in fact."

"Definitely not a good sign," he said, shaking his head with concern as he stepped closer, closing the gap between them. Both of his hands cupped her face, his gaze intense. "Any nausea?"

She put her hand on her belly. It was a nice touch. "Maybe a little."

"Hmm." He lowered his head and looked deeply into her eyes while stroking her cheek with his thumb. "Double vision?"

"Yes," she said breathlessly. "Lots of that."

He bit back a smile and gave her his best stern doctor look. "Maggie, I don't think I should leave you alone tonight."

Her eyes swirled and flashed. "It would totally go against your Hippocratic oath."

He smiled slowly. Her lips, parted slightly, were impossible to resist. He dipped his head, and when she stretched toward him, there was no reason to deny the invitation. The moment his lips touched hers, he was lost. They were so soft, so welcoming, and felt so good against his own.

Michael inhaled her sweet breath, took it into his body. It was like a drug, intoxicating and highly addictive. When her lips parted further, he reveled in the taste of sweetness and cinnamon. Someone moaned, but whether it was him or her, he didn't know.

Maggie's arms snaked up around his neck when he deepened the kiss, his hands finding their way downward to her lower back, pulling gently. She responded, pressing her body against his.

An eternity later, Michael somehow found the strength to pull away, though he kept his arms around her. His heart pounded; his breath came hard and fast. Never had a kiss had such a complete and devastating effect on him. Maggie's arms clung to his neck, her lips red and slightly swollen from his kisses, head tilted to him in surrender, eyes closed. The image of her, just like that, would forever be burned into his mind.

MAGGIE WAS glad Michael was holding her because her legs had gone weak, threatening her ability to stand on her own. *Lord, but the man knew how to kiss!* She no longer had to pretend she was feeling dizzy; Michael and his kisses had shattered her internal sense of balance. She tried to remember the warning symptoms he'd told her to look out for, those that might indicate a serious concussion, but her mind could think of nothing but him.

She opened her eyes slowly to find him staring at her, looking every bit as surprised as she felt. She took great personal satisfaction in that; clearly, she was not the only one affected.

"No one has ever kissed me like that before," she whispered, her gaze dropping to his mouth. "Would you mind very much if I asked you to do it again?"

Thankfully, he was eager to comply.

"MICHAEL," she murmured sometime later.

She was snuggled in his lap in front of the fire, his arms around her, his hands roaming lazily over her back and shoulders along with the outside of her thighs and calves as they made out like teenagers. His hands felt so good, so warm and strong and capable. Even though he kept his caresses to "safe" areas, they ignited a slow burn that heated her from the inside out. The man must have incredible self-control; other than an occasional deep-throated growly sound and nibble, he'd kept his kisses above the shoulders and his fondling PG. She knew he was aroused—she could feel the hardened proof of it beneath her bottom—yet he made no move to take things further. It was both a relief and a disappointment.

"Hmm?" he answered, his voice muffled as he pressed his lips to the underside of her jaw. Each time he did, it elicited a shiver that ran from the top of her head to the tips of her toes.

"I think we lost power."

The only light in the room came from the dwindling fire. The steady background hum of appliances and radiators was noticeably absent with only the muffled pelting of snow and ice against the side of the sturdy house.

He chuckled into her neck, sending vibrations against her throat. "It went off over an hour ago, Maggie."

"Did it now?"

"Mmhmm."

"Michael?"

"Hmm?"

"Thank you for staying."

Maggie's body was on fire for him. Her breasts were swollen and painful, begging to be touched. Though he'd come close several times, he'd redirected his hands at the last second. As he kissed her expertly, she couldn't help but wonder what it would be like if he took one of her breasts in his mouth, teased her with that wicked tongue of his, and nipped at the hardened points like he was doing to her neck.

She shifted in his lap, a subtle attempt to relieve some of the ache in her center. It was agonizing and electric at the same time, a rhythmic pulse extending down into her wet, throbbing sex. For the first time in her life, Maggie felt empty. Along with that thought came the certain knowledge that Michael could easily remedy that with the impressively large, hard bulge currently pressing against her bottom.

Maggie shuddered at the low growl that rumbled through his body and into hers, intensifying her desire to have him inside her. To cradle his narrow hips between her thighs and welcome him into her body. Judging by his erection, he wanted her, too, yet he made no move to progress beyond kissing.

It's ironic, she thought vaguely, *that the first man I would say yes to isn't asking.*

"Are you cold?" he asked in that deep voice when she shivered again.

"No." She felt unbearably warm in fact, and some

parts felt *hot*. Those shivers and that tremble in her voice were solely a result of her burning desire, desire that he had stoked to dangerous levels.

MICHAEL INHALED SLOWLY. Deeply. This woman set him on fire from the inside out. He had to get a grip on his control before he flipped her over the sofa and pounded into her like his body wanted to. God help him, his dick was like cast iron, his balls tight and aching. She was so deliciously soft, every lush feminine curve and swell begging for his attention. As much as he wanted to be inside her body, he wanted to be inside her heart as well—and for a lot longer than one night.

Ian had tried to explain to him once what it felt like when he first met Lexi. "It's like when you finally return after being on a mission for weeks. You come over the crest of the mountain, and everything's dark. Then, suddenly, you see a million twinkling lights in the valley, welcoming you, and you just know you're *home*, where you belong, and there is nowhere else on earth you'd rather be."

Yeah, thought Michael, staring into the sparkling eyes of the woman in his arms, *it's like that exactly*.

He'd never felt anything remotely similar for a woman, and it was staggering. From the moment he'd laid eyes on her, she'd called to something deep within him, awakening a need he hadn't even realized he had.

He wasn't about to do anything to jeopardize that even if it meant standing outside in the frigid temperature to cool himself off.

With great reluctance, he called upon his will while he still had some remaining. "I'll put a few more logs on the fire." With another lingering kiss, Michael eased her from his lap.

She stared at him in the firelight, her eyes luminescent, her hair mussed—all his doing, of course. She looked at him with so much hunger, so much possession, that his heart skipped a beat. He imagined his eyes looked very much like that as well, if the need coursing through his body and pulsing in his groin was any indication.

"It's late," he said, a husky rasp to his voice. "You should rest."

Maggie nodded. Her dreamy expression transitioned to uncertainty before it evened out into something less readable. Surely, she couldn't believe he'd *wanted* to stop?

She wrapped her arms around herself. "It makes sense to camp out in here, I think. There won't be any heat upstairs. It's what I usually do when the power goes out."

The reds and golds of the flames reflected in the clear green of her eyes, creating stunningly beautiful shades of gold and brown.

"Does that happen often?"

She shrugged. "Often enough. It's an old house."

Michael made a mental note to check the circuit

boxes first thing in the morning. At that moment, the most important thing on his agenda was getting Maggie to rest.

Maggie created a cozy nest of blankets and pillows in front of the fireplace while Michael brought in enough firewood to last through the night as well as the overnight bag he'd stashed in the truck. Satisfied that everything was in order, he sank down, wondering just how he was going to manage being in the same room with her all night without touching her. Even time in the snow and icy wind hadn't diminished his arousal. Not to mention, her scent permeated the space. And he couldn't be held responsible for his actions if she continued to look at him with those big green eyes—eyes that begged him to take her. Clearly, she had no idea that beneath his calm, controlled exterior lay a beast that wanted nothing more than to ravish and claim her in the most primitive way possible.

He swallowed hard when she reentered the room. She wore the same flannel shirt he'd wrapped her in at the pub with fleecy ankle socks, and she smelled of vanilla-mint toothpaste. The shy way she looked at him from beneath her long, dark lashes with the firelight reflected in her hair had him spellbound. He'd always considered himself a strong-willed man, but then again, he'd never known the likes of Maggie Flynn.

As if it was the most natural thing in the world, she curled up next to him on the floor. Her hair, now freed from the clips that had held it in place, fell over his arm like crimson silk. Her warmth seeped into him, making his cock pulse beneath the sweats he'd changed into.

"Maggie?" He was about to suggest she move up to the sofa, where she would be more comfortable.

She lifted her head, pinning him with a gaze that nearly rendered him helpless.

"Is this all right?" she asked, a doubt in her voice that hadn't been there before. "I just thought ..." She didn't finish, casting her eyes downward, her face flushing a furious dark pink as she began to push away, mumbling an apology.

"Maggie," he said softly, his arm reaching out to coax her back into him. "No more thinking." He tucked her against him, relishing the perfect fit of her body to his. He would find some way to tether his surging lust if it meant being close to her like this.

He felt, rather than saw, her relief as her body melted into his.

"Good night, Michael."

She snuggled back into him, and within minutes, her deep, even breaths told him she was asleep. He curled his arm around her protectively, drifting off himself a short time later.

CHAPTER ELEVEN

Maggie awoke with a terrible ache that had nothing to do with her recent injuries and everything to do with the hard male wrapped around her. Her face was tucked into his neck, her leg nestled between his powerful thighs. Something long and thick pressed into the soft flesh of her belly, no doubt a major source of her lusty discomfort.

She rocked slightly against him, silently delighting in his response—a deep, low-throated groan and the flex of his large hand on her behind. No man had ever inspired such carnal desires in her before. Fevered and anxious, a hungry need clawed in her core so deeply that it bordered on frightening.

She'd experienced arousal before but nothing even remotely close to this. Reading Salienne Dulcette's steamy novels didn't compare to the reality of Michael's hot, hard body against hers. Beneath the soft flannel, her breasts swelled, and her sex grew wet in blind, hopeful anticipation. She rocked again, relishing the delicious grind where she needed it most.

A tiny part of her was ashamed by her lack of self-control. Even when they'd been making out earlier, she'd boldly straddled his lap. If he'd tried to take things further, she wouldn't have stopped him.

But he hadn't. While his kisses had been filled with passion, he'd kept his touches frustratingly tame.

There could be many reasons for that—several of them honorable. He'd certainly seemed interested enough, so she decided to be cautiously optimistic. At that moment, however, there was little chance of her getting any sleep unless she found some way to relieve the worst of the ache. Rubbing against him like a cat in heat, while pleasurable, was only stoking the fire within.

Under normal circumstances, she wouldn't even consider what she was about to do, but she was desperate. And really, it was all his doing. If he wasn't so damn gorgeous; if his body hadn't been made for hot, sweaty, epic sex; if he hadn't nearly brought her to orgasm with little more than his kisses and deft caresses ... what woman wouldn't be just shy of a core meltdown?

She had to do *something* if she wanted to get any rest. Jumping the man in his sleep probably wasn't the best idea. Clearly, he wasn't ready to go there yet. That left only one viable alternative.

She carefully extracted herself from his hold. He

frowned in his sleep, reaching for her as she pulled away. She whispered against his ear, promising to return soon, and stroked his hair until he relaxed. Given the intensity and sense of urgency simmering in her blood, this wouldn't take long. He wouldn't even know she was gone.

MICHAEL'S first thought when he woke was how cold he was. Maggie had been like a perfect little heater, warming him from the outside in. Of course, no other form of heat had made him ache quite so fiercely.

He reached out and ran his hand over the blanket where she had been. The spot beside him still held warmth, so she hadn't been gone long. He rose to add a few more logs to the dwindling fire. George was snoring loudly in front of the hearth, but Maggie was nowhere to be seen.

Outside, the blizzard continued to rage mercilessly. Some nor'easters could last up to several days, and this one appeared to have that kind of staying power. Not that he minded. Being stranded with Maggie was the best possible way to ride out the storm.

After ten minutes passed and she still hadn't returned, Michael's unease grew. The kitchen was dark, and the door to the downstairs bathroom was wide open, the candles she'd lit flickering softly. A check of the other rooms on the first floor came up empty as well.

He grabbed a flashlight and went toward the entrance to the basement. Perhaps she'd gone down to check the circuit breaker.

"Maggie?" he called softly, opening the door.

There was no answer, no telltale glow down below, only silence and darkness.

He closed the basement door and then made his way up the steps on silent feet. He didn't want to startle her or impose on her privacy. He just needed to make sure she was okay, and then he would slip back into the living room to wait for her.

Michael ran one hand through his hair. When had he become so protective? What was it about this woman that turned him inside out?

The wind howled. Snow and ice pelted noisily against the side of the house. Below, the fire crackled and sizzled as the sap from the new logs heated and popped. But there was another sound too. A low, barely audible hum. He turned at the top of the stairs, trying to pinpoint the source.

There! The soft glow of candlelight was visible in the slight opening beneath one of the closed doors.

Like a ghost, Michael drifted silently down the hallway. The closer he drew, the more fixated he became on the sound. Laying his ear against the door, he heard the muffled hum, along with another sound. One that had his heart beating frantically and his lungs incapable of drawing a full breath.

His hand turned the knob slowly so as not to make a sound. The door swung open noiselessly. Michael flicked off the flashlight and stepped inside. A candle in an old-fashioned holder, complete with looped handle and drip tray, burned atop a dresser just inside the door. The hum came from the far corner, back in the shadows, beneath a pile of blankets.

Dear God, he prayed fervently, *don't let that be what I think it is.* He wouldn't survive it.

The top of Maggie's head was barely visible, but her soft, whispered moans were as loud as if someone had hardwired an amplifier directly into his brain. Each one was like an erotic stroke right where it had the greatest impact.

His feet carried him forward without conscious thought, his eyes adjusting to the darkness. Her body undulated rhythmically beneath the blankets, unaware of his presence. Eyes closed, lips parted slightly, she was the sexiest thing he'd ever seen.

Suddenly, her eyes flew open and locked on his. She froze, the horror of being caught evident in her eyes.

"Don't stop," he begged, his voice as rough as sandpaper as he tried to speak through his tightened throat. "Please, Maggie, don't stop."

She eyed him warily as he reached out and pulled the covers away, sucking in a breath when he found her hands between her thighs, panties pulled to the side, the gentle hum of her mini vibrator unmistakable.

He'd been so good. He was a strong man. But this was just too much.

"You're beautiful," he said in awe as he eased down beside her. He placed one of his hands over hers and cupped it over her sex. "Don't stop," he whispered again, the wonder in his voice unmistakable.

Slowly, tentatively, she obeyed him. He watched, fascinated, as she sought to satisfy her own need. Her eyes widened when he slid his hand down into the waistband of his pants and gripped himself. With a new hunger sparkling in her eyes, she boldly threw her head back and arched before him. He groaned.

"Jesus," he muttered, unable to tear his eyes away from her. "That is the hottest fucking thing I've ever seen."

"Show me," she commanded softly, her husky voice a hard tug on his cock.

That voice was pure fantasy. Deep and throaty, breathless and thick with desire.

Her gaze dropped from his face to the hand concealed within his pants. Obediently, he pulled them down over his hips. Her eyes widened at the sight of his fully erect manhood straining toward her. He began to stroke himself in synchronization with the subtle rise and fall of her hips.

Michael leaned over and single-handedly unbuttoned the flannel shirt—*his* flannel shirt—to reveal her creamy skin and lush breasts. Unable to resist, he took one hard nipple into his mouth. Her whispered moan became a soft cry that nearly did him in. He scraped the diamond tip with his teeth and then sucked. *Hard.*

IT FELT SO GOOD, so damn good. Her initial embarrassment fled, shoved aside with brutal force by the wave of desire Michael had created. It continued to build, lifting her higher and higher. The need grew more urgent, obliterating rational thought until all she could do was *feel*. Feel his lips. Feel his teeth. Feel the press of his heated flesh in the chill of the room.

He tortured her with his mouth, sucking and biting with stinging nips that made her cry out, followed by long, languorous licks that made her shudder and moan. There was no doubt about it—this man knew more about what she needed than she did, and she would willingly surrender to his expertise.

She felt the wave beginning to crest, but it was so much more powerful than anything she had experienced at her own hand. The tension, the pressure, continued to rise, and she was afraid to open her eyes. Her movements became erratic, her breaths shallow and ragged. And then, just when she was about to break into a thousand tiny pieces, that was when, in one swift motion, he pulled the vibrator from her hand and ripped her panties away, burying his face, nose to chin, against her sex.

She cried out again in surprise but welcomed him by burying her fingers in his hair and pulling him closer. No man had ever gone down on her before. She'd read about it, dreamed about it, imagined it, but the reality was so much better. He murmured against her, a litany of curses and praises that only partially registered in her fevered brain.

"Ah, Maggie," he moaned. "That's it, baby. So sweet."

He pulled her legs up over his shoulders for a better angle as he flattened his tongue and gave her a long, slow lick. Her entire body shuddered beneath him, and he smiled wickedly. Michael glanced up at her face, saw her looking at him with half-lidded eyes heavy with desire and desperate with need. He knew then that it was a look he wanted to see over and over again.

"Michael," she gasped. The sound of his name in that breathless, pleading voice sent a fresh wave of need through him. "Michael, please. Don't stop."

Happy to oblige, Michael dipped his head and continued where he had left off.

Ah fuck, he thought as he greedily lapped at her. She tasted like candy. Like some decadent dessert. Like *his*.

Possession fired through his body. *His* Maggie. Her scent, her taste were a part of him forever now, burned into his senses like a brand.

His lips kissed hers, tugging lightly. His tongue dipped inside her, coating itself with her sweet cream. His long arms reached around her legs and fondled her breasts, so full and heavy, spilling over his palms.

"Oh God, Michael, I'm coming … I'm coming …"

Her cry was a desperate plea, accentuated by the sharp pull on his hair.

He redoubled his efforts, sliding his tongue across and around her most sensitive spots and then dipping inside her as he felt the first tremor. Refusing to let up, he continued his feast until her legs squeezed hard and began to shake. Her entire body arched and then seized as the powerful orgasm overtook her, but not once did she release her hold, taking him along for the ride.

She was beautiful in the throes of her climax, her response raw and primal. As she rode the crest, he placed himself between her legs, his thick, swollen head pressed against her entrance. Her eyes widened again, but she reached for him. He pushed into her, inch by glorious inch as she stretched around him, thankful for the deluge of wetness that eased his passage.

Finally seated balls deep, Michael slipped his arms beneath her while she continued to squeeze around him. Each contraction was powerful, gripping him in a series of rippling waves. He clenched his back teeth and remained still, fighting against the seed rising within him. *Just a little longer.* He needed to last just a little longer.

Relishing the perfect way she sheathed him, he kissed her until she stopped shaking. Then, he met her eyes, humbled by the desire he saw there. As if reading his thoughts, Maggie reached her hands up and grasped his shoulders.

There, in the sweet cradle of Maggie's embrace, he was on the brink of paradise.

Michael remained still, fighting the urge to pound into her. He hung heavy against her slick folds, filled to bursting, tight with need, and aching for release. But not yet. He wanted to savor the moment. To bask in the feel of her around him. To memorize the image of her just like this—sated and anticipating his pleasure.

He raked his eyes over her. No hard, tight body here, just lush feminine curves that made his heart pound and his cock harder than iron. Round, full breasts that spilled over his palms—breasts that he could spend hours, days, nuzzling and fondling. A curvy waist with the tiniest swell that trembled when he kissed it. Perfectly proportioned hips that he could grab on to while he took her repeatedly.

He loved that he could grasp her flesh in his hands, that he could squeeze and knead and nibble. Her soft swells and dips yielded to his harder planes, allowing his body to sink into hers. This—*this*—was a woman made for pleasing a man, for making him forget everything, except the most basic and primal of urges. He wanted to possess her so fiercely and thoroughly that no other man ever entered her thoughts again. Even now, he continued to swell and harden, anxious to get on with it, but he refused to hurt her. He would allow nothing to mar this perfect union.

She rolled her hips, just a tiny movement but one that let him know it was okay for him to continue. With care, he pulled back, his muscles tense from the effort of restraint, then eased forward slowly, deeper and deeper until his tip hit her cervix. He followed that with another stroke and another, measured and controlled, until she became accustomed to his girth. Despite the chill of the unheated room, sweat broke out on his brow. When seed began to pool in his shaft, he forced himself to stop once again.

Maggie cupped his head and looked into his eyes. "Don't stop," she whispered.

Did she have any idea what she was asking? Did she know just how hard it was not to pound into her, the need to claim and brand her as his own a tangible thing?

"Take me," she begged, saying the words he needed to hear. "Take me like you need to. Like I need you to."

Something snapped inside him then, and the last of his control shattered. He pulled out and slammed into her, hard and commanding.

"Yes!" she cried out, not in pain, but in encouragement. "Yes, Michael, like that, just like that." Her nails dug into his shoulders, marking him, demanding more.

Hearing his name on her lips in the throes of passion, feeling her score his flesh with her nails as she welcomed him into her body, did something to him. He pulled out and slammed into her again and again, gratefully accepting everything she offered. He would care for her later, pamper her and soothe her and coddle her, but now, he just *needed*.

"Take me," he rasped, his voice barely recognizable. As she'd begged him to take her, so he did the same. "Take me, Maggie, please. Oh *fuck* ..." His plea broke off in a gasp as he felt his seed rising. He couldn't stop it this time.

"Yes," she whispered and tilted her hips, accepting him. She wrapped her legs around him and cried out his name.

Michael felt her clamp down around him, milking him, drawing him into her as she was consumed by a second powerful orgasm.

With a final thrust, he let himself go. It was impossible to get deep enough, to hold her close enough. Her body arched and convulsed against his in rapturous bliss, the ecstasy nearly unbearable.

An eternity later, his cock drained, her cries now reduced to sated purrs against his ear, weakness overwhelmed him. He shuddered and collapsed, barely catching himself on his elbows as her arms and legs clutched him to her.

In those moments, Michael knew true happiness. His mind, body, and soul were in perfect harmony as he lay in Maggie's arms. Her heart beat strong against his chest; her breath feathered warm air across his skin. Aftershocks rocked through his body, the searing euphoria settling into contentment.

He rolled to the side, taking Maggie with him until he was beneath her and she was spread atop him. He pulled the covering over her and cocooned them both in warmth. He loved the way her body blanketed his, loved the way his hands fit perfectly over her shapely ass.

Eventually, his mind began to function again along with his capacity for speech.

"Maggie, are you okay?"

In response, she hummed against him, a half-purr, half-moan, and flexed her sheath around him in a gentle but firm squeeze. Clearly, she had not yet regained her ability to speak.. A surge of pure male satisfaction ran through him.

When he felt strong enough, he bundled her up in the comforter to carry her back to the warmth of the fire. As he lifted her from the bed, his heart clenched, for there, upon the sheets, was evidence of the innocence he had just unknowingly shattered.

Christ, he should have known. He was a doctor, for God's sake. And he'd ravaged her like a beast.

"Maggie, why didn't you tell me?"

CHAPTER TWELVE

S he looked deep into his eyes. "I needed you, Michael. All of you."

"I was too rough. I should have been gentler with you."

She put a finger to his lips. "I'd been waiting a long time, dreaming of what it would be like. You made it real for me. You made it better than anything I ever could have imagined."

If he hadn't already lost his heart and soul to her, he would have in that moment. Unable to reply with words, he kissed her deeply, passionately, with the certain knowledge that he would never be the same again.

He carried her back downstairs, returning to the warmth of the fire. No words were necessary. Michael lay on his back with Maggie's soft, sated body nestled against him. Her arm rested on his chest, her leg draped over his thigh. Peace and contentment settled over him as he gazed into the flames. Before long, Maggie drifted off to sleep.

Now that he was coming down from those incredible heights and capable of rational thought, his analytical mind set to work. The first question that came to mind was, *What the hell just happened?* The second was, *Why?*

What had happened? That one was relatively easy. He'd just had the most amazing sex of his life with a woman who had given him the gift of her innocence.

Why? Well, that one was a bit harder to answer.

Yes, Maggie was beautiful. Soft and feminine, generally shy—the last two hours notwithstanding. He also found her to be smart and witty, funny, resourceful, and passionate. Slightly clumsy perhaps, but in his eyes, that only added to her charm. All very attractive things, to be sure, and Michael was a fit, healthy man. It was only natural he wanted to be with her, right?

Except that Michael had been with smart, funny, beautiful women before, and none of them had ever made him feel like *she* had. None had ever made him lose control or neglect to use protection. None had brought him to his mental and emotional knees by screaming his name in the throes of passion.

And, he thought as he curled his body protectively around hers, *none have ever filled me with such a strong need to protect and possess.*

Unlike much of his family, Michael tended to be on

the quiet side, more apt to think a situation through thoroughly than act on impulse. He was the least likely to jump in bed with a woman he'd just met or to exhibit what he often half-jokingly called *innate caveman tendencies*. Except here he was. He'd known Maggie less than forty-eight hours, and he'd already laid claim. God help any man who even thought about looking at her.

He believed he already knew the answer. Like two of his brothers before him, he had found his *croie*. His heart. His perfect woman. His soul mate.

Maggie let out a mild protest in her sleep, rousing him from his thoughts and making him realize he was clutching her too tightly. He forced himself to relax his hold and was rewarded with a contented sigh as she burrowed into him further. For some reason, that simple action/reaction seemed incredibly profound.

Michael closed his eyes and soaked in the feel of her naked skin against his. As he finally drifted off, he couldn't help but think that there was no place in the world he would rather be.

IT WAS INSANE—THAT was what it was. Maggie drank in the sight of the beautiful man beside her, his large hand clasped possessively over her hip. His other arm sat beneath her cheek, serving as the most wonderful, warm pillow. In sleep, his face had an angelic quality, as if it had been carved by skilled, inhuman hands. A hint of dark shadow dusted his jawline, lending him a slightly dangerous air.

As gorgeous as he was, if anyone had told her she would jump in bed with a man she'd just met, she would have thought them a few bricks shy of a load. That wasn't her. Maggie was solid, cautious, almost prudish with her old-fashioned values. A good Irish girl, clever and self-sufficient, unwilling to lower her standards for the sake of male company.

But here she was. Forty-eight hours after meeting him, she was buck naked beneath the covers, pressing herself against him. One leg was bent, resting atop his hip, as though in open invitation to slide himself deep inside her once again. She could summon none of the shame she *should* be feeling. There was only the potent desire to have him again.

Her hand traced upward from his forearm along his formidable biceps—hard even in the midst of slumber—and over his broad shoulder before dipping down to his neck. Here, she paused, feeling the strong, steady pulse beneath her fingertips. The rhythm carried through into her own body, coaxing her heart to beat in the same tempo.

With no other movement to indicate he was awake, Michael opened his lids. His eyes were so lovely, so deep, and filled with enough power to steal her breath away.

"Michael," she whispered his name as she cupped his cheek.

He caught her hand with his own and turned his head to lay a kiss on her palm.

"Yes, sweet?" His voice was husky and deep.

She wondered if it was always like that in the morning or only after nights filled with passion. Hopefully, she'd have a chance to find out.

So MUCH WAS GOING on behind those eyes. He watched, fascinated, as they swirled and lost focus, only to return with more clarity than they'd had before. He waited patiently, content to memorize the feminine contours of her face as she lay, warm and soft, in his arms, unable to accurately express the depth of what was happening between them.

"I know," he whispered as his thumb tenderly caressed her cheek.

She had given him a tremendous gift. He wished he could tell her how much it meant to him, how she had already crawled into his heart and soul, but he couldn't find the words. Instead, he kissed her forehead and pulled her closer to him.

She sighed, and he knew she understood.

THE STORM LASTED for three days. When all was said and done, nearly thirty-six inches had been recorded officially, though it was not uncommon to find drifts that topped the six- or seven-foot marks. Highways had been shut down, airports had been closed, and parts of the northeastern United States had been declared disaster areas. But in one isolated farmhouse, Michael Callaghan and Maggie Flynn remained blissfully removed from all of it.

They spent long, luscious hours making love. They heated water over the fire and gave each other erotic sponge baths by candlelight. Toasted sandwiches and roasted marshmallows on sticks. Ate canned brandied peaches off of each other. Made love some more. When the wind finally died down and the snow stopped falling, neither was particularly pleased to return to the outside world.

Michael dug out his truck, but while the roads in town were reported passable, the mountain roads remained in bad shape. He was quite happy staying right where he was, but Ian's increasingly aggressive texts insisted Michael had to attend the final tux fittings for the wedding, making it clear that those were Lexi's orders, not his. Maggie, unfortunately, agreed.

Now, they were awaiting the Hummer, and Michael was making the most of every moment by holding her in his lap in the big picture window seat. He hadn't even left yet, and he was already trying to figure out how quickly he could get back to her.

"When will I see you again?" she asked, mirroring his thoughts.

Michael pulled her into his arms, devouring her mouth with his own. "Not soon enough," he growled. "Sure you won't come back with me?"

"I'm sure."

It wasn't the first time he'd asked. She'd explained that she needed to stay at the farm to keep the fire going, so the ancient pipes wouldn't freeze. Plus, there was George to think of. She couldn't leave him alone in this weather with the power expected to be out for several more days. They had debated back and forth, but Michael had discovered that Maggie, while soft-spoken, was every bit as stubborn as he was.

"Maybe I should stay," he said, hesitating. "At least till the power comes back on."

"No," she told him firmly. "You need to be there for your brother. This isn't just about tuxes, you know."

He arched a brow, wondering at the certainty with which she spoke.

"Besides," she continued, "I can fire up the generator if I need to."

Michael's jaw dropped. "You have a generator? Why didn't you say something?"

She gave him a slow smile, one that had him hardening again despite the fact that, physiologically speaking, he should be sated for days. Apparently, his vast medical knowledge of human anatomical needs hadn't quite made it down to his penis.

"Because you are one gorgeous, sexy man," she said, pressing her palms against his chest, flexing her fingers just slightly, like a cat curling her claws. "But by candlelight, you are a god."

Michael felt the familiar warmth spread through him. Jesus, his toes actually *tingled*. He groaned. "You are a wicked woman, Maggie Flynn," he lamented. "I have half a mind to carry you back in there and—"

MAGGIE LEANED into him and pressed her lips to his, effectively putting an end to his description of exactly what he was going to do, and it was a good thing too. Over the last few days, Maggie had discovered just how explicit and descriptive the good doctor could be.

"I think your brothers are here."

Michael cursed under his breath in Irish. Maggie wasn't quite sure what he'd said, but she'd heard her grandfather utter something similar enough times to get the gist.

Through the frosted window, they watched as the powerful H2 pushed through the snow, the V-shaped plow mounted in the front making a clean path down the long lane to the house. Maggie heard the earsplitting thump of bass well before they drew close. Michael shook his head but smiled.

Michael identified each one as they became visible. Ian was the first to pop out, followed by Kieran, Sean, Shane, Jake, and Kane. Dressed in black coveralls from head to toe, they looked more like a black ops team from Call of Duty than brothers heading for a tux fitting. Maggie said so jokingly to Michael, but he barely cracked a smile. When his eyes met hers, the intensity she saw in them shocked her.

"That is the last time you drive the Hummer," the one she thought was Sean shouted vehemently, clutching his stomach as they moved en masse toward the house, but even Maggie could see that he was hamming it up.

"True that," his twin agreed.

The youngest looking one roared with laughter, a smile on his boyish face so bright that it would have been blinding had the snow not been so white. The three others, who looked slightly older and maturer, just shook their heads. It was clear to see the blizzard had been nothing but an excuse for them to get out their big toys and have some fun.

"Mick!" The shout was accompanied by an insistent pounding on the front door. "Come out, come out wherever you are!"

Another round of laughter reached them inside. George, coaxed from his doggy bed in curiosity, ducked his head behind the couch.

Michael opened the door with a look of complete martyrdom. "Jesus, grow up, will you?"

Their grins grew wider. Maggie shrank back. The closer they were, the bigger they seemed. Had they been that large the other night?

Grinning boys in the bodies of massive men. She

wondered absently if her old porch could withstand the weight of them all without collapsing.

"Come on, Mick. Invite us in. Where is she?" one of them said. It would take time for her to be able to identify who was who. They all shared the trademark jet-black Callaghan hair, blue eyes, and general build.

"Yeah, we want to meet her," said another.

"Fuck off." Michael slammed the door in their faces and looked apologetically at Maggie, whose expression must have been somewhere between amused and terrified. "Sorry about this. I didn't know they were *all* coming."

"They're, um ..." Words failed her. Gorgeous, big, loud, forces of nature ... all seemed applicable.

They hadn't seemed so large, nor had they seemed quite so intense when they were sitting down and behaving themselves—of course, the several shots she'd had that night to calm her performance anxiety might have skewed her perception.

"Yeah, that pretty much sums it up." He leaned down and gave her a tender kiss.

And just like that, she was tempted to change her mind and convince him to stay.

"I'll call you, okay?"

"Okay." The word came out sounding breathy, making him smile as a familiar heat filled his eyes.

She loved that look and wished fervently he could stick around to see it through.

Maggie rested her back against the door as it closed

behind him, listening to the good-natured ribbing Michael was taking, her cheeks blushing on his behalf. When she heard the Hummer start up again, she crouched down to give George a reassuring rub along the back of his neck.

The sudden knock startled her so much that she unintentionally pulled George's ear, making him yelp. She rose slowly and opened the door a crack. A glance up the driveway revealed Michael being physically held back by five of his brothers. The sixth was at her door, one striking blue eye peering at her through the narrow opening.

This brother had eyes just like Michael as well as the same lopsided grin. He held out a small envelope, made even smaller by the sheer size of the man who wielded it. She glanced at it and then at the man, who she guessed was the groom-to-be, Ian.

"Here," he said, his eyes twinkling with amusement and curiosity. "I'm under strict orders to deliver this personally."

He extended the envelope, pushing it at her through the door. When she finally took it, his grin widened, and he winked. "Great cookies, by the way." Then, he turned around and jogged back to the vehicle.

Maggie watched as Michael was unceremoniously tossed into the back of the Hummer, and they sped off. Only then did she consider what was in her hand.

It had a satiny feel and was intricately embossed

with pearl and gold. With shaking fingers, she lifted the flap and extracted a card with a matching design.

You are cordially invited
to attend the wedding of

Alexis Cassandra Kattapoulos
and
Ian Patrick Callaghan

Saturday, the twenty-seventh of February
One o'clock in the afternoon

St. Patrick's Roman Catholic Church

Reception immediately following.
Celtic Goddess, Grand Ballroom

Maggie sucked in a breath and reread the contents several times.

Well, damn.

CHAPTER THIRTEEN

"I can't."

Maggie lay beside Michael, her back to his front, before the blazing fire.

Michael had brought food and flowers and wine, professing his intent to spend a nice, romantic evening together before climbing into bed. But two days without seeing or touching him had taken its toll. She'd had the front door open before he got out of his truck. He'd barely stepped inside when she'd thrust herself into his arms, effectively derailing his plan.

"Why not?" Michael trailed light, moist kisses along her shoulder while one hand stroked her belly possessively.

"How many reasons do you want?" She placed her hand over his, relishing his touch, every skillful stroke soothing and exciting her at the same time.

When Michael touched her, her body's response was immediate, arching shamelessly for more. Her insides still ached slightly from his thorough and branding lovemaking, but it was a good ache.

"I'm a reasonable man. One good one should do it."

She took a deep breath. "Well, for starters, I don't even know them."

"You've met Ian twice."

"Technically, I haven't." Erotically stripping at a bachelor party and accepting an envelope through a crack in the door didn't exactly qualify as valid introductions in her book.

"It doesn't matter. You'll be with me, and I know them quite well, so that's not a good enough reason."

He gave her a long, slow lick from her collarbone to her neck, sending delicious shivers through her entire body. When he did that, it was hard to imagine why being with him anywhere, anytime, for any reason would be a bad thing.

"Besides," he added, the timbre of his voice making her sex ache and throb, "they're dying to meet you. I'd just as soon rather it be all at once when they're dressed up, in public, and behaving themselves."

Given the brief look she'd had at his brothers, she could understand his point. Not that it did much to alleviate the anxiety she felt at the prospect.

"But, Michael, I *danced* at his *bachelor party.*" Which, as she saw it, was a perfectly good reason the bride would not want her there.

He laughed when she explained this, causing parts of his body to move against hers. *Dear Lord, the man was hardening again.* Either he was naturally virile or he really, really liked her. She hoped it was the latter because the feel of his erection pressing against her backside was making her feel needy all over again. *When did I become such a wanton woman?* She'd managed thirty years of abstinence, and now, she found it hard to go thirty minutes without him inside her.

"Clearly, you don't understand my family. That only elevates you in their eyes." His teeth raked the bottom of her ear while his hand skimmed the underside of her breast. "As a matter of fact, I overheard Lexi say that Ian's, uh, performance after your dance has her considering signing up for belly dancing lessons. If anything, I bet she'd thank you and ask you to teach her some moves."

Maggie sincerely doubted that. The real question was, could she face them? Even now, her cheeks flamed at the thought of the seductive dance she had done. Granted, she hadn't stripped entirely, and the men had been absolute gentlemen, really, but still.

She snuggled her backside against him in a bold enticement. He groaned and grasped her hip, pulling her closer.

"I have nothing to wear."

He nudged her upper thigh with his knee and smoothly slid into her from behind. They moaned simultaneously as she stretched to accommodate his thickness. "So, we'll go shopping."

With the arm that was beneath her, he fondled her breasts, alternating between gentle, kneading squeezes and light pinches of her tight, hard nipples. His other arm was draped over her hips, his thumb and fingers swirling expertly—though with maddening slowness—over the outside of her sex. The result was a flood of sensation across her entire body that threatened to burn her to ash. She moved with him, against him, into him, desperately needing more.

GODDAMN, the woman was hot, driving him crazy as no one else ever had. The mere sight of her flipped a switch inside him, turning him into a man possessed. Minutes after he'd arrived at her door, they'd been at it, hot and heavy with no concern for finesse. Now that the edge was off, he wanted to take it slow and make it last, but she was making it damn hard. He began with long, deliberate strokes meant to maximize her pleasure. Within minutes, Maggie was panting, crying his name in those breathless, husky whispers, and he couldn't help himself. His thrusts became harder; his fingers moved faster. When she came, it was even more intense than the first time. She tightened around him in rolling spasms that felt like heaven along his cock, and impossibly, he found himself releasing inside her once again.

For a long while afterward, their heavy breathing mingled with the crackle of the fire as they drifted back to earth together. It was Michael who spoke first.

"I really want you there, Maggie," he said, returning to their previous conversation.

He'd been thinking about it since he'd first realized what Ian had handed her. Ian's wedding was the perfect opportunity to introduce her properly to his family. That was best done sooner rather than later because he already knew that she was someone very special. To spend the evening in her company—talking, laughing, dancing, and celebrating—was preferable to counting the minutes until he could make a respectable exit to be with her again.

Still, it was a lot to ask for a "first date." He wished he could have taken her to dinner a few times, maybe a few movies first, but sometimes, he just had to work with what he had.

"But I understand why you might not want to," he added, his fingers twitching on her hip.

"Why?" she asked.

"Well, I know my family can be overwhelming. I can see why you'd prefer to be exposed to them in small doses."

"No," she interrupted. "Why do you want me there?"

Michael was stunned. *She doesn't know?* Reluctantly, he withdrew from her, only so he could turn her around and see her face.

Christ, he thought, looking into her eyes. *She really doesn't know.*

He saw hope and fear and uncertainty and genuine puzzlement.

"Because I am falling hopelessly, desperately in love with you, Maggie Flynn."

Her eyes widened; her lips parted. "You are?"

"Yes," he confirmed, stroking her cheek with his hand. "I know it's fast, but that doesn't change the fact that it's true."

He hoped she was feeling the same way. It was hard to believe otherwise, given the way things were between them. The thought of her smiling at anyone else the way she smiled at him was just wrong. Hell. Thinking of her doing *anything* to anyone else made him ten ways to crazy.

"Okay," she said finally.

"Okay what?"

"Okay, I'll go."

Michael's heart swelled. She hadn't returned his declaration and told him she loved him, but she wasn't running away either. And she had agreed to go to the wedding with him. Michael was a patient man. For the right woman—for *Maggie*—he could wait for the words he believed were inevitable. When they did come, they would mean that much more.

At that moment, however, they had more pressing concerns. The unmistakable sound of Maggie's stomach growling made him grin.

"Hungry?"

She smiled shyly. "A little."

Michael got up and pulled on his jeans. "Good. I brought dinner. Hang on. It's probably cold, but ..."

He disappeared into the foyer and returned with

two huge bags. Maggie was donning a flannel shirt. He smiled when he realized it was the same one he'd put on her that first night—another positive and encouraging sign.

"I think we're going to want to heat this up," he said, his eyes sparkling as he looked at her.

Her hair was messed up (his doing), her skin flushed (he took credit for that as well), and she practically glowed with the look of a woman well sated (obviously).

"But we can come back in here for dessert."

Oh yeah, he knew exactly what he was going to do with the strawberries, chocolate, and whipped cream he'd brought along.

For the first time that night, Michael noticed Maggie was favoring her right leg. Not that he'd really had much of a chance to notice earlier—two feet inside the door, and he'd swept her into his arms and carried her into the living room.

"Maggie, is your ankle still bothering you?"

She deliberately averted her eyes, reaching into the cupboard for plates. "No, not really."

"Maggie."

"I'm fine."

He recognized the tone, and it chilled his blood. That familiar unease washed over him again—the one that told him, without a doubt, that she was hiding something.

"*Maggie.*" He put the food down on the table before

his hands gently took her around the upper arms, and he guided her onto the nearest chair.

She sighed heavily in resignation, and a feeling of apprehension came over him.

A flesh-colored bandage covered the skin several inches along the side of her shin, midway between her ankle and knee. He hadn't paid much attention to it before—he'd just assumed she'd wrapped her sore ankle, and he'd been concentrating on other parts. Now that he looked closer, however, he could see that the wrap wasn't down around her ankle; it was higher than that.

"What happened?" he asked, his fingers reaching for the edge of the bandage.

"It's nothing." She attempted to swing her leg under the table, out of sight.

Michael's grip was gentle but firm, holding her leg in place between his knees. His warning look suggested she not even try.

She inhaled deeply but stopped resisting.

Michael pulled away the bandage and found an ugly gash several inches in length, surrounded by swollen, bruised flesh. "Jesus, Maggie! What did you do?"

Instead of waiting for an answer, he was on his feet, retrieving the first aid kit he'd seen in her kitchen.

Maggie hissed as he poured antiseptic over the wound. "I did that already," she bit out through clenched teeth.

Michael's face was hard. "*What. Did. You. Do*?!"

"Nothing. It was just a little accident—that's all."

His heart pounded against the walls of his chest, but his well-trained hands were steady, providing care with rote, practiced movements. It was a good thing, too, because he wasn't thinking clearly.

"*Maggie.*"

"I was chopping wood, aimed wrong, and struck a glancing blow. End of story. I'm fine."

"What?! You did this with *an ax*?" His voice was sharp, making her flinch. "What the hell were you thinking? And why in God's name didn't you say anything?"

"Stop yelling at me!" she shot back, her tone wounded.

Michael felt a slight pang of regret but not enough to quell the uneasiness within him. He'd treated hundreds of patients with injuries more serious than this without batting an eye, but this was *Maggie*.

"I was thinking that with the ice accumulating on the power lines, I might lose electricity again, and I needed to split a few more logs. And in case you've forgotten, I've been a bit busy since you got here."

Michael took a deep breath, praying for patience. He wasn't sure who he was more upset with—Maggie, for doing something that had gotten herself hurt and not telling him, or himself, for not double-checking the wood supply before he'd left and for not noticing that she was wounded because he was too busy slaking his lust.

His jaw was clenched so tightly that she must have

heard his teeth grinding, but he refrained from making any further comment while he redressed the wound. He felt Maggie's fingers gently threading in his hair. It soothed him. Slightly.

"Michael," she said softly, "I'm all right."

The hell she was. At least she'd had the good sense to clean it out well. It looked as though she'd applied some kind of poultice too. He would have to remember to ask her about that later when he could think logically again.

"Get dressed. We're going to the hospital. You need stitches. Definitely a tetanus shot. And maybe an X-ray because it looks like you might have clipped the bone."

Her hand stilled in his hair, and he felt her tense. It was as if a field of static electricity had suddenly powered up around her as she pulled away from him.

"No."

He tilted his head up and pinned her with a warning glare as he fastened the bandage. "I'm not kidding around, Maggie. Get dressed."

"Neither am I. I am *not* going to the hospital. Now, stop overreacting, and let's eat. I'm starving."

Michael felt like a wire strung so tightly that it was in danger of snapping. The feeling was so alien that it was difficult to get control of it. The woman had no sense of perspective whatsoever.

"*Overreacting*?! Maggie, you put a fucking ax blade into your leg!"

She winced at his words, at the authority that had rung through his tone. He was a man used to being obeyed. Unfortunately for him, she was not a woman accustomed to being told what to do. Her eyes narrowed, and her chin lifted defiantly.

"You'll not be getting me into any hospital, is that clear?" The faintest hint of an accent colored her words, a shadowy echo that was probably a direct result of growing up with her Ireland-born grandmother.

"*Maggie.*"

He saw real fire in her eyes then, which took no small amount of courage. He towered over her, his expression as fierce as it got, every muscle in his body tensed. In contrast, Maggie seemed to shrink before him, all but for her eyes, which held absolute conviction.

"Don't *Maggie* me, Michael Callaghan. I will not be bullied by the likes of you. Accept that I am a grown woman, capable of making my own decisions."

"When you start acting like a grown woman instead of a stubborn child, I might be more inclined to do just that." His lips thinned, clamping shut before he said anything else.

He leveled a gaze at her, one that would have most men looking away and snapping to execute their orders. But not Maggie. She met his intense stare with one of her own, her green eyes luminous. She clasped her hands together in her lap but not before he saw them tremble.

The face-off continued for a full minute before Maggie spoke again. In a softer voice but with no less conviction, she said, "I am not going, Michael, and that's final. I'd like you to stay. Eat with me. Make love to me again." She took a deep, steadying breath for her next words, which were spoken even more softly. "But if you can't accept my decision, then you should leave now, before this goes any further."

A war raged within him. His medically trained, rational side said she needed more care than he could give her here in her home. His heart balked at doing anything that would put distance between them.

It made no sense to him—this aversion Maggie seemed to have toward hospitals. He tried to look deeper, tried to understand. She'd been just as adamant about not going to the ER the night she fell. She had refused to take any of the meds he'd left for her. The vehemence with which she reacted went way beyond typical anxiety, especially in an age when medical care and modern pharmaceuticals were so advanced and readily available.

Yet her eyes were worried, pleading. She wanted him to stay, but she was not going to back down. If he continued to push her on this, it would drive a wedge between them, and the damage could be irreparable. But if he didn't and her leg got worse, he wouldn't forgive himself because he had known better and could have helped her.

It was a hell of a choice—force the issue and risk losing her, or respect her wishes and go against his medical instincts, which, so far, had never been wrong.

"Damn it, Maggie," he said, blowing out a breath,

running one hand through his already-messed-up hair. "I'm worried about you." That was putting it mildly.

The intensity of his feelings, the powerful need he had to care for and protect her, was so strong. But hell, he'd already admitted he was falling in love with her. If he tried to explain this compulsion, obsession—whatever it was—to care for her, she might get spooked and end up kicking his ass out anyway.

Her face softened, and she reached out to touch his cheek. "I love that you care for me, Michael, and I understand that you are a doctor and that my behavior makes no sense to you. But it is my decision, and I need you to decide if you can accept that."

"Can you explain it to me, Maggie? Can you help me understand why you have such an aversion to things like stitches and X-rays and shots?"

"Maybe," she said carefully. "When you are of a mind to listen. But this isn't just about a little cut on my leg."

Michael was about to point out that her injury was a hell of a lot more than "a little cut" but thought better of it when he saw the seriousness of her expression.

"It's about whether you see me as one of your patients or as the woman who is falling in love with you too."

His heart stuttered. He blinked. For several moments, he forgot to breathe. She'd said it. She'd admitted that she was falling in love with him too. Everything else could wait. He went to his knees and kissed her as if his life depended on it.

"Does this mean you'll stay?" she asked breathlessly, her eyes slightly unfocused.

"I'll stay. But I want you to promise me that if this leg doesn't look any better tomorrow, you will let me take you to the hospital."

"Michael ..."

"Maggie, you have to meet me halfway on this, sweetheart. We'll do this your way for now but only because it looks like you did an excellent job, treating that wound. If it gets worse or shows any signs of infection, we do things my way. I might be falling in love with you, but I will not sit idly by and watch you hurt yourself. I care far too much for you to allow that to happen. And whether you like it or not, I do know more about injuries and treatments than you do."

He cupped her face in his hands and prayed she would be reasonable. "Do you think *you* can accept *that*?"

She bit her bottom lip, her eyes swirling again until, finally, she nodded. "I do."

Those two words, coming out of her mouth while she was looking at him, had the oddest effect. His mind filled with pictures of Maggie in a flowing white gown, looking up into his eyes with so much love that it made his heart feel as though it would burst. Maybe it was all the talk and planning for his brother's wedding, but the thought of marrying Maggie made everything click into place.

It took him a moment or two to find his voice, but

when he did, he was once again without words. So, he kissed her instead.

Maggie's stomach picked that moment to growl again. He chuckled and then rose to get what he needed to feed his woman. He brought the take-out containers to the table, along with plates and silverware, while insisting she remain seated.

"This is incredible," Maggie said between bites. "Where on earth did you get this?"

It pleased Michael to see her eating, even if she was only sampling.

"Lexi. She's been cooking up a storm all week. I think she's anxious about the wedding."

"A woman after my own heart," Maggie said.

An idea popped into his mind. "You know, as good as this is, I bet it would taste even better with some of your homegrown ingredients. Would you mind if I took some back to Lexi? She's always looking for healthy, organic things to put into her creations."

"No, I don't mind. Take whatever you want. Lord knows, I have more than I'll ever use."

"Great. Why don't you try to eat a bit more while I go down into the cellar and grab some?"

"Everything is wonderful," she said too quickly. "It really is, but I don't think I can."

Michael frowned. Something seemed off. Perhaps he was just feeling especially paranoid, but he didn't think so. "Maggie, do you always eat so little?"

"No," she admitted. "I just haven't been that hungry lately." She gave him a sly smile. "I think it's all the sex.

You have me feeling so satisfied that I don't need to compensate with food."

Michael couldn't help the grin that spread across his face. He loved satisfying her needs. But deep inside, something was bothering him. He just couldn't put his finger on it.

"I'm flattered. But you need to keep your strength up because I've got plans for you, sweetheart." He winked and gave her a smile filled with wicked promise. "And I'd hate to have to withhold sex just to get you to eat."

"You wouldn't!" she exclaimed, her expression a combination of mock and genuine horror.

"I would if it meant preserving those luscious curves I love sinking myself into."

She blushed as Michael pulled her into his arms, letting his hands roam down over her behind.

"I'm serious, Maggie. I can't help it. I'm worried about you."

CHAPTER FOURTEEN

Maggie snaked her arms up around his neck, loving that she could touch him like this. The truth was, she was becoming a little concerned herself. The dull headache persisted, and sometimes, it was difficult to focus. Her depth perception seemed especially affected, which was why she'd miscalculated that ax swing earlier. She wasn't going to tell him that though. Their fragile compromise would fall by the wayside, and he'd have her admitted within the hour.

She couldn't let that happen.

It will pass, she told herself. After all, she had taken a nasty fall. It was only natural to expect some lingering effects, right? And it wasn't keeping her from doing what she needed to do. It was more annoying than anything, really. Like a tiny pebble in her shoe.

Unfortunately, Michael was too perceptive. He sensed something—she knew he did. It was in the way she'd catch him watching her intently or the discreet way he'd let his fingers pause in his caresses.

Or the way he was looking at her right now.

"Maggie, is there something you're not telling me?"

"You worry too much."

"Where you're concerned, I'm not certain I worry enough."

Her shoulders stiffened at the insinuation that she needed a keeper. "And yet, somehow, I've managed to make it to this point all by myself."

"Maggie, I didn't mean it like that."

"I know what you meant," she exhaled. "Now, go on down and pick out some things while I try to be a good little girl and finish my plate."

His lips thinned, but thankfully, he did as she'd asked. Maggie quickly scraped the remains of her dinner into George's bowl.

By the time Michael returned from the basement a short time later with several baskets of various canned and dried items, Maggie had everything cleaned up and was waiting for him in the living room. The lights were off, and she was in the process of lighting the scented candles she'd placed on nearly every available surface.

"What's all this?" he asked.

"Ambiance."

"Ambiance. Hmm. What exactly do you have in mind?"

Maggie felt her cheeks burn hot. This had been

much easier when she envisioned the scene in her mind. "I want to try something."

"I'm intrigued."

She cleared her throat. "I want to pleasure you."

He smiled indulgently. "Sweetheart, you do that all the time."

"Not like that," she said, clasping her hands together to hide her sudden case of nerves. Fantasizing about bringing him to his knees with pleasure was one thing; actually pulling it off was something else entirely. She was already bungling this royally. What had made her think she could do this? She was no smooth seductress. "I mean, um, orally."

Michael went still; the smile faded from his face, but hunger blazed in his eyes. "You don't have to do that, Maggie."

She wrapped her arms around his waist and laid her face against his chest. "I know. But I want to. I want to give you the same kind of pleasure you give me. I'm just … I've never …"

Maggie closed her eyes and took a deep breath to summon her courage. This was something she'd been thinking about for the last two days, and she wasn't about to back out now. She tilted her head and looked up into his face. It was the barely banked fire in his eyes that strengthened her resolve. He wanted this too.

"I mean, theoretically, I know the basics, of course, but I want to know what *you* like. Please, Michael, let me do this."

WHEN HE DIDN'T REFUSE—HOW could he possibly refuse when she looked at him like that?—Maggie began to unfasten his jeans. He hissed when he felt her hands against his skin, coaxing both his pants and his boxer briefs down over his hips. His erection sprang forth, as hard and thick as when he'd first arrived. She hummed in approval and then continued to work downward, lightly scraping her nails against his skin on the way. When he stepped free, Maggie pushed the jeans to the side and went to her knees.

"Maggie ..."

She took him in one hand and then two, exploring his length with tentative, curious half-strokes. "So warm and silky," she murmured, more to herself than him. "And yet ... so ... hard." She drew a circle beneath the broad head and traced along the veins, as if committing every inch to her tactile memory.

Michael watched in awe as she fondled him, resisting the urge to buck into her hands. He had to be patient, had to savor every possible moment. This was one of his secret fantasies—to have a woman learn on him. To teach her everything that drove him insane, brought him to the very edge. Could she have sensed that? Or was he just the luckiest son of a bitch in the universe?

One hand caressed down his length, fingering him along the base before cupping him further below. Michael sucked in a breath. One thing was for certain:

if she continued doing things like that, he wasn't sure he'd have the strength to stop if she changed her mind.

"Maggie"—his voice was rough, raw—"are you sure?"

She tore her eyes away from his package and looked up. "Very sure. Unless you don't want me to."

He groaned in response.

"Do you want me to stop?" she pressed.

One hand encircled his shaft, moving up and down with featherlight caresses. The other held his balls, rolling them lightly from pinkie to index finger and back again. He wasn't providing much in the way of useful information; she seemed to instinctively know what to do. Or maybe it just felt so good because it was Maggie doing it.

"No," he managed. "Fuck no. Please don't stop." Of their own accord, his hands buried themselves in her hair; it ran like silk through his fingers.

She pushed him backward until he felt the sofa at the backs of his knees. "Sit down, Michael," she whispered in a soft tone. "Sit down and let me discover how to pleasure you."

As if he could deny her. Michael did as she'd asked, leaning back. Maggie positioned herself between his legs, pressing his thighs open, exposing him to her. So intense, she ran her fingernails lightly along his inner thighs, smiling when his cock bobbed for her.

"Touch me, Maggie."

Without hesitation, she wrapped her hands around

him and began stroking again. "Like this?" She looked up into his face expectantly.

"Perfect."

She smiled and licked her lips.

He held his breath as she leaned in closer, close enough that he could feel her hot, moist breath on him. Her hands never stopped moving in an easy, teasing rhythm while she studied him from all angles.

"Where shall I start?" she whispered, licking her lips.

"The tip," he bit out.

She pressed her lips to him in a chaste kiss.

The muscles in his leg tensed and bunched, but he forced himself to remain still. He didn't want to do anything that might scare her away because he already knew he wanted her to do this again and again.

She kissed around the tip first. Michael nearly passed out when she pulled back slightly and licked her lips again, giving a breathy exclamation of delight when she spotted the drop of pre-cum. She ran her tongue along the slit, then paused.

"Mmm," she hummed softly. "So, this is what you taste like."

He thought he might just lose his mind.

Maggie held him loosely with one hand; the other continued to work him as she kissed her way down his cock. Her lips were wet; every now and then, he would feel her tongue come out to moisten them. She took her time, her lips and tongue retracing the paths her fingers had taken earlier, leaving no part of him untouched or untasted.

She reached the base, and her tongue dipped lower. One hand pushed back lightly, giving her mouth full access to the area below. Half-lidded eyes looked up at him, questioning, seeking approval.

"Yes," he breathed. "Fuck yes."

Her tongue came out again and licked along his seam while her hand continued to work his shaft. Michael's hand covered hers, tightening her grip, guiding her. She parted those incredible lips and took his balls in her mouth, rolling them over her tongue, savoring. Her unengaged hand shifted lower; her thumb pressed lightly, making little circles on the area just below her lips.

Where the hell had she learned that? Michael had never felt anything like it. It was insane. It was beautiful. And the best part? She was loving every minute of it.

"Damn, Maggie. Suck my cock, please." His voice was strained from the effort of holding back, but he was at his limits. If she didn't take him in her mouth soon, he was going to lose it.

He felt her smile against him, taking great pleasure in his response to her attempts. Maggie released his balls from her mouth, giving them each one last loving lick. As soon as she pulled back, her hand cupped him again. It was incredibly arousing to be fondled and sucked at the same time. The woman had natural, intuitive skills.

She rose up onto her knees. He could feel the rock-hard tips of her nipples through the flannel. He wanted her naked, wanted to feel her bare skin against the insides of his thighs, but he couldn't bear the thought of losing contact for even the few seconds it would take to pull the shirt over her head. Instead, he grabbed the shirt and wrenched it apart, sending buttons flying across the room.

Her grip was firmer and more confident now. Maggie was a quick learner. In no time at all, his tip was glistening again. Michael groaned when he saw the hungry smile on her face.

All at once, her mouth descended upon him. She sucked him tentatively at first, letting her tongue swirl around him.

"Ah, baby," he gasped in encouragement. "That's it. Just like that. Just like that."

She experimented with hard pulls and tender licks, adjusting her assault based on the quickness of his ragged breaths and the way he rippled beneath her.

"More," he pleaded, pushing down on her head as his hips rocked.

Her hand dropped down to the base of his shaft. She took more of him into her mouth, her head bobbing in rhythm with his thrusts.

It was too good—too fucking good—watching himself disappear into her mouth over and over again. Her tongue was wicked, swirling; she pressed the underside against him, mimicking the sensation of being inside her.

"Relax your throat," he rasped, feeling his control slipping even further. "Take me deeper, Maggie."

She did. She tilted her head and opened for him, until he was able to slide in far enough to feel the back of her throat. Tiny, careful movements—he didn't want to overwhelm her—sent colored lights bursting behind his eyes; his balls began to tingle with the warnings of his rising seed. He pulled back, and she clamped down around him with her lips in response, sucking hard.

"Fuck!" he cried out, grasping her head. "Maggie, stop. It's too good, sweetheart. You're going to make me come."

She didn't stop, the defiant little wench. She sucked him harder, dropping down over his shaft and taking him deep again, snuggling her body closer against the inside of his legs.

"Sweetheart, stop, please. I'm going to come in that mouth … that sweet fucking mouth …"

One hand continued to stroke in time with her pulls; the other stopped fondling to give a gentle tug on his balls, followed by a light squeeze.

He couldn't stop it now; it was coming—*he* was coming—and it was going to be hard and fast. Afraid that it might be too much for her first time, he tried to pull back, but she fought him. The first jet hit the back of her throat, and she swallowed. The second hit the roof of her mouth as he held her head in place and retracted his hips. The third covered her lips. Still, she struggled against him, reaching greedily for more.

"Maggie ..." he moaned her name in agony, in ecstasy.

When he finally released her, shuddering as he fell back, she took him in her mouth again, more gently this time, and cleaned him from base to tip.

He reached down and pulled her onto his lap; she curled immediately against his chest. He held her tightly, afraid to let go for even a moment because she was the only thing anchoring him. His mind, his heart, and his soul were soaring somewhere far away, but as long as he held Maggie, he knew he would find his way back.

So beautiful, he thought later as he kissed the top of her head.

She'd fallen asleep in his arms, the hint of a smile curving her lips.

Like an angel. An angel who, only a short time earlier, had taken him into bliss.

It wasn't the act itself that had awed him. It was the selflessness, the way she had completely given herself over to pleasing him. He'd felt not just her hands and mouth, but the love and need she had for him as well, and it had been his undoing.

There were no words he could speak, nothing he could say that could begin to express what he felt in his heart at that moment. He knew only that he would never let her go.

CHAPTER FIFTEEN

"Well?" Maggie asked the next morning as Michael inspected her leg.

"It doesn't appear to be any worse," he said finally. Reluctantly.

He'd wanted to find something, anything that would give him a reason to make her uphold her end of their bargain. She'd had a restless night, yet when he'd asked her about it, she'd refused to admit anything was wrong.

"What did you use in the poultice?"

"Slippery elm, marsh pennywort, and vervain."

Michael was grudgingly impressed. Each of those things had been utilized for their healing properties for generations. He'd been doing a lot of research on organics over the past year on Lexi's behalf. Lexi suffered a rare blood disease that made even the simplest injuries life-threatening. The medicines she had to take were sometimes worse than the disease itself, but she was thriving on ancient homeopathic remedies consisting of exotic-sounding roots and extracts.

"You have all that?"

Maggie nodded. "My grandmother didn't put much faith in the modern healthcare system. She kept her own garden and taught me to do the same."

He was beginning to understand where Maggie's aversion to medicine had originated. A sudden memory struck him. "Wait a minute. Your grandmother ... she was the healer, wasn't she?"

"She never claimed to be a healer," Maggie said carefully, "but many came to her for help when traditional medicine didn't work."

"My father used to swear by a paste; he called it Angels and Demons or something ..."

"Probably a mixture of angelica and devil's claw," Maggie said thoughtfully. "Gram used to make a compress that was good for things like arthritis or deep bone and joint injuries. It's quite popular."

Michael's jaw dropped. "Do you know how to make it?"

Maggie shrugged. "Sure. I make it regularly for some of Gram's old friends. Takes a bit of time though. You need to extract the oil from the angelica and steep the devil's claw for the better part of a day. Why?"

"My father said, sometimes, it was the only thing that helped."

The corners of her mouth quirked. "Was it now?"

For some reason, that hint of an Irish brogue that slipped into her speech occasionally drove him wild. He resisted the sudden urge to toss her onto her back and give her a good, old-fashioned tuppin', as she would say. Instead, he offered her a rueful grin, and adopted a brogue of his own. "Aye, Maggie, 'tis true enough."

She laughed, sending waves of warmth through him. "That's hard for you to accept, isn't it?"

"Not as much as you might think," he answered honestly. "I'd choose a natural remedy over an artificial one every time, providing it works." He placed his hands on the bed at either side of her hips, effectively caging her in while he pinned her with that clear blue gaze. "But my father let me run tests to properly diagnose the problem first."

Maggie wiggled free. "I bet he just did it to stop you from nagging him constantly."

It was Michael's turn to laugh. "You might be right." He turned, reaching out and pulling her back. "I don't give up easily, you know."

She leaned heavily against him, avoiding his eyes, but he was not fooled by her easy submission.

"Please, Maggie. Just let me take you in and give you a thorough exam for my own piece of mind."

"A deal's a deal." False brightness colored her tone. "You wouldn't go back on your word now, would you?"

His lips thinned. "No, but—"

"Good," she said, interrupting him. "Then, that's

settled, and we don't have to speak of it again. Now, don't you have somewhere you need to be?"

"Yes, but I don't want to."

"Go!" she said, playfully swatting him. "I'll meet you at the wedding tomorrow."

"Are you sure you don't want me to swing by and pick you up?"

"I'm sure. You'll be too busy. I'll be fine. Quit stalling."

Michael left with a growing feeling of unease, exacerbated by the fact that Maggie seemed to be hurrying him along.

THE MOMENT MICHAEL LEFT, Maggie sagged against the closed door. The migraine that had begun the day before hadn't gone away as she'd hoped. It had continued to build and was now almost unbearable. It had been all she could do not to let Michael know. He'd suspected something, she was sure of it, but thankfully, he had been reluctant to push too hard.

With her hand on the wall for support, she made her way to the bathroom. Thus far, she'd avoided taking the pain pills he'd left for her but no longer. She poured a few into her palm and gulped them down with a cup of water, then sat down in the shower stall and turned on the water as hot as she could stand. The excessive heat and steam dulled the pain temporarily until the meds had a chance to work. When her eyelids grew heavy and her skin numb, she turned off the water and half-walked, half-crawled into bed, where she buried herself under covers that still smelled of Michael and sex and lost herself to the blessed darkness.

SATURDAY DAWNED CLEAR AND SUNNY. After sleeping for nearly twenty hours straight, Maggie forced herself out of bed. She was moving slowly, but she was moving. The pain in her head had reduced to a dull, manageable ache. Her vision was somewhat blurry, but she chalked that up to the meds. Whatever they were, they were powerful. In retrospect, she shouldn't have taken as many as she had, but there was no sense in worrying about that now. Her intent had been to sleep away the worst of the headache, and she had. Strong coffee and another shower would dispel the remaining fog.

She was just pouring herself a cup when the phone rang.

"Hello?"

"Maggie? Maggie! Are you all right?"

She yawned. "Michael?"

"Damn it, Maggie. Why haven't you been answering your phone?"

"I just got up. You should have warned me how potent those pills were."

"You took pain meds?" He sounded surprised.

Probably because he knew she wouldn't unless it was bad. "I'm on my way over there right now."

"Don't be silly." Another yawn. "I feel much better. Refreshed even. I'll see you at the wedding, okay?"

Silence hung heavy over the line.

"Michael?"

"If you're not there, I'm coming for you, Maggie, wedding or not."

She sighed, sensing it was no empty threat. As much as she didn't want to go, she wouldn't be the reason he skipped out on his brother's wedding. "I'll be there."

"Maggie?"

"Hmm?"

"I love you. I'll be waiting for you." Michael hung up before she could reply, leaving her to stare at the phone.

That cut through the fog.

MICHAEL PACED BACK and forth along the vestibule. He and his brothers, Ian and Jake excluded, were seating the guests as they arrived.

"Relax, Mick," Kane said under his breath. "You're acting like you're the one getting married."

Michael checked his watch. Twelve fifty-five. Far above, the church bells tolled a last call for late arrivals. The wedding would be starting in five minutes. He saw the priest signaling them to the front.

"She should be here by now."

He scanned the packed church again. Finally, he spotted her. Somehow, she'd slipped in along the side, and was quietly making her way into the back pew. She caught his eye and smiled apologetically. He took one step toward her before Kane caught his arm.

"That her?"

"Yeah."

"Thank God. Now, let's go."

Kane forcibly guided Michael toward the front of the church, where the groomsmen were lining up— not an easy thing to do, but Kane was the oldest and biggest among them. Michael looked back, but Maggie had already vanished in the crowd.

It took a while for him to find her again. She was in the back corner, sitting in the shadows of the alcoves. Throughout the ceremony, Michael kept her in his peripheral vision, afraid that she might attempt to sneak out before he could get to her. Even though she'd come, he knew she wasn't comfortable. That was understandable but something he could work with. His gut told him there was more to her discomfort than social anxiety, and he wouldn't be satisfied until he could look into her eyes and see for himself that she was all right.

At the conclusion of the Mass, Michael made a beeline for that section. He caught her just as she tried to slip out one of the side doors.

"Going somewhere?"

She turned, a mixture of surprise and guilt on her

face. He was momentarily stricken. She was *beautiful*. Her hair was drawn up, held in place by antique silver combs that allowed narrow waves of dark red to cascade around her face. Her eyes were lightly outlined in a dark charcoal gray, accentuating the crystalline green. Her skin was pale and flawless. The dress she wore was simple but exquisite—a sheath of dark gray silk that fit her like a glove from the hips up, falling into an irregular cascade just below her knees.

MAGGIE FOUND it hard to form a coherent thought. From a distance, he'd looked stunning. Close-up, he took her breath away. In jeans and flannel, Michael was a good-looking man, but dressed in his black tux, he was devastating.

He held out his hand; she had no option but to take it.

"Come with me." His soft, commanding tone sent shivers through her, and she found herself wanting to obey without question.

"Don't you have, uh, wedding stuff to do?"

"Yes, but I want you with me." He smiled, and her knees went weak.

"I don't think that's a good idea."

He placed his hand along the small of her back and his lips close to her ear. "Don't think. Just be with me. Otherwise, I'll be forced to do something that will end up embarrassing us both." His voice was low, silky, and so suggestive that it had her damp between the thighs.

Maybe it was the look in his eyes, maybe it was the tone of his voice or the expression on his face, but she didn't argue. He led her into a quiet room and closed the door behind them. Before she knew what was happening, his mouth was on hers, and he was kissing her as if his life depended on it.

"Don't scare me like that again," he said finally, pulling away and allowing her to catch her breath. "Please." He stepped back enough to study her from head to toe, running his fingers over her, as if checking for further injuries.

His kiss had been so possessive, so commanding, that she was unable to reply. He didn't seem to be expecting a response anyway. He took her hand and led her back into the church, now mostly empty.

"Please wait here. We need to do some pictures, okay?" He nudged her into a pew.

She nodded.

With one last quick kiss, he joined the rest of the party in front of the altar. One by one, they glanced her way. The bride smiled warmly and said something to Michael. He nodded, and the groom laughed, clasping him on the shoulder.

"So, that's my future sister-in-law, huh?" Lexi asked, looking at the woman trying unsuccessfully to blend into the shadows but it was impossible. The woman was strikingly beautiful.

"Welcome to the club, brother." Ian laughed softly, his hand falling on Michael's shoulder.

"Another one bites the dust," Kieran lamented, reiterating Shane's earlier assessment.

CHAPTER SIXTEEN

The Celtic Goddess was one of the most opulent structures Maggie had ever seen. Huge white columns and arches divided the massive space. Built in the style of an ancient Greek temple, it boasted a restaurant made up of several levels that looked out over the valley through floor-to-ceiling glass panels, as well as several ballrooms for private functions. It was in one of these where the reception was held.

The Grand Ballroom was filled to capacity. The blizzard earlier in the week didn't seem to have kept anyone away. People were everywhere. For someone as accustomed to solitude as Maggie, it was a bit over-whelming. Everyone seemed so happy though, and that helped. Being surrounded by friendly, smiling faces eased her nerves somewhat, as did the abun-dance of laughter, ranging from low chuckles to loud, raucous bellows. Arms were raised in toasts or clasping another's back. Maggie had never seen anything like it.

"Are they always so happy?" she asked.

Michael's fingers flexed lightly on the small of her back as he navigated them through the crowd. He seemed content as long as he was touching her, and she took comfort in that. His smile was genuine and relaxed.

"Usually, yes," he told her. "But this is an especially happy celebration."

They stopped at the open bar and he got a brandy for her and a beer for himself. They continued to one of the few empty tables, which she appreciated. After holding the seat for her, he took the one next to it.

Michael gave her an abbreviated version of the past year, explaining how they'd almost lost Lexi, how it had nearly torn Ian apart, and her miraculous recovery. Maggie listened with rapt attention.

"If Lexi had been upfront with Ian," Michael concluded in a soft voice, "she could have saved everyone a lot of heartache. It nearly killed Ian. And her."

Maggie looked down at their joined hands. When she spoke, her voice was even quieter than his. "If she had, then she wouldn't have experienced half the things she did. Ian wouldn't have allowed it, would he?"

"Of course not! She could have died, Maggie, and she would have taken Ian with her. Nothing is worth that."

"Some things are," Maggie countered.

Michael opened his mouth, but before he could respond, another voice piped up, "She's right, you know."

They turned, startled to find Lexi and Ian behind them. Lexi wore a warm, gentle smile, but Ian's expression more closely resembled the denial on Michael's. Maggie was mortified to realize they'd overheard them.

"I'm so sorry," Maggie sputtered. "I didn't mean—"

"It's all right," Lexi said, placing her hand on Maggie's arm. "You're probably the only one here who didn't know." She leaned closer with a conspiratorial smile. "There aren't a lot of secrets in this family, you'll find."

Lexi went up onto her tiptoes and kissed Michael on the cheek. "Except maybe where this guy is concerned," she amended, a twinkle in her eye. "He's the strong, silent type. Definitely not one to kiss and tell."

Maggie felt the heat rise in her cheeks, wishing her skin tone wasn't quite so pale.

"Ah, she blushes." Ian chuckled. "She's a keeper, Mick."

"Way ahead of you," Michael said, smiling easily as he formally introduced Maggie to the bride and groom.

"Mind if I sit for a bit?" Lexi asked.

Before she got the words fully out, Ian had pulled out a chair and eased her into it. Maggie marveled at the way he looked at her. Like she was everything to him. She saw the same look mirrored in Lexi's eyes.

"How are you holding up, Lex?" Michael asked.

Maggie instantly recognized the look of genuine concern and affection in his voice as he slipped into his "doctor mode." Rather than being annoyed by it, as Maggie would have been, Lexi seemed appreciative.

"Good," she answered. "But I'm slowing down. I could use a little help."

Maggie was amazed at how easily Lexi asked for help. She would have found it next to impossible. Michael's response was immediate.

"You got it, Lex," he said with a dazzling smile. "Anything for my favorite sister."

"Hey, I thought I was your favorite," a female voice said with mock hurt as another couple joined them. The man, Maggie recognized from the bachelor party. Jake. She assumed the beautiful woman by his side was his wife.

"She's nicer to me than you are," Michael said seriously, but his eyes were dancing.

The woman laughed, stretching up onto the tips of her toes to give Michael a kiss on the cheek, as the bride had done. "I love you, too, big guy."

Apparently, both women were quite fond of Michael. A slight stab of jealousy went through her. They were obviously close. Then she noted the look of total possession in their husbands' expressions, as well as the way the air practically sizzled between the couples, and she knew she had no reason to feel that way.

"Maggie, I need to get something for Lex," Michael said. "Will you be okay for a few minutes?"

"She'll be fine, Michael. We promise we won't corrupt her while you're gone. *Much*," said the newcomer. Turning to Maggie, she said, "I'm Taryn, by the way. This is Jake."

"We've met," Jake said, his eyes twinkling.

Now that she wasn't a bundle of nerves, she could assess him more accurately. He looked remarkably like Michael and Ian with blue-black hair and clear blue eyes, but he was a bit stockier and probably had a good twenty pounds of lean, hard muscle on them. This, Maggie knew instinctively, was not a man to trifle with. Yet as he greeted her, he had a boyish grin that she couldn't help but like.

Michael looked uncertain about leaving Maggie, but she mustered what she hoped was a reassuring smile.

"I'll be fine. Go."

Very deliberately, Michael leaned over and kissed her. Then, he looked pointedly at Taryn. "Behave yourself."

Taryn's eyes opened wide, and in the span of a heartbeat, her face became the picture of innocence. As soon as he took two steps, Taryn plopped down next to Lexi and winked at Maggie. "But seriously, if you ever have to get a shot in the ass, Michael's your man."

"Amen to that, sister," Lexi said, giving her a high five.

"Taryn!" Michael growled in warning, but she shooed him away with a lighthearted wave as Lexi succumbed to a laugh.

Maggie caught the hint of a smile on his face as he turned away once again, and had the distinct impression that this was a recurring joke among them.

"Did you hear what your wife just said?" Ian asked Jake in feigned disbelief.

"Yeah, and *your* wife agreed with her."

"I think we should kick his ass."

"Copy that."

"Be nice, boys," Taryn warned as the two men followed Michael toward the exit. "Maggie likes him."

Boys? That's the last word I'd use to describe the Callaghan brothers, Maggie thought. Even *men* seemed too mild a word for them. The phrase *lethal alpha males* was more accurate, though that didn't quite capture the dark, natural beauty that seemed to surround them. Or their innate intensity and power. Or their raw, base sexuality.

Maggie forced herself to take a slow, deep breath. Clearly, the brandy Michael had ordered for her was some potent stuff.

Since Michael had just finished telling her, she knew about Lexi's condition. Looking at her now though, she never would have guessed it. The woman was strikingly beautiful. She'd heard it said that every woman looked stunning on her wedding day, but

Maggie sensed that Lexi looked just as breathtaking in jeans and a T-shirt.

"Thanks," Lexi said to Maggie.

Maggie was caught off guard. "For what?"

"For surrendering Michael for a few minutes. Honestly, I don't know what I'd do without him. Has he told you about my challenges?"

"A little. I hope you don't mind."

"Not at all," Lexi told her. "It is what it is. If you're going to be a part of this family, you should know."

Maggie blinked.

Taryn chuckled. "Uh-oh, Lex. She's got that *deer caught in the headlights* look. I don't think she knows."

Before Maggie could respond, two more women made their way over to the table. One was a gorgeous blonde with multihued hair in streaks of gold, platinum, and bronze; the other was equally attractive with dark hair and cherry-red highlights. The dark-haired one walked with a cane.

"Is this the girls' table?" the petite blonde asked, sinking down before waiting for an answer.

"Oh, thank God," the brunette said, joining them. "I think I'm OD'ing on male hormones here."

Taryn laughed. "Tell me about it. I think it should be illegal to have this much testosterone in an enclosed space."

Maggie couldn't help it. She smiled, having had similar thoughts only a few minutes earlier. The room was filled with more stunning alpha-male types than she'd ever seen in one place before. Well, excluding the time Sherri had talked her into seeing the Chippendales show when their tour took them to Philadelphia. But even those men couldn't compete with these guys. The Chippendales put on a show. The Callaghans were the real deal. The thought of Michael giving her a private lap dance sent a delicious shiver up and down her spine.

Taryn's grin grew wider, as if she knew what Maggie was thinking.

Lexi took care of the introductions. "Maggie, this is Lina."

The pretty blonde gave a warm smile.

"And this is Stacey."

The brunette offered a friendly wave.

"Maggie's here with Michael," Taryn explained, exchanging a glance with the others.

"Ooh, he's a good one," Lina said, slipping out of her shoes and rubbing her feet. "Honestly, how do women wear heels all day long? Barefoot and pregnant is a walk in the park compared to this." She turned to Maggie. "So, how did you guys meet?"

Maggie felt her cheeks flame again and shot a quick glance toward Lexi, who laughed and patted her hand.

"It's okay, Maggie. Michael said you might feel weird about it, but honestly, I think it's awesome. After all, you did all the work, and we got all the benefits." She winked.

At Lina's and Stacey's puzzled looks, Lexi asked, "Can I tell them?"

Maggie nodded, though she wasn't convinced it was the best of ideas.

Lexi leaned forward and dropped her voice. "Maggie is the woman who danced at Ian's bachelor party."

Maggie braced herself for condescending looks and catty comments, so she was unprepared for their reactions.

"Oh. My. God," Lina said, her eyes growing large. "That was you?" When Maggie indicated that it was, Lina leaned forward excitedly. "Can you teach me?"

"Me too," Stacey chimed in. "Whatever you did, woman, it had our husbands in thrall."

Maggie was stunned. There had to be some mistake. "You must have me confused with my friend Sherri. She dances all the time. Professionally. I'm sure she'd be very flattered."

But Taryn was shaking her head, smiling. "No, Maggie. It was you. Jake told me everything."

"And anything that got Michael to spend three days holed up in your house during a blizzard? Honey, you've got yourself pure magic right there," Lexi added.

"Oh, I don't think he meant for that to happen," Maggie said quickly. "It's not like it was planned or anything."

Lexi was shaking her head, her expression more serious than it had been. "Maggie, I'm not sure how much you know about these guys, but you need to trust us on this. Everything they do is intentional, down to the smallest detail. Nothing is left to chance.

Michael knew when that storm would hit to the minute, I'd bet. If he was at your house, it was because he wanted to be. And believe me, if he didn't want to stay there, he would have found some way to leave, blizzard or not."

"It must have been so romantic," Lina said with a sigh. "Just the two of you in the middle of a blizzard, cut off from everything ..."

"That sounds like a great story line," Stacey said, her eyes glittering. "What was it like?"

Under normal circumstances, Maggie wouldn't even consider talking about the time she and Michael had spent together with women she'd just met. But there was something about them that pulled her in and made her feel like she was one of them. It was not something she was accustomed to, and it felt kind of nice. Maybe it was the brandy, maybe it was the romance of the wedding, but Maggie found herself sharing. Not the intimate details, of course, but she couldn't help but gush a little. It *had* been pretty romantic.

"Well, we lost power early on. Thankfully, it's an old house with a huge fireplace, and I had lots of candles on hand."

"That sounds awesome," said another voice from just behind her. "What are we talking about?"

"Ah, Keely, there you are. Maggie was just telling us about being trapped in a blizzard for three days with Michael. Her Michael—not your Michael, of course," Lina said.

Keely pulled up a chair between Maggie and Stacey. "Ooh," she said, pouring herself a drink from the bottle she'd brought with her before passing it around. "Michael is yummy and a total sweetheart. Do tell."

Maggie didn't go into explicit details, but they did seem really interested and asked lots of questions. By the time her glass had been refilled several times—as had theirs—they were all sighing.

"I always knew he was a hopeless romantic," Lexi said.

"I am so pulling a couple of fuses when we get back tonight," Keely murmured.

"Michael is going to make an awesome husband, Maggie. Good catch, girlfriend," said Stacey.

"Yeah, and you're cool too," said Lina. "We were afraid Michael would end up with someone a little more ..." She scrunched up her nose, searching for the right word.

"Stuck-up," Taryn finished.

The rest of them nodded in agreement.

Maggie's eyes opened wide. "Oh, we're not ... I mean, he hasn't ..." she stuttered, unable to stammer her way into clarification. "We've barely known each other a week."

They smiled, as if they knew a secret she didn't.

It was Lexi who spoke first. "Trust us on this, Maggie. Michael plans on marrying you."

"How could you possibly know that?"

"Because we've been in your shoes, Maggie. It's fast,

it's furious, and you can't believe it's happening, but it is. And you know in your heart that it's right even if your mind can't quite wrap itself around the idea."

It was as if they *knew*.

Maggie had refused to let herself think too much about it. About the feelings she had when she was with Michael. About the way he'd wrapped himself around her heart and commanded her soul. Things like this just didn't happen, except maybe in books.

"There's one way to know for sure," Taryn said quietly.

The other women nodded somberly, knowledge in their expressions.

"How?" Maggie wondered how her voice could tremble so much on a single word.

Keely tipped the brandy into Maggie's glass and nodded slightly, encouraging her to sip. Maggie gratefully raised it to her lips.

Taryn leaned forward and dropped her voice, so only those at the table could hear. "Our men, they aren't choir boys, not even Michael."

Maggie had suspected as much but had been afraid to ask.

"Among other things, they've had their fair share of women. But they are careful men, Maggie, and like we said before, they leave nothing to chance."

Taryn paused, searching for the right words. "Jake told me once that they are of the belief that there is but one woman fated for each of them. They even have a name for her. They call her their *croie*."

Maggie's mind translated the word. "Heart?"

"Heart, soul mate. When they find her, their heart and body will recognize her, even before their mind does. When they find her, Maggie, they will not use protection. It goes against every instinct they have, and these men live and breathe by their instincts. *That's* how you know if you're the one." Taryn took a deep breath and sat back.

Several emotions hit Maggie one after the other in a multi-feeling pile-up; the resulting wreckage was a jumble of hope, denial, shock, and fear. Maggie tipped the glass and downed the rest of her drink in one swallow.

Lexi placed her hand over Maggie's. Keely did the same on the other side.

"It's okay, Maggie," Lexi said. "These are good men. Michael's a good man. You'll never find another man who will care for you the way he does."

"She's right, you know," Taryn said. "We all tried fighting it, but in the end, it's pointless. You need him as much as he needs you."

"Like all great love stories," Lexi added.

"But those are just stories," Maggie murmured, feeling numb and dizzy. "They're not real."

"More real than you'd think," Lina said.

"And your story, that is pure gold right there. Do you mind?"

Maggie looked at Stacey and blinked. She didn't have a clue what Stacey was talking about.

"Stacey's an author," Lina explained. "She's always

looking for ideas. I think we've all contributed in one way or another."

Stacey grinned. "With a family like this"—she spread her hands out, encompassing the entire room—"I have enough material to last me a lifetime."

"What kind of stories do you write?"

"Romantic, erotic fiction."

"Like Salienne Dulcette?"

The women exchanged knowing glances.

"You know Salienne's work then?" Lina asked.

"I love it," Maggie confessed somewhat shyly.

Why did she have the feeling she was missing something? Her mind was still reeling from Taryn's bombshell and buzzing comfortably from the brandy she'd been sipping. When she spoke, it was as if someone else were speaking for her.

"As a matter of fact, I posted a thank-you note on her website yesterday," she added. "Her books can be very, um, educational."

Maggie was shocked by the words that came out on their own, but the other women nodded in ready agreement.

"Which book did you find especially helpful?" Stacey asked.

"The one set along the beach, where the woman takes charge and surprises the man by sneaking into his room and waking him in the middle of the night ..."

"Oh, I love that one!" Taryn exclaimed. "Jake was appreciative too," she added with a wink.

"One of my personal favorites," Stacey said.

"Though I must admit, that one required extensive research. There's so much mystery there, you know?"

"I'll bet Johnny didn't mind helping you solve that particular mystery," Keely said with a laugh.

"No"—Stacey grinned—"he didn't at that."

"Wait a minute," Maggie said, finally catching on. "Are you telling me that you are ..."

"Salienne Dulcette, in the flesh," Lexi finished.

"So, what do you think, Maggie? Would you mind if I used the blizzard theme in my next novel? I'll send you the first copy."

"Uh, no, not at all," Maggie said, her head swimming.

CHAPTER SEVENTEEN

"**N**ow, that looks like trouble," Jake said when they reentered the room and spotted all of the women at one table.

Michael was thinking the same thing.

"Ready, Lex?" Michael asked when he reached the table.

What had he been thinking, leaving Maggie alone with them like that? It had taken longer to get back than he'd thought; his brothers had had several things to discuss.

"Just do it here," Lexi said, pulling one side of her gown up to her thigh. "I'm too tired to make it up to the office."

Taryn scooched over, allowing Michael access. Because of the way the table was positioned, no one besides those already there were privy to what was happening.

It only took a few seconds to give her the shot, and the guests were none the wiser.

Lexi closed her eyes and patted his arm. "Thanks, Michael," she said warmly.

Once Lexi was taken care of, Michael turned his attention back to Maggie. Her eyes were unfocused, her expression somewhat shell-shocked. He narrowed his eyes when he saw Maggie reach for her glass and miss. She didn't even seem to notice that he'd returned.

"What did you do to her?" Michael asked.

Five pairs of female eyes locked on him.

Taryn smirked. "The question is, Michael, what did *you* do to her?"

"Ah fuck," Jake muttered. "Should have known better. Sorry, Mick."

Jake signaled toward the bar, where the other husbands were wisely keeping their distance.

"Maggie?" Michael asked. "Dance with me, sweetheart."

She slowly lifted her eyes. The look she gave him shook him to his core.

What exactly had they been telling her?

She took his hand and stood slowly. She said nothing as she shuffled to the dance floor behind him.

The band was playing a slow ballad, for which he was thankful. Maggie leaned into him and laid her head against his shoulder, so he was unable to see her expression. They swayed to the music, her movements more mechanical than natural.

"You okay?" he asked quietly.

"I'm not sure," she answered.

"Talk to me, Maggie."

"I think I'm going to visit the ladies' room," she murmured. Her voice sounded eerily distant. "It's quite warm in here."

"Of course."

Michael led her from the reception out toward the center of the complex. The ballrooms were arranged in a semicircle around a huge lobby. Restrooms appeared on the other side.

"I'll wait here," Michael said.

"I'll be fine." Her lips curved slightly.

He had no idea what was going through her mind, what she was thinking. Her emotions, usually so evident in her eyes and her expression, were unreadable. He didn't like it, not at all.

"Please. Go back to the reception. Give me a few minutes to regroup. A little air and a splash of cold water, and I'll be right as rain."

He opened his mouth to argue, but she pressed a finger to his lips.

"Please, Michael. Do this for me."

He searched her eyes but found nothing that gave him a clue. "What's going on, Maggie?" he asked.

"Nothing," she said evenly. "I had too much brandy —that's all. I'm just asking you to give me a few minutes to catch my breath and pull myself together before I end up embarrassing both of us."

Something didn't feel right, but he was hesitant to say so. People were streaming around them, coming and going. It was neither the time nor the place to push the issue.

Finally, he nodded. "All right. If that's what you want."

Her shoulders sagged in relief. "It is. Thank you."

He released her reluctantly and then watched as she made her way into the ladies' room. The fact that she held her hands away from her body a bit, as if to balance herself, did not escape him.

Michael returned to the Grand Ballroom, as she had asked, but stayed at the arched entryway, so he could watch for her and escort her back to the reception. Or, if she preferred, he'd make their excuses and take her home. Minutes passed, feeling longer than they should have. Michael paced back and forth, worry growing with each tick of his watch.

"Mick," Jake said, appearing behind him. "Is she okay?"

"I don't know. What the hell happened?"

"I'm not sure," Jake said slowly. "Taryn's not talking, and neither is Lexi. They just keep saying to give her some time and space, something about shock and denial being the first stages."

Michael ran a hand through his hair, his expression flustered. "What the hell does that mean?"

"Damn if I know. Want me to ask one of them to go in and check on her?"

Michael nodded. He'd been on the verge of

heading in himself, but Jake's suggestion was better and less likely to draw attention.

Just as Jake left to deliver the message, Maggie emerged from the ladies' room. She didn't even glance his way, her expression one of extreme concentration. She moved slowly, her hand on the wall, as if she was feeling her way. Dread settled in the pit of Michael's stomach as he started toward her, praying that she'd just had too much to drink, but the feeling of unease that had been plaguing him was now roaring in his ears.

STAYING upright and putting one foot in front of the other required all of Maggie's concentration. With each passing moment, she felt increasingly worse. If she could just make it outside to the fresh air, she could text Michael and ask him to bring the car around. She hated the thought of making him leave his brother's wedding early on her account, but she needed to get home and lie down for a while.

Without warning, a man came out of the men's room and plowed right into Maggie. With quick reflexes, he shot his arms out and caught her before she hit the ground, apologizing profusely.

"Maggie, is that you?" the man asked as he tried to steady her.

Maggie tried to focus, but it was difficult. Her head was spinning, her vision blurry. The voice was familiar, but it definitely wasn't Michael's, and it took her a moment to place it.

"Spencer?"

"God, Maggie, you look stunning." Spencer Dumas held her at arm's length and looked her up and down appreciatively.

Maggie tried to take a step back, but Spencer had a firm grip on her upper arms.

"Excuse me, Spencer. I was just on my way out." She felt something warm trickling above her lip and self-consciously reached her fingers up. When she pulled them away, the tips were stained a dark red.

"Get your hands off of her, Dumas," said a deep voice.

Suddenly, Maggie was tugged backward, vaguely recognizing the warmth of Michael's hard body and the clean male scent that was uniquely his.

"Callaghan?" Spencer blinked and then narrowed his eyes at Maggie. "You're with *him*?"

Maggie tried to answer, but somewhere between her brain and her mouth, the message became garbled. She leaned heavily into Michael, grasping at his arm for balance.

"I've got you, Maggie." His voice sounded distant, but she could feel the rumbles through his chest as he spoke.

She heard Spencer's voice again, angry and insistent, and then another voice—Jake's?—warning him off.

Suddenly, she was weightless and moving quickly.

It was getting harder to stay awake. Every now and then, she'd hear Michael calling to her, but she couldn't answer.

Bright lights flashed through her closed lids, and then there was only darkness.

CHAPTER EIGHTEEN

Maggie opened her eyes, but her view remained dark and murky. Occasionally, she thought she'd glimpsed a flash of light but no clear shapes or images. Sounds, too, were muffled. Low ones, high ones, rhythmic ones.

She shivered, her body cold and uncomfortable. Cool air blew over her skin. Something squeezed her arm tightly and then released. She couldn't move. *Why can't I move?*

"I think she's coming around," said an unfamiliar voice.

"Maggie, can you hear me, sweetheart?" *Michael.*

She wanted to answer, but she couldn't. Nothing was working. *Why isn't anything working?*

Ow! Something stung her arm. She tried to jerk away but was stung again.

"*Maggie.*" Michael spoke again, more urgent this

time. "Don't fight this, baby. I've got you. Everything is going to be all right."

Maggie turned toward the sound of his voice.

"She hears you, Doctor," a woman said. "Keep talking. Maybe I can get a line in."

A line? What the hell were they talking about? Where am I? Who is that woman, and why is she talking to Michael?

"Maggie, you are in the emergency room of Pine Ridge Medical Center. You collapsed at the reception. We're going to take care of you, sweetheart." Michael's voice was soothing, but his words terrified her.

A hospital? No!

Michael knew how she felt about hospitals. She started fighting again.

"Maggie, calm down. I've got you, baby."

"No!" She forced a scream, but it came out as a rasping shriek.

With everything she had, she tried to sit up, to turn, to do something. She had to get out, had to get out *now*. Panic gripped her heart, and it was hard to breathe.

Strong hands pressed down on her shoulders, her arms, her legs.

"Maggie! Maggie, stop. It's okay."

∾

MICHAEL TRIED to keep his voice even, but it was difficult. She was scared and panicking, and it was ripping him apart inside.

"Doctor?"

"Use the restraints. I want her sedated *now*."

For one horrible moment, Maggie seemed to look right at him, but it quickly became apparent she could not see him.

"Michael, no. Please, don't do this ..." She started sobbing hysterically.

The others looked to him for direction, hesitant to do anything that might land them in a lawsuit. Providing emergency care in a life-or-death situation was one thing, but there was no doubt Maggie didn't want treatment. Rendering care to an adult against his or her wishes was against policy, no matter how much they might want to help. Unfortunately, healthcare had become more about litigation than doing what was best for the patient.

Icy-cold fear continued to claw at his chest. Michael had seen his share of blood, but the trickles from Maggie's nose, right eye, and ear had terrified him more than any other. He'd held her tightly in his arms as Jake rushed them to the hospital. At first, she was disoriented, but at least she seemed to recognize him on some level. Then, she'd been totally unresponsive, limp in his arms. Now, she was coming out of it, confused and in the midst of a full-blown panic attack.

He cursed himself repeatedly. He'd *known* something was wrong. He'd ignored his instincts, afraid of alienating her. Now, he prayed fervently that it wasn't too late.

They no longer had the luxury of choice. His inaction and Maggie's refusal to seek treatment might have already cost Maggie her sight, and with or without her permission, he was going to make damn sure she didn't lose anything else.

"Get out, all of you," he ordered the ER staff.

He saw the relief, the uncertainty in their eyes, but they did as he'd said. All except one nurse, who had worked with Michael on a number of occasions. Michael acknowledged her with a brief but grateful nod.

"Jake," Michael barked to his brother, who'd appeared at the doorway. "Get over here and secure her."

Jake moved without hesitation, using his long arms and strength to keep Maggie from thrashing around.

"Nancy, call Radiology and tell them we're on our way up. Full head series, stat."

Maggie's screams reduced to pitiful whimpers that broke Michael's heart.

"Sweetheart, shh. I'm going to make you sleep now. I promise, I won't leave you."

He nodded to the nurse. "Do it."

Within seconds, Maggie's cries ceased, and she went still.

～

"YOU SAVED HER LIFE," Lexi said quietly. She'd come by Maggie's private hospital room to check in and provide encouragement and support. They all had.

Michael didn't respond. He checked the monitors for the hundredth time. Adjusted the IV lines. Tucked the blankets more snugly around her.

"You didn't have a choice, Michael. She'll understand that."

Michael smoothed the hair back from Maggie's forehead, wondering how much longer he'd have the privilege of doing so. How much longer would he be able to hold her hand and whisper soothing words into her ear? How long before she told him to get out of her life and never come back?

He'd replayed the last few weeks in his head, wondering what he could have done differently, and kept returning to the same conclusion. If he had pressed Maggie to seek medical attention, she would have pushed him away and not gone. Yes, he regretted that he hadn't listened to his instincts, but at least he had been there when she really needed him.

He couldn't bear to think what might have happened if he hadn't been there.

He didn't understand Maggie's fears, but he understood his own. He loved her, and he'd done what he had to do. She might see it as a betrayal, but maybe someday, she'd find it in her heart to forgive him. If not, well, he'd have to live with the consequences. If he had chosen to respect her wishes, he'd have been making funeral arrangements instead of sitting at her bedside, waiting for her to awaken.

The neurosurgeon had been very clear. Had the smaller of the two hematomas not burst first, Maggie wouldn't have survived. In treating the first, they discovered the second and were able to take care of it before it came to that. The specialist had pointed out, however, that had she come in earlier, they might have spotted the clots and been able to provide treatment.

Michael hoped Lexi was right, but his gut told him otherwise.

"THERE IS NO IMPROVEMENT," the neurosurgeon said several days later, clicking off his silver penlight and slipping it back into his front pocket.

Maggie, now awake, didn't flinch. She was as still as marble, no expression on her face, yet Michael felt her disappointment keenly, as if his heart was linked directly to hers.

"Prognosis?"

The surgeon checked his watch. Michael had always respected James Roberts for his unparalleled skill with a scalpel. The other man's coldness hadn't registered before.

Is this how physicians come across to most people? he wondered. *Impersonal, unaffected, uncaring?*

"Hard to say. Vision might return as the swelling recedes."

"What do we do now?"

Roberts was already at the door. He hadn't spoken once to Maggie other than to issue short commands. "She can go. I've already signed the discharge papers. No heavy lifting, no bending. Have her schedule an appointment with my office for a post-op in two weeks."

Michael placed his hand on the door, preventing the other man from leaving. "That's it?"

"I'm due in surgery." When Michael pinned him with an unwavering stare, the man sighed. "I wish I could be more optimistic, Michael, but you of all people know that there are no guarantees. There's a chance. That's all the hope I can give you. I'm sorry."

Michael let him leave, resting his head on the door for a moment. That was not what he'd been hoping to hear.

He turned his eyes to Maggie. She looked so fragile, so small there in that hospital bed, pale skin against the stark white coverings. She stared at the hands in her lap with unseeing eyes, broken. His chest ached.

Somehow, he would find a way to make her whole again.

"Looks like you're good to go," he said, forcing a cheerfulness into his voice he didn't feel. "I'll call Ian while you get dressed. He can meet us at your place."

Ian and Lexi had volunteered to take care of George while Maggie was in the hospital. Their young son, Patrick, had fallen in love with the basset at first sight.

Maggie had yet to speak to him since waking up. She had answered some basic questions in the recovery room after emergency surgery to remove the clots, enough for them to know that her speech and mental functions were intact, but had been silent since. He wished she would yell at him, scream at him, vent the frustration and anger and fear she must be feeling. He would bear it; he would gladly take it all. But she didn't. She remained silent, stoic, and refused to acknowledge him.

She was almost dressed when he returned, finishing the last of the buttons on her shirt. He looked around, gathering the personal items he'd brought for her—her hairbrush, her toothbrush, the flannel shirt of his she liked to wear at night, now folded neatly and placed off to the side. She'd refused to wear it, opting for the backless hospital gown instead. It hurt more than he cared to admit.

A nurse came in with a wheelchair. Michael guided Maggie into it, though she pulled away at the first possible moment.

"I'll take her from here, Sally, thanks."

The drive to Maggie's was a silent one. When they arrived, he noticed that the walks and driveway had been cleared. Logs had been split and were stacked neatly off the porch. A roaring fire blazed in the hearth; the inside of the house was warm. The refrigerator was freshly stocked with prepared meals, enough for a week at least. Not for the first time, Michael was grateful to his family for taking such good care of everything.

"Who did all this?" Maggie asked quietly. She didn't need her sight to know that she hadn't had to trudge through snow or that her house was warm and filled with the scents of food. She knew it wasn't Michael. He hadn't left her side for the past three days.

"Lexi and Taryn did the inside stuff. My brothers took care of the outside."

Maggie felt the walls starting to crumble. Keeping herself together had been much easier when she was in the hospital. That was such a cold, sterile place, filled with strangers. This was her home. And Michael's family had gone to so much trouble.

"Please thank them for me."

"You can thank them yourself."

She felt his hand at her back, hating it and loving it at the same time. One part of her longed for him to hold her in his arms and shut out the rest of the world. To make love to her until she forgot everything else. Another part wanted nothing to do with him. He had done the one thing she could not forgive—he had taken away her choice.

Decision made, she stepped away from his touch.

"Thanks for bringing me home."

"You're welcome. Maggie—"

"I'd like you to leave now."

Michael's jaw clenched. For one brief, hopeful moment, she'd looked as if she might be softening toward him, but then her features hardened again, and she moved away.

"I don't think so."

She sighed in resignation, as if his response was no less than what she'd expected. With one hand on the wall, she proceeded carefully down the hallway, just like she had that first night he brought her home. Except then, he'd been on the brink of something new and wonderful, tingling with anticipation, knowing that he'd found someone special.

That night, she'd seemed pleasantly surprised by his desire to care for her. Now, that same desire had erected a huge wall between them, one that he wasn't sure he'd be able to find his way over.

Instead of continuing into the kitchen like she had then, Maggie went for the stairs. She took them slowly, one at a time. At the top, she turned left, entered her bedroom, and closed the door.

Michael exhaled heavily. This was not going to be easy.

"She'll come around, Michael," Taryn said, patting his arm.

They were sitting at Maggie's kitchen table,

drinking coffee. Taryn had brought over additional meals, though there was more than enough in the fridge. Maggie had been eating even less than before, and Michael couldn't seem to summon much of an appetite these days either.

"The only time she leaves her room is when she thinks I've gone outside," he said, the sadness in his voice unmistakable. "It's gotten so that I open and close the door and then sit off to the side, just to see her. She hasn't spoken to me since I brought her home."

Taryn was quiet for a few minutes. "Maybe you should give her some space."

"I don't want her to be alone."

"I know. And I know you don't want to hear this, but … if Jake hadn't let me go, I never would have had the chance to realize how much I love him. I think Lexi would say the same thing about Ian." She paused, letting that sink in.

Michael shook his head. "I don't think I can do that."

"I don't know that you have a choice."

THE NEXT DAY, Michael knocked softly on Maggie's bedroom door. He tried the knob and found it unlocked. Opening the door, he asked, "Mind if I come in?"

Maggie sat on her bed, George in her lap. She didn't protest, so he took a step inside.

He cleared his throat. "Maggie, I'm, uh, leaving. Please call if you need anything, anything at all. Taryn wanted me to tell you she's there for you, if you want to talk."

She might have nodded slightly—he couldn't be sure.

"I don't know if you'll ever forgive me. I hope you can someday. If you do, I'll be waiting, forever if I have to. But I'm not sorry, and you need to know that I'd do the same thing again in a heartbeat. I love you, Maggie. I can live with you hating me, but I don't think I could live in a world without you in it."

He turned and left then, quietly closing the door behind him.

A few moments later, Maggie heard the front door close. Heard the rumble of his truck starting up and driving away.

Then, there was silence.

And Maggie cried.

CHAPTER NINETEEN

Hours turned into days. Days turned into weeks. It snowed a few more times before the weather began to grow warmer. Maggie's vision had been improving slowly but steadily. After two months, it was close to being back to normal.

She hadn't bothered making follow-up appointments with the neurosurgeon; she wouldn't have gone anyway. She couldn't drive. Her pride and stubbornness wouldn't allow her to ask anyone for help even though someone called at least once every day to ask if she needed anything. She appreciated their offers—she really did—but they only reminded her of how much she'd lost. Eventually, she'd stopped answering the phone, letting their well-intentioned calls go directly to the machine.

It was more than stubborn pride that kept her from visiting the specialist. The man was as cold and caring as a block of ice. He'd already informed her that there was nothing more he could do for her. Either her vision would improve on its own over time or it wouldn't. She didn't need to pay upwards of two hundred dollars a visit—which she didn't have—for him to tell her what she already knew.

The house felt empty without Michael. Even George missed him. He hadn't been by once since he'd left. His brothers had come by occasionally, despite her refusal to pick up the phone. She watched them from behind the curtains as they walked around, checked things out, and scraped away bits of snow and ice she hadn't managed to clear herself. Taryn and Lexi stopped over every few days, too, but Maggie couldn't bring herself to face them. Shortly after her sight had begun to return, she had written an apology to Lexi and Ian, saying she was sorry for what had happened the night of their reception and thanking them for taking care of George while she'd been in the hospital.

Their calls, their visits, went unanswered.

What could Maggie say to them? That she loved Michael so much that it hurt? That, incapable of taking one day at a time, she had broken each day into hours, surviving from one to the next without believing she could? Of counting the seconds in her head when she was certain she simply could not bear another minute?

What would they tell her? That Michael loved her? Maggie already knew that. That he'd only done what he did because of that love? She knew that too. But it didn't excuse him. She had given him her heart, her very soul. Had done so willingly and without reservation. But that night in the hospital, Michael had taken her choice away from her. He'd stripped away her freedom, made decisions for her.

And that was unacceptable.

Maggie had seen firsthand what happened to a woman who surrendered her free will to those who claimed to have her best interests at heart. Her entire life had been shaped by one well-meaning but tragic event. After a difficult pregnancy, Maggie's mother had begun hemorrhaging a month early. She was rushed to the hospital, where a doctor made the decision—against her wishes—to deliver her early. As a result, Maggie's mother was left unable to have more children, and Maggie almost died. Her father was devastated. For five years, they'd tried to get past it, but Maggie and the care she required were constant reminders of everything they'd lost. Unable to cope, they'd left Maggie in the care of her grandparents and returned to Ireland.

Maggie's hand reached protectively around the slight swell of her belly. She would allow no one to risk her life or the life of the child growing within her, regardless of their intentions. *Ever.*

The starkness of winter slowly began to give way to the promise of spring. Maggie began plowing the fields, pruning the orchards. It was a long, arduous process, especially without her full vision. Even simple tasks, like getting the tractor key into the ignition, had to be done more by touch than by sight. But at least it kept her busy. She fell into bed each night, completely exhausted, where her dreams would take her back to Michael, to a time when she'd believed she had found true happiness.

One night, her dream turned into a nightmare. She dreamed that Michael was dying. With astounding clarity, she saw him, heard his brother's voice in her head.

"Hang on, Mick. Don't you fucking die on me, man, you hear me? Lexi's going to kick my ass if anything happens to you."

Maggie's dream self identified the voice as Ian's.

"And I'm not telling Taryn you got your sorry ass shot on my watch." That was Jake. "Mick—goddamn it, Mick! Stay with us!"

The image was blurry around the edges, but Maggie could see Michael and his brothers clearly, as if her vision were perfect once again. They were dressed in black, like the day they'd come to pick him up at her house. Jake was holding Michael in the back of a vehicle—a van maybe— while Ian was pressing something to his chest. Another man was driving. Though they hadn't been formally introduced, Maggie recognized him as Michael's older brother. She thought his name might be Kane.

Jake was trying to hold Michael as still as possible as they bounced along, swerving from side to side, moving at great speed.

"ETA?" Jake yelled up.

"Five minutes," Kane responded.

"Too long."

Kane cursed and the van lurched forward at an even greater speed.

"We're losing him," Ian said, pressing his fingers to Michael's neck.

The entire front of Michael's chest was wet. With growing horror, Maggie realized it was blood.

"Michael." Maggie's voice echoed throughout the back of the van.

The others didn't seem to hear her, but Michael did. His eyes popped open and sought her out, trying to focus.

"Maggie," he gasped.

Jake and Ian exchanged a glance.

"Yeah, that's right, man. Maggie's waiting for you. You can't let her down," Jake said.

"Come back to me, Michael. I need you." Maggie reached out with her hand. The moment she touched his face—it felt so real!—his eyes went wide. "I love you, Michael," she whispered. "You promised you'd wait, forever if you had to."

The van squealed to a stop, and they ripped Michael out of the van. Maggie tried to follow, but she couldn't, forced to stay behind and watch as they carried him out of sight.

Maggie woke with a start, covered in sweat. The clock read two twenty-two a.m. She could see the clock! Grabbing the phone, she dialed Taryn's number. Taryn picked up on the first ring, sounding wide awake.

"Taryn, it's Maggie. I need to speak to Michael."

Maggie clearly heard Taryn's sharp intake of breath over the line.

"Maggie, are you okay?"

"I'm fine, but I need to talk to Michael—right now."

There was a slight pause as Taryn put her hand over the phone and spoke quietly to someone.

"Michael's not here, Maggie."

Dread curled in her stomach, writhing like a nest of snakes. Her nightmare couldn't have been real; it just couldn't have been.

"Then, let me talk to Jake or Ian. Please, Taryn. It's important."

The long pause made her stomach roil.

"They're not here either."

The truth came crashing down around her. "Michael's hurt, Taryn. Badly. He's dying."

"How could you possibly know …"

Maggie didn't want to take the time to explain, not now. Besides, Taryn would probably think she was crazy. "I don't know. I just do. He can't die, Taryn—he *can't*—because he doesn't know that I still love him."

Another pause, another muffled exchange.

"Maggie, Lexi's here with me now. I'm going to send someone to get you, okay?"

BY THE TIME Shane arrived a short time later, Maggie was dressed and waiting by the door with George.

"Have you heard anything?" she asked as he carried George to the truck for her.

Shane studied her intently, as if deciding whether

to answer or not. "Not since you called," he said carefully.

"And before then?"

Again, Shane seemed reluctant to reply.

"Please," Maggie pleaded.

Shane studied her stricken face and took pity on her. "Michael's alive, last we heard."

She opened her mouth to say something, but Shane held up his hand.

"Please. No more questions until we get back to the pub."

She nodded. It was enough—for now. It would have to be.

An hour later, Maggie sat, dumbfounded, in the communal living room, stroking George. Taryn and Lexi were there, as were Shane, Sean, Kieran, and the Callaghan patriarch, Jack. The men were sitting in front of several laptops, wearing partial headsets, while Taryn and Lexi took turns explaining.

Maggie was taking the news rather well, though if she was honest with herself, she had suspected Michael and his brothers were more than they appeared to be on the outside. She still remembered the look Michael had given her when she made that quip about them looking like a black ops team.

"Why didn't Michael tell me any of this?" she asked.

"It is forbidden," Taryn said.

"I'm sure Michael wanted to tell you," Lexi added,

"but he couldn't, not until he got permission from the others."

Maggie caught the guarded glances of the brothers. They didn't trust her.

"So, why are you telling me now?"

Taryn looked at Lexi before turning back to Maggie. "You dreamed of him, didn't you? That's how you knew Michael was in trouble."

"Yes."

Taryn shot an *I told you so* look back at Shane. "You and Michael were meant for each other, Maggie. You were the only one who couldn't see it. But now, you do. And Michael needs you."

"I want to go to him."

Shane stood up abruptly, shaking his head. "No."

Maggie stood up too. "Why not?"

"Absolutely not. It's completely out of the question."

Kieran held up his hand for silence, pressing the receiver closer to his ear. "Hang on. Something's coming in from Ian." Kieran's expression barely changed, though it was obvious the news was not good by the subtle tightening of his jaw. When he turned to face them, his expression was grave. "Mick's asking for her. Maggie goes," he said.

Once the decision was made, things moved quickly. Maggie was rushed to a private airfield, where Sean ushered her onto a waiting plane. He shoved a bundle into her hands and told her to change and try to get some rest while he piloted the craft. Maggie did as he'd asked, pulling on the dark camo pants and shirt over her own clothes and tucking her hair securely under the cap he'd provided.

It was still dark outside when they landed, but from the few glimpses Maggie was able to get of her surroundings, she had the distinct impression they were on some kind of military base. With orders to keep her head down and her mouth shut, Sean took her arm and led her quickly into what looked like a two-seater military jet, much bigger than the small plane they'd started off in.

"You get airsick?" Sean asked as he belted her in securely.

"A little late to ask me that, isn't it?"

Sean smiled grimly. "This next leg is going to hit different."

"I'll manage," she told him.

He replaced her cap with a helmet and placed a bag into her hands. "If you feel sick, lift up the face plate before you hurl."

"Thanks for the tip."

It was by far the most breathtaking experience of her life, and by the end of it, Maggie was quite sure she didn't want to do it again. Thankfully, she had not embarrassed herself, though she was pretty shaky when they landed a second time. Even though Sean was forced to put an arm around her to keep her moving in a forward direction, he seemed relatively impressed.

From the jet, they were whisked away in a black

sedan, which Maggie found infinitely preferable. This time, someone else was driving, and Sean was in the backseat with her. He studied her intently.

"What?" she asked finally.

"You haven't once asked where we're going or why."

"I've been too busy trying not to vomit," she said, only half-joking. "But the where of it doesn't really matter as long as Michael's there, and I already know the why."

Sean pulled no punches. "Michael's in bad shape, Maggie."

"I know."

"There's a chance he might not—"

Maggie hit Sean with a look that stopped him from completing that sentence, her green eyes fierce. "Don't even *think* about saying it, Sean Callaghan, because if you do, I will completely lose the very thin thread of control remaining, and you will have a hysterical female on your hands. Michael is going to make it through this because I am going to make sure of it. Are we clear?"

"Yes, ma'am," Sean said, biting back a smile.

She pulled the bag he'd given her from her pocket and waved it in his face. "Call me ma'am again, and I'll shove this barf bag right up your arse."

The driver coughed, though it sounded suspiciously like a laugh.

The car wound through narrow streets, working its way up a mountain. In many ways, it reminded Maggie of the mountains at home. The temperature was on the cool side with the slight hint of rain in the air. Eventually, they pulled up to what looked like a modest castle, set far back from the road and hidden among the swells.

Jake was waiting outside. His face was grim, but he offered Maggie a brief smile.

"Thanks for coming, Maggie. I want to hear how you knew about this but later."

He guided her through a labyrinth of corridors, each heavily secured. Large, intimidating soldiers nodded to Jake as they passed.

They stopped outside a closed door, and Jake put his hand on Maggie's shoulder—a silent warning for what she would find on the other side.

She thought she'd prepared herself, but she hadn't. Michael lay on a hospital bed, perfectly still. His eyes were closed, a white sheet drawn up just above his hips. He was heavily bandaged across the chest. His breathing was labored.

"Why isn't he on oxygen?" Maggie asked quietly.

In answer, Jake pointed to the yellow paper taped on the wall above Michael's shoulder. Maggie read it, paling as she did so. It was a DNR—Do Not Resuscitate—order, a mandate to take no artificial measures to save his life. Maggie yanked it off the wall and ripped it into tiny pieces.

"Maggie, you can't—"

"The hell I can't," she snapped, her eyes flashing dangerously. "He didn't give me a choice. I'll not give him one. Did you hear that, Michael Callaghan? I'm here because of you, and you'll not be leaving me alone just yet."

At the sound of her voice, Michael's eyelids fluttered.

"Did you see that?" whispered Ian, who had been sitting quietly in the shadows.

"Say something else, Maggie," encouraged Jake. "I think he can hear you."

Maggie pushed a lock of hair away from Michael's forehead. "Michael, you can rest now. I'm here."

She leaned down and pressed a kiss to his forehead. Amazingly, his body relaxed a little, and his breathing eased just a bit.

"That's it, Michael," she said softly as she stroked his hair with tenderness. "That's it. I'm here now, and I'm not going anywhere."

Within a few minutes, Michael seemed to be resting comfortably.

"That's the most amazing thing I've ever seen," Jake said, shaking his head.

Keeping the same calm, soothing voice, Maggie asked, "If I give you a list of things, can you get them?"

"What kind of things?" Jake asked.

"A few herbs, some teas, things like that."

"We'll get it," Ian said confidently. "Just tell us what you need."

CHAPTER TWENTY

Michael knew he was close to death. He'd heard enough people describe the sudden feeling of peace that came over them. How they heard the voices of the ones they loved, easing them through the process, before they were brought back. It wasn't that he had doubted them, but he wasn't sure the same thing would happen to him.

He always wondered though ... if it did happen, whose voice would he hear? He thought it might be his mother's. It had been so long since he'd heard it; she had died nearly twenty years earlier when he was still a boy. Yet he knew he would recognize it instantly.

Whenever he had been sick, his mother would sit on the side of his bed and speak softly to him. It was as if she had known the sound of her voice was what he needed more than anything else. Sometimes, she would read him a story, and sometimes, she would talk about anything and nothing at all until he fell into a restful sleep. She would stroke his hair, just like she was doing right now ...

Except that it wasn't his mother's voice he'd heard, he realized. It was Maggie's. And her soft, lilting voice was getting an edge to it.

"JUST WHAT DO you think you're doing?" Maggie asked the young nurse who had entered the room and was now setting up a tray with a basin of water, pH-balanced cleanser, and a sponge. In Maggie's opinion, she was looking far too happy about it.

"I must ask you to leave," the nurse said with an accent Maggie couldn't quite place. Russian possibly? "It is time for his sponge bath."

Maggie's eyes narrowed; her hand stilled momentarily. Jake, who was sitting in the corner—one of Michael's brothers was with him at all times—was biting the inside of his mouth, presumably to keep the smile off of his face.

Maggie failed to see the humor. She did smile, however. It was a wide smile, one that showed quite a few teeth, and it did not reach her eyes. "Oh, I don't think so."

The nurse hesitated but then got a determined look on her face.

She began to argue, but Maggie cut her off immediately. "Sorry, honey, no playtime for you today. I will give him his bath."

The nurse looked from Michael, to Maggie, and back to Michael again. She was several inches taller than Maggie, but Maggie had the mother-bear look about her that said it would be no contest. If the nurse was smart, she'd turn quietly and leave. She wasn't, apparently deciding that sponge-bathing Michael would be worth the trouble.

"That is not acceptable. You are not qualified."

Maggie's smile grew as she stood.

Thankfully, Jake chose that moment to speak up, "Actually, nurse, she is. And I'm afraid you do not have the necessary clearance."

Ignoring her protests, he took her lightly by the arm and escorted her to the door.

"I could have taken her," Maggie said when Jake pulled the door closed again.

"Of that, I have no doubt," Jake said, grinning. "Removing her from the room was for her protection, not yours."

Maggie's face relaxed as she grinned back at him. Her expression turned to a look of surprise when she felt a tug on her hand.

"*Maggie.*"

Michael's eyes were open. His voice was rough, raspy.

Maggie took a cloth and dipped it in ice water, holding it to his lips. He swallowed gratefully.

"Michael," she said, tears forming in her eyes. "I knew you wouldn't leave me just yet."

"You shouldn't be here. It's not safe. You need to go." He sounded so weak, as if the effort it took to speak cost him greatly.

"You need to be quiet," she told him. "I'm not leaving without you, so you can just forget that."

"Need to go. Tell Jake. Get home."

He was getting himself worked up, and Maggie knew that was not a good thing.

"Michael, if you continue to fight me on this, I'm going to have your brothers put you in restraints, and I'm going to stick a needle into your arse to put you out, just like you did to me. And unlike you, I'm not very good with a needle. I might have to jab it in there several times until I get it right."

Michael glared at her but kept his mouth shut.

"That's better," she said. "Now, listen to me. If you want me out of here, you're going to have to get your arse out of that bed and drag me, kicking and screaming, out the door yourself. Until then, I am afraid you are stuck with me."

Michael looked pleadingly at Jake, who held up his hands.

"I'm not taking her on," he said. "Especially after what she almost did to that nurse who tried to give you a sponge bath."

The tiniest hint of a smile curved Michael's mouth. "Sponge bath?" he said, his gravelly voice sounding hopeful.

Maggie bit her lip. "Uh-huh."

"I'll wait out in the hall," Jake said wisely. "Yell if you need me."

MAGGIE LAVISHED constant attention on Michael over the next week, refusing to accept the lodging the brothers had offered her. She spent her nights at Michael's side, her days bathing him, massaging him, reading, and talking to him. She made him special teas and spent hours stroking his hair and pampering him.

More than once, Ian suggested that Michael wasn't half as sick as he pretended to be, just so Maggie would fuss over him some more. In response, Michael generously offered to shoot him so that Lexi might give him the same treatment, but Maggie discouraged it, saying that Lexi had enough on her plate already.

Between Maggie's attention and the medical care, Michael improved rapidly. The doctor cleared him for transport back home, but insisted he would have to take it easy for a while.

SEEING the lights of the Pine Ridge valley as they topped the crest of the mountain and began their downward descent was the second most beautiful thing he'd ever seen. The first had been waking up to Maggie's face in the hospital.

A low-key welcome-home celebration was awaiting them. Maggie was awed by the love and support of Michael's family.

All families should be like this, she thought, *and the world would be a much better place.*

There was a substantial amount of appreciation for Maggie as well, though the attention made her uncomfortable. Several times, she tried to slip into the shadows to turn the focus back onto Michael. He never let her stray far, his eyes ever watchful.

No matter how many times they asked, she couldn't give them the answers they sought. She couldn't explain the dream she'd had any more than they could.

"Some things," she told them quietly, "should simply be accepted and not questioned."

"Have you told him yet?" Taryn asked during a quiet moment when everyone else was otherwise occupied. "About the baby, I mean?"

Maggie thought about pretending she didn't know what Taryn was talking about but decided against it. It seemed pointless. Taryn had already proven that she was light-years ahead of Maggie on the understanding scale.

"How did you know?"

Taryn smiled. "Because I was in your place once." The smile faded. "I lost our first baby. Jake doesn't think I know, but I do. I was attacked, you see, and ended up in a coma..." She shook her head. "It's a long story, one for another time. The point is, maybe if I had been upfront with him instead of running away, trying to fool myself into thinking that I didn't need him ..."

"I'm so sorry," Maggie said sincerely.

"Thanks," Taryn said. "We have Riley now, and she's wonderful, but I'll always wonder, you know? What would her big brother have been like? Would he have had Jake's eyes and the cockeyed Callaghan grin?" She paused as her voice broke slightly, taking a moment to regain control. "Anyway, I just wanted to say that if you're waiting for the right time, or the right place, or for things to be perfect, don't. Because like it or not, tomorrow is not guaranteed, not for any of us."

MICHAEL GLANCED over at that moment and caught the seriousness of Maggie's expression.

"What was that all about?" he asked when they were on their way back to Maggie's house, where Michael would continue his recovery under Maggie's watchful eye.

"What was what all about?" Maggie asked, but given the way she avoided his eyes, she knew exactly what he was talking about.

"The little chat you had with Taryn."

"Oh, that. It was nothing."

"Usually, when you say something is *nothing*, it turns out to be a very substantial *something*," Michael said.

"There's a lot we need to talk about, Michael, but not tonight, okay?"

"Not tonight," he agreed. Tonight, he needed to be with Maggie, to lose himself in her and forget everything else.

Maggie's house was dark, but as before, plenty of firewood was stacked neatly, and a nice pile had been assembled in the fireplace, waiting only for a match to set it ablaze. The fridge was full, a bowl of fresh fruit was on the table, and the cupboards were packed with Michael's favorite snacks.

"I could really get used to your family," she said approvingly. "They're spoiling me rotten."

"Family takes care of family," he said simply. It was how things were done. They didn't question it; they just did it.

"But I'm not family, Michael."

Michael pulled her into his arms. "Yes, Maggie, you are. You belong to me, as I belong to you. Surely, you know that by now."

Michael lowered his head and kissed her fully, passionately. There was no gentleness, no easing into it. It was a kiss of possession, a kiss of forgiveness, and she gave herself up to it completely. Maggie took his hand and led him up to the bedroom.

∾

"Maybe it's too soon," she said hesitantly after unbuttoning his shirt and seeing the bandages that still covered the wound.

Michael's eyes had become a deep sapphire blue. He undid the clasp of his belt, letting the sides hang freely. "Come here." His voice was low, husky, filled with hunger. It made Maggie's insides tighten and ignited the inner burn she always felt around him, stealing her breath away.

Dutifully, Maggie placed her hands on his jeans and unsnapped the fastening, subconsciously licking her lips in anticipation as the tip of him strained over the top. Pleasuring Michael had become somewhat of an obsession for her; she loved the control, the power she had over him.

Before she had a chance to lower his zipper, he grabbed the sides of her shirt and pulled, sending buttons flying as he exposed her. Before the startled cry left her lips, he was on his knees, sucking her through the satin and lace bra while his hands traced her curves from hips to breasts.

"So pretty," he murmured, torturing first one breast and then the other until her knees went weak.

Her hands tangled in his hair, longer than it normally was, holding him close. She had forgotten how devastating Michael's touch could be.

"Do you know how much I've missed this?" he murmured against her. "How, every night, I woke up, reaching for you, Maggie?"

With a snap of his fingers, the front clasp of her bra was undone, and he was peeling it away, pushing the straps from her shoulders. The searing, wet heat of his mouth against her bare skin made her whimper.

While his mouth worked her breasts—her incredibly sensitive breasts—his hands slipped between them and went to work on her jeans, skillfully undoing them and coaxing them down to her ankles before she kicked them away.

"I need to taste you," he said roughly, his words muffled against her skin.

He cupped her behind and guided her back onto the bed.

"Maggie ..."

He lay down and firmly grasped her hips, pulling her up until she straddled his face. A cry ripped from her throat when she felt that first glide of his tongue. His arms locked like iron bands around her hips, taking control, holding her exactly where he wanted her.

He ravaged her with his mouth. He licked. He bit. He sucked, groaning when she spilled over his tongue.

"Michael," she screamed, her hands clutching at the headboard. "Oh, Michael, don't stop!"

Her pleas inflamed him; he attacked with renewed vigor, plunging his tongue deep and true. She tried to squirm against the onslaught of sensation, tried to ease some of the shooting bolts of white-hot pleasure he was sending through her with every touch, but he held her firm. He was relentless, pushing her further and further. Each time she was on the verge of coming, he would pull back, over and over again until she swore she couldn't take another second.

"Ride me, Maggie," he said against her sex.

He had to repeat the command three times and physically tug her hips downward before her fevered mind was finally able to comprehend. As she positioned herself over him, he held himself ready. She impaled herself, taking him all in one downward glide, relishing the stab of pain as much as the ecstasy of having him inside her again.

She was nearly beyond rational thought, but the urge to protect Michael was strong. Mindful of his wounds, she leaned over, placed her hands on his biceps, and let her nails curl like claws into his skin. It was both a warning and a promise that *she* would be in control.

Michael groaned. "Ah, baby, it feels so good to be inside you. Fucking heaven. Ride me, baby."

It was all the encouragement she needed. She began to roll and lift her hips, taking him even deeper, mindful to keep weight off of his chest and abdomen. Her inner muscles clamped down around him, protesting every time she pulled away, rejoicing every time she took him again.

After so much time without him and with his torturous preparation, it took mere minutes for her to reach climax. Michael cursed when her muscles tightened around him, pulling, milking, squeezing. He grabbed her hips and held her in place while he thrust upward. She screamed again, begging for mercy as he continued to pound up and into her, forcing her beyond anything she'd ever experienced, beyond bliss, beyond pain. It was too much. Too intense. She couldn't imagine another second, yet he continued until she exploded again. Michael shouted her name as he found his own release, shattering what remained of her mind, body, and spirit.

Maggie's bones had become liquid, her capacity for rational thought gone. Michael caught her and held her close.

"Shh, baby," he whispered as she cried against his shoulder. "I've got you." One arm locked her to him while the other ran up and down her back.

As much as she wanted to, she couldn't stop. She cried harder as the reality of the last two weeks—the last two months—crashed around her. She'd come so close to losing him. She clutched at him, holding on to him hard.

MICHAEL HAD BEEN WAITING for it. She'd been so strong, so capable, but he knew it was only a matter of time. He'd had plenty of opportunities to get used to the idea of death. Had seen it many times. Known that with each mission he and his brothers accepted, there was a chance he would not return. But Maggie hadn't. She hadn't been prepared for this.

He let her cry it out, doing the only thing he could —he held her until there was nothing left.

Eventually, the tears stopped. She relaxed her desperate hold but didn't let go. That was okay with him. He had no intention of letting her go ever again.

CHAPTER TWENTY-ONE

"Don't let him overdo it," Maggie instructed Kieran when he came to pick up Michael.

Kieran managed a fitness and rehab center in town, where Michael would be doing his physical therapy.

"Relax, Maggie. We know the drill," Kieran reassured her. "This isn't the first time one of us has been shot."

It was the wrong thing to say. Immediately, she felt the color drain out of her face and her lip began to tremble. Michael shot Kieran a withering look.

"It's okay, Maggie," he said, his voice softening.

She nodded, but it wasn't okay, not really. Now that Michael was home and recovering, she had to face the awful truth that if she stayed with him, this might happen again. And next time, he might not come home at all.

"How do you do it?" Maggie asked quietly later that afternoon.

After Michael had left with Kieran, she'd phoned Taryn. Taryn had picked up Lexi, and they had been at Maggie's within the hour.

"It's not easy, but doing this is part of who they are." Taryn sipped her coffee, her violet eyes clear, her expression serious. "It's one of the things that attracts us to them in the first place. We crave their intensity, their sense of honor. Regular men just won't do it for women like us."

Maggie wasn't sure she agreed with that. She had fallen in love with Michael when she thought he was just a doctor, and she relayed as much.

"Maybe you didn't know up here," Taryn said, pointing to her head, "but you knew here." She pointed to her heart. "You can't tell me you didn't sense it, Maggie. It reaches out to you, calls to you, and if you're the one, you can't help but respond to it."

Had she known? If she was honest, she had to admit that she'd been instantly drawn to Michael, feeling a connection she'd never felt with anyone else, even when her brain had tried to convince her that she was imagining it, that such things didn't really happen. The ferocity of her feelings for him defied all logic, all the rational expectations she'd ever had. That was some scary stuff.

If anything happened to Michael, it would destroy

her. The past few weeks had proven that beyond a shadow of a doubt. The pain of missing him but knowing he was safe and well was nothing compared to what she would face if he …

Her mind refused to complete the thought.

"I just don't know if I can bear sitting around, waiting for that phone call or knock on the door," Maggie said, wrapping her arms around herself. "I'm not that strong."

"You'd be surprised what you can do for the love of a man like that," Lexi said with quiet strength. "And you won't be alone. You have us. We know what you're going through, and we help each other through it."

"Besides," Taryn pointed out, "nothing in life is guaranteed. How many people die every day? People who wake up one morning and never see it coming?"

"True," Maggie admitted, "but let's face it—what our guys do is pushing the envelope, don't you think?"

"We know what they face, as do they. They are good at what they do, Maggie. The very best. And they leave absolutely nothing to chance," Taryn replied.

"All the more so, if they have a reason to come home," Lexi added.

The words were left unspoken, but Maggie sensed the implication easily enough. She'd overheard enough of Jake's and Ian's exchanges with the others to glean that Michael had taken chances he shouldn't have. Had it been because of her? Had it been because he thought he'd lost her forever? Because Jake and Ian had wives and babies waiting for them and he didn't?

"Michael was *shot*," Maggie said firmly, suddenly feeling restless again.

She got up and absently started collecting the ingredients for a coffee cake. Thinking better of it, she put everything away and pulled out items to make a sweet dough, so she could knead some of her stress away. Every time the image of him lying there came into her mind, she felt like part of her was dying all over again.

"Have either of you had to look at your husband lying in a hospital bed, wondering if he was ever going to open his eyes again?" She spoke the words not with accusation or sarcasm, but with a deep-seated need for someone to understand what she was feeling.

"No," Taryn admitted. "But each of them has had to sit beside *our* hospital beds, wondering the same thing of us."

Stunned, Maggie stilled for a moment and then turned slowly.

"It's true," Lexi admitted. "And I thank God every day that Ian didn't walk away because of it."

"Me too," agreed Taryn. "Jake was there for me every step of the way. And Michael was there for you, Maggie."

"But that's different," Maggie insisted defensively. "I didn't purposely place myself in danger."

"Didn't you?" Taryn asked quietly.

Maggie froze. Had she? By ignoring her symptoms, by refusing to listen to Michael's pleas to be checked out, hadn't she done just that? Yet Michael hadn't given up on her. He'd stuck by her even though he was worried about her. Even though his doctor's instincts had been telling him that something was wrong despite her stubborn insistence otherwise.

"You're a strong-willed woman, Maggie. What if, when you left the hospital, Michael had decided he couldn't handle the possibility that something like that would happen again and left you forever?" Lexi offered gently.

Maggie sank down in the nearest chair as the bitter truth dawned on her. "Oh my God," she whispered.

"And your baby?" Taryn pressed. "If you walked away, believing you couldn't handle a life with Michael, could you look into your child's eyes, knowing that your love is what brought him into this world?"

"Our baby," Maggie repeated softly. "Michael doesn't even know about our baby."

"You haven't told him yet?" Lexi asked. "Why not, Maggie?"

"I'm so scared," Maggie said, losing the battle to stay strong before them as tears began to fall, unchecked. "What if there's something wrong?"

"Because of the surgery?" Lexi asked.

"I had all those drugs. What if they hurt the baby?"

Lexi nodded. "I know exactly how you feel. I had the same problem. I didn't think I could get pregnant, and when I did, I was afraid my medical issues might have harmed Patrick in some way. I didn't want to tell Ian until I knew everything was okay."

There was tremendous comfort, Maggie had to admit, in having someone who understood exactly what she was going through.

"So, we'll take you for tests," Taryn said reasonably. "Not here though. The boys would find out before we even had a chance to get there."

Maggie shook her head. "I can't."

"Why not?"

Maggie exhaled, embarrassed. "No insurance. And I can't afford to pay cash."

Taryn and Lexi exchanged a look.

"And before you even think of suggesting it, I will not accept charity."

"Tell her," Taryn prodded Lexi. "Tell her what you were telling me on the way over."

"Tell me what?"

"Well, a couple of months ago, Michael brought me some of your home-canned stuff. I loved it! So much so that I gave some to my partner, Aidan, and he loved it too. We've had a difficult time with getting quality organic products for our menu, and he wants to talk to you about a possible business agreement."

"What kind of agreement?"

"We contract with you for organic produce and ask you to oversee the harvesting and canning processes. It would be a term type thing, so after a year or two, if you felt it wasn't in your best interests, you could opt out. Aidan is extremely flexible and fair-minded about that sort of thing."

"My land?" Maggie asked warily.

"Would remain yours. There would be occasional inspections and whatnot, as required by federal regulations, of course. Although, I'm sure that Aidan would ask that you agree to provide exclusively for the Celtic Goddess and not any other restaurants."

Maggie was stunned. "But I couldn't possibly do all that."

"You wouldn't have to do it alone. You'd have a staff, equipment, whatever you needed. Delegate as much or as little as you wanted."

It was too good to be true.

"An added benefit is that you would be required to have meetings with Aidan and me, especially in the planning stages. Some of those would undoubtedly be at our corporate offices in Benton, Georgia." Lexi paused. "I know some great specialists down there. No one else would have to know, not unless you wanted them to."

Maggie couldn't help it. She started to cry. "Why would you do all this for me?" she asked tearfully.

"Because, Maggie, like it or not, you're one of us now," Taryn said with a smile. "And we take care of our own."

"Explain to me again why you think I shouldn't go with you." Michael pouted as Maggie packed a small overnight bag.

If she hadn't been so nervous, it might have been

funny. But she *was* nervous, afraid that she would give something away. So far, she hadn't had to lie to him. Everything she'd told him was one hundred percent true even if it wasn't one hundred percent complete.

"You're supposed to be recovering, remember? It's only for a day or two," Maggie told him, keeping her voice light. "Ian's not going either."

"I'm not sure I like this, Maggie."

"I know, Michael, and I'm sorry about that. I'm going to miss you terribly, but I'd be lying if I said I wasn't looking forward to a little girl time with Lexi. I haven't done anything like that in a long while."

Michael shifted uncomfortably, his eyes watching her every move.

"You trust Lexi, don't you?" She refrained from asking him if he trusted *her* because either way, she didn't want to hear the answer. An affirmative would rack her with guilt, and a negative would crush her.

"Of course I do." To a point, that was.

Lexi would never do anything to intentionally cause harm to anyone. She was quite possibly the gentlest soul he'd ever met. On the other hand, there was nothing Lexi would not do to help someone else she cared about. If she believed she was helping Maggie in some way—even if it was something she knew he would not agree with—she wouldn't hesitate.

Michael was pleased by the fact that Maggie was

growing so close to Taryn and Lexi. The more she became part of his family, the better, as far as he was concerned. And he certainly wouldn't begrudge her a little "girl time," as she'd called it. But there was something else there—something unspoken, something vague and undefined—that made him uneasy.

"Lexi told me about this great spa down there. She said she'll take me if we have enough time." Maggie let the genuine excitement creep into her voice. "I've never been to a real spa before."

Yeah, Michael had heard about that place from Ian. Lexi hit it every time she traveled down that way. Ian had said she came back smoother and softer than silk. Just thinking about Maggie returning to him, all buffed and waxed, had him hardening painfully.

Maybe he was being paranoid. Maybe this trip really was only about meeting with the board of the Celtic Goddess Corporation and some feminine pampering on the side. He took one look at those big, pleading green eyes and felt bad for doubting her.

"Come here," he commanded, using that low, deep voice that she'd said made her tingle in all the right places.

She obeyed him without hesitation. His suspicion immediately rose up again.

"That was too easy," he said when she straddled his lap, locking his arms around her. "What are you up to?"

"I'm going to be gone for almost two days," she

said, licking beneath his jaw, burying her hands in his hair. "I need a little extra to hold me over."

How could he argue with that? Michael growled as his hands found their way beneath her shirt, skimming along her waist. He kept his hands there, gently kneading the soft flesh. She sucked in a breath, her hands freezing momentarily.

"I love how you're filling out again," he breathed against her ear before all thoughts but one fled his mind.

"They're up to something," Michael said to Ian for the tenth time. "I'm sure of it."

Now that Maggie and Lexi were gone, it seemed much clearer to him. Whether it was a sixth sense or subtle changes in her behavior—or possibly both—Michael believed Maggie hadn't told him everything. The more he thought about it, the more certain he was. It was the same gut feeling he'd had when she was experiencing warning signs after her fall and didn't want him to know. Michael had sworn he would never ignore that feeling again.

Maggie had seemed preoccupied and distracted that morning. She'd tried to pass it off as a fear of flying. Since her first experience in a plane had been with his adrenaline-junkie brother, Sean, that seemed believable enough, but Michael had been with her on the much gentler trip back, and she hadn't seemed bothered in the least. Maybe she'd been too worried about him at the time to give it much thought, but he wasn't entirely convinced.

And she'd picked at her breakfast. No big surprise there if she was truly nervous about the flight and subsequent meeting, but he'd caught her absently placing her hand over her stomach while she appeared to be a million miles away. It was her reaction when he asked her about it that had the warning bells sounding an alarm in his head. She looked almost afraid, as if she'd been caught doing something wrong, and from that point on, she made an obvious effort to keep both hands on the table.

At the time, he'd thought she was feeling self-conscious about gaining a few pounds. It was why he'd made sure he told her how much he loved her lush curves. But now, he wasn't so sure that was it at all.

And then there was the packing issue. Luckily, he'd double-checked her overnight bag; otherwise, she would have found herself in Benton with four shirts, two bras, and no pants or underwear when she went to change that night. She tried to laugh it off, saying that with him around, she was so used to going without clothes that the thought of having to wear them all day was foreign to her. To prove her point, she lifted her skirt to show him that she wasn't wearing anything underneath. That distracted him for a while, as he'd had the sudden urge to bend her over the bed and investigate her claim thoroughly.

But again, the moment Aidan's limo arrived, the unease began to resurface.

In the back of the limo, the atmosphere was tense. It was subtle, but it was there. Several times, Michael caught the furtive glances between Maggie and Lexi when they thought he wasn't looking. The rest of the time, Lexi went out of her way not to look at him directly. When she spoke with him, her focus had been on a point in the middle of his forehead rather than his eyes.

Kind of like Taryn was doing right now.

Michael had mentioned this to Ian, but his brother hadn't seemed quite as concerned at the time.

As the day progressed, Taryn retreated into the shadows several times to text. And while behind the bar, Taryn seemed distracted enough that he had to repeat himself on multiple occasions about the simplest of things. By mid-afternoon, Ian began to suspect something as well.

"You know something, don't you?" Michael blatantly accused, blocking Taryn's exit to the quieter back room when her phone sounded out the tolling strains from "Hells Bells," announcing yet another incoming message.

The look she gave him was too perfect, too innocent, to be believable. Taryn didn't do innocent.

"I don't know what you're talking about."

"Taryn ..."

"I'd love to stay here and chat, really, but ... I'm not

going to." A moment later, she ducked under his arm and was gone.

"Okay," Ian said, watching her retreating form. "Now, I believe you. Jake, watch the bar, man. Mick and I have some research to do."

CHAPTER TWENTY-TWO

"Okay," Ian said, lacing his fingers together and stretching them wide. "Let's see what we can find, shall we?"

He began by pulling up the travel itinerary.

"Looks like Aidan's private jet landed outside Benton, just as they'd said it would. This log shows them being picked up in the company limo and taken directly to Lexi's penthouse."

Next, he brought up a custom search engine. He typed in several pieces of information, including Maggie's and Lexi's first and last names, cell numbers, Social Security numbers, a location code, and a range of dates covering their planned time down there.

"This will search every online database in the Benton area and give us a listing of anything that references their information—appointments, reservations, et cetera."

Michael was impressed. "When did you set all this up?"

"When Lexi was hiding out in Benton," he replied without apology.

At the time, Michael had thought Ian was being too intrusive of Lexi's privacy. Now, he wanted to buy his brother a beer for having the foresight to create such an intricate and thorough system.

Within seconds, a list began to appear. The flight schedule. The limo log. The big corporate meeting. The day spa.

"Wait," Michael said when an unexpected entry popped up. "There. Elena McKenzie, two p.m. What the hell is that?"

Ian frowned. Elena McKenzie was one of the specialists Lexi had seen when she was pregnant with Patrick. She was also the one who had worked with Michael to discover the most effective combination of organics to treat Lexi's blood disease. Since Lexi's dramatic improvement on the organic program Michael had developed, Ian and Lexi had begun trying for a second child.

Ian's face lit up with hope and fear. "You don't think she's pregnant again already, do you?"

As Ian's fingers flew across the keyboard, new information flashed upon the screen. It soon became clear that it was not Lexi who had been subjected to a battery of tests.

"Oh, man," Ian said softly as he pulled up the series of ultrasound images.

Michael finally knew with certainty what his subconscious had been trying to tell him.

MICHAEL COULDN'T TAKE his eyes off Maggie. They sat at a cozy corner table at the Celtic Goddess, enjoying a quiet dinner for two. She looked so beautiful. Her skin was radiant, her eyes were clear and sparkling, her dark ruby hair lustrous and shiny.

"What?" she asked self-consciously, lifting her hand to her face. "Do I have lipstick on my teeth or something?"

"No. I just can't seem to stop looking at you. You're glowing. It must have been a good trip."

"It was," Maggie agreed with a smile. "But I think this glow is more from my homecoming than it is a result of my travels."

A smug grin slowly curved across Michael's face.

Aidan's limo had dropped her off at the house, and the moment she'd stepped through the door, he'd swept her into his arms and spent the next several hours making love to her. Thoroughly. Passionately. Possessively.

"What can I say? I missed you."

"I MISSED YOU, TOO." That was an understatement.

From the moment she'd left his arms to board the

plane, all Maggie wanted to do was get back into them again. To have his strength and support as she underwent test after test, scared beyond belief. To listen to his calming voice as he explained everything, soothing away the fear. As it was, poor Lexi was probably being fitted for a hand splint. She'd stayed with Maggie through everything, holding her hand and offering support whenever she could.

Throughout the entire trip—thirty-six hours, which had felt more like hundreds—Maggie had gone back and forth in her mind. One minute, she was convinced she had done the right thing by not telling Michael about their baby yet. He would have been beside himself with worry, and she didn't want to do that to him, not with him still recovering from a near-fatal chest wound. No, it was better that she carry the weight of not knowing alone. If the tests revealed that there was a problem, then they would face it together. If not, then she wouldn't have worried him unnecessarily.

In the next minute, her heart would ache so badly that she could barely breathe, and she'd be just as certain that keeping the truth from Michael was the worst thing she could possibly do. There were already some trust issues between them. She took full responsibility for those even though, at the time, she'd thought she was doing the right thing. He wouldn't be happy to learn that she'd kept this from him, no matter the outcome.

And she was feeling so close to the edge right now —Lexi blamed hormones—that she simply could not bear it if he was angry with her. What if he decided that he'd had enough? That he was tired of worrying about whether or not she was keeping something from him?

The waiter came by with a bottle of wine.

Maggie politely placed her hand over the top of her glass. "No, thank you."

"Are you sure?" Michael asked. "Perhaps some wine will help you relax."

"I'm fine."

"Would you like a mixed drink instead?" He lifted his hand, as if to call the waiter back.

"No, no. I'm good, thanks."

"Iced tea then?"

"Um, no. Maybe just some water."

"With lemon?"

"Yes, please."

MICHAEL WONDERED AGAIN how he hadn't seen it before when, now, it seemed so blatantly clear.

For the past several weeks, Maggie had been avoiding alcohol and caffeine. She'd even been declining the morning coffee she loved so much, saying that she was too jittery even though most of the time, she looked as if she could fall asleep where she stood. Breakfast consisted of only dry toast—when she ate it at all. When he asked, she'd blame it on the lingering headaches that continued to plague her, sometimes making her nauseous. He hadn't hounded her about it because she would eat heartily later in the day.

"You're awfully quiet tonight," Michael said as the remains of their meal were cleared away.

For the entire evening, Maggie had been distracted, her mind a million miles away. Several times, he'd caught her staring at him, looking as if she was about to say something. Then, her lashes would drop down, and she'd take a sip of water instead.

Maggie had yet to tell him he was going to be a father. He could sense the undercurrent of anticipation though, and he knew she *wanted* to tell him. He was giving her every opportunity, but so far, no admission was forthcoming. Her eyes were doing that swirling thing again, almost constantly now. There was so much going on in that stubborn, proud mind of hers. When would she learn to open up to him? To believe that she didn't have to handle everything on her own?

She loved him—he had no doubts about that. He saw it in her eyes every time she looked at him, felt it in her touch. His brothers had told him how fiercely she had guarded him in the hospital, how she had threatened anyone, without regard to size or gender, who dared approach him. The thought made him smile.

Yes, she was strong and capable and smart and funny with a kind and generous heart. Ironically, it was her capacity to love that scared him the most because he knew she would protect him and their child without a thought to herself. It made his own protective instincts all that much stronger because he knew that he would do the same.

Even as he worried for Maggie though, he could barely contain the primal joy he felt at the knowledge that he was going to be a father. His elation was tempered only by the fact that she had gone through those tests without him. He should have been there, damn it. Nothing would have kept him from her side, had he known.

The irritation he'd felt at her silence drained away rapidly as he mentally scanned the myriad of tests she'd gone through. Some were relatively innocuous; others, brutally invasive. He hated the thought of her having to face that on her own. It would have been bad enough for any woman under any circumstances, but this was his woman. A woman terrified of medical procedures in general.

God, he thought once again, *she must have been beside herself.*

As it was, he'd had to use every last bit of self-restraint not to say something and admit that he knew of the pregnancy. All but one or two of the tests had come back negative for any indications of a problem—a hopeful sign that all was well. He'd hoped Maggie would've said something upon her return, dropped some hint at least, but she hadn't. Was she waiting until the last results were in to tell him?

During those intimate hours they'd spent together upon her return, he'd found it impossible to keep his hands from her abdomen and the slight baby bump she'd developed. Or to break his mouth away from the fuller, more rounded breasts that had already begun preparing for their child. Just knowing his baby was growing inside her had him nearly insane with the visceral need to protect and possess, no matter what the tests revealed.

But how could he make her see that? He thought he might have an idea.

"Maggie, I've been thinking," he said slowly. She hadn't responded to his previous comment, once again lost in her own thoughts. This time, however, his quiet, serious tone captured her attention immediately.

"Yes?" she prompted when he failed to expound. She hoped the single word hadn't sounded as shaky as she thought it did.

Michael pulled a small velvet box from his jacket and knelt beside her chair. "Maggie, I love you, and I can't imagine my life without you in it. Will you do me the honor of becoming my wife?"

Maggie gasped. Her eyes grew wide as she gazed upon the most stunning diamond she'd ever seen. At least a full carat, it glimmered as if it held its own source of light deep within. The setting was just as stunning, done in intricate white gold.

"It's beautiful," she whispered.

"*You're* beautiful," he responded, taking her left hand in his. "Say yes, Maggie."

"I want to," she said, her voice barely above a whisper. "More than anything."

"Then, say yes, Maggie. Say you'll marry me." His eyes, so clear and blue, implored her.

"I ... I can't. Not yet." It was so hard to get those words out when every fiber of her being was screaming, *Yes! Yes!*

"Why not?" he asked, bemused.

She took a deep breath, steeling herself to do what she must and dreading it because it might drive the final wedge between them. "Because there's something I haven't told you. Something that might change your mind."

"Nothing you say could change my mind," he said firmly, shaking his head.

God, please let that be true, she prayed.

"Please, Michael. Hear me out."

He slowly released a controlled breath and placed the ring box on the table. He rose from his knees and returned to his seat, then extended his arms and took both of her hands in his. "All right."

"Not here."

His eyes pinned her with his stare; she could feel him looking right down into her heart, her soul. She felt herself unraveling, losing the battle to stay strong. Michael had that effect on her, making her believe he would protect her, take care of her, ease any pain she might be struggling with. The longer she was with him, the more she felt her natural resistance weakening. She wanted to melt into his arms and let him take over. She only prayed she could keep it together a little while longer.

CHAPTER TWENTY-THREE

B y the time he pulled into the driveway, Maggie was a nervous wreck, her eyes shiny with unshed tears. She blinked rapidly in an attempt to keep them from spilling over.

"Maggie, sweetheart, what is it? Baby, come here."

He tugged gently on her arm until she leaned into him, needing his warmth, his comfort. She blinked a few more times, letting herself look into his eyes. The love and concern she saw there, the quiet strength of the man she could not live without, calmed her soul. Michael loved her. He would always be there for her, no matter what. The thought was humbling.

"I love you so much, Michael," she finally managed, her voice thick with unshed tears, choked with emotion.

"I love you too, Maggie."

She moved closer, letting his arm curl around her,

resting her head on his shoulder. "The dinner was wonderful."

"Yes, it was."

"I'm pregnant."

There was only a brief pause before he responded, "I know."

She pulled back enough to look at him. His face— so beautiful, as if carved by angels—smiled patiently back at her. His eyes—a bright, luminous blue— pierced her all the way to her toes.

Her eyes widened in stunned surprise. Her mouth opened and closed several times before she managed to get the words out. "But how? Did Lexi tell you?"

"No," Michael assured her, raising her hand to his lips and tenderly kissing her fingers. "Lexi told me nothing. You seem to keep forgetting that I'm a doctor, Maggie." There was only a trace of admonishment in his voice; he couldn't, in good conscience, summon more since he hadn't put the pieces together until he'd seen the ultrasound.

With a pang of guilt, he also neglected to confess that the images on Ian's computer had nearly stopped his heart or that he'd spent the rest of that night and the following morning berating himself for not recognizing the now-obvious signs for what they were.

When it came to Maggie, it seemed, his wealth of

knowledge, his ability to think clearly, and his common sense took a backseat to his baser nature. Love. Claim. Possess. Protect. As much as he'd like to believe otherwise, that was what she'd reduced him to. In that respect, he was no better than his caveman ancestors.

A bit humbling perhaps, but it was what it was.

The truth was, he *should* have known. Maybe he had, somewhere deep down. The images, as startling as they were, were more of an affirmation than a revelation. From the moment he had seen them, everything had just clicked into place.

She sniffed. "You didn't say anything."

Was that accusation in her voice?

"Neither did you," he pointed out. His thumb brushed away the tears that now spilled freely over her cheeks. "Come on. Let's go inside."

Maggie let him lead her into the house, crouching down to greet George.

"Michael ..."

"Shh. It's okay, Maggie. It's been a long day, and you need to relax. We'll talk later."

With a hand upon her lower back, Michael guided her upstairs, where he ran a warm bath for her. He undressed her and then waited until she was safely ensconced in the tub. Leaving her to soak and unwind, he went back downstairs to let George out, fed him the leftovers they'd brought back for him, and closed up the house for the night.

Only once she was properly dried and tucked into

bed beside him would he allow her to bring up the subject again.

MICHAEL MOVED to the other side of the bed and began to remove his clothes. Maggie lowered her eyes, resisting the urge to watch, knowing the distraction would sap her courage. Not to mention, it was difficult to focus on anything else when she saw his hard, muscled body. Just knowing that he was getting naked was enough to have her tingling in hopeful anticipation.

"Is that why you want to marry me? Because I'm pregnant?"

Michael lifted the sheets and slid in beside her, his arms immediately reaching for her, pulling her close. "It's one of a thousand reasons, Maggie," he said in that gentle, thoughtful way he had. "I'd be lying if I said I didn't want our child to carry my name. Or his mother for that matter. But it's not the primary reason. I've known from the first night we met that you were the one I'd been looking for. You are the only woman I dream of spending the rest of my life with, of growing old with. And I would have asked you to marry me whether or not you were pregnant."

She settled against his chest, her body melting into his as she inhaled his clean male scent. She'd barely slept while she was away. Now, she realized that at least part of the reason was because the pillows hadn't had his scent. She wondered if he knew that he had left behind one of his shirts several months ago, and that she kept it tucked safely beneath her pillow. That she'd buried her face in it and cried countless times when she thought she'd lost him forever.

Now, he was telling her that he wanted to spend the rest of his life with her. Dare she even hope?

"You're not upset with me?"

Michael ran one hand lazily up and down her back, closing his eyes. "Upset with you? Your warm, naked body is against mine. You are in my arms, where you belong. And my child is growing inside you. The only thing that could possibly make me happier is if you agreed to marry me."

She picked her head up, gazing at him doubtfully. Michael was a wonderful man, but even he had his limits.

"But I didn't tell you."

Michael opened one eye, continuing the tender strokes from her shoulder to her hip. It felt so good that she arched into it, needing, wanting more. She understood why George liked being petted so much.

"You would have," he said confidently. "You've been trying to tell me for a while now, haven't you?"

Maggie laid her cheek back against his chest, muttering, "You could have told me, you know. Saved me a little anxiety."

Had she still been looking, she would have seen the slight quirk to his lips.

"Consider it penance for not trusting me enough to tell me."

"It wasn't a matter of trust. I didn't realize I was pregnant until after you left. I thought maybe I was late because of the surgery, but then it still didn't come, so I bought one of those at-home tests."

Michael closed his eyes again. "You could have called me."

Should she tell him how many times her hand had been on the phone? How many times she had dialed the number at the pub, only to hang up after the first ring?

"I was afraid to. Afraid of what you might say. Of what you might want me to do." The slight tremor in her voice was unmistakable. "Because no matter what the tests say, Michael, I want this baby."

Michael stiffened. "You think I would be capable of that?" he asked, his voice rough. "That I could ever suggest such a thing?"

"Not under normal circumstances, no," she said quietly.

"Not under *any* circumstances."

"But I had the surgery, the anesthetic. What if it hurt the baby?"

"Then, we would deal with it. You and I. Together." He stroked her hair and kissed the top of her head. "But if it makes you feel any better, the hospital performs a pregnancy test before any procedure as a standard practice. It doesn't eliminate the risk, but it does reduce the possibility of harmful side effects."

"They did a pregnancy test? Don't they need consent?"

"In an emergency situation, technically, no, they don't. As long as they can prove they had the best interests of you and your unborn child at heart, they would not be held liable. At the time, you were semiconscious and hysterical, incapable of making any rational decisions. But to be clear, *I* gave consent."

It was her turn to stiffen, but she relaxed again almost instantly. While she had been furious at the time that he'd gone against her wishes, she now understood why he'd done what he did. Just as she had ripped his DNR to shreds without a second thought.

"So, you knew before I did?"

"No. They didn't tell me the results of the test, and I was too distracted to ask. Since Roberts performed the actual surgery, I was not informed." The disapproval—or disappointment—was evident in his voice. "But if they had, Maggie, you have to believe that I would never have left. And that I want you and our baby, no matter what."

"Everyone says that, because that's what we like to think. But none of us knows for sure how we'll react until we're actually in that situation."

"*I* know."

Maggie stayed silent, the pads of her fingers sliding in small circles over his chest.

"We're not talking about me anymore, are we, Maggie?"

Her fingers stilled; her breath hitched.

"Tell me."

And so she did. She told him about her mother's pregnancy, how the doctor had run tests and prescribed medications that resulted in hemorrhaging and early labor. How an unnecessary hysterectomy had been performed, robbing her parents of the opportunity to have the big family they'd always dreamed of.

How, as a child, she'd been in the hospital more than out of it until her parents couldn't even look at her without overwhelming grief and sadness.

She went on to say how the last time she had come home from the hospital, her parents were gone. Her grandparents had told her that they'd returned to Ireland for a while to "rest and heal." But they never came back. And slowly, it was her grandmother's remedies and unconditional love that had made Maggie whole again.

Michael tightened his arms around her. "Oh, baby. I'm so sorry. I didn't know. No wonder you hate hospitals."

"It's not your fault. You couldn't possibly have known."

"Well, I know now," he said. "And I promise you, I will never let anything happen to you or our baby."

She felt his words and the absolute conviction with which they had been spoken. And she believed him.

"I saw a specialist in Benton," she continued, watching him closely. She didn't want to hide anything from him anymore. It wasn't fair to either of them.

"Lexi pulled a few strings and got me in to see the woman who had cared for her during her pregnancy."

To his credit, Michael kept his expression and his voice calm, though she felt him subconsciously tighten his hold while concern deepened his eyes to sapphire. "Are you having problems with the pregnancy, Maggie?"

"No," she answered honestly, hoping he would believe her, knowing she hadn't given him reason to. "Lexi and Taryn assured me that everything I was feeling was perfectly normal. But I was afraid that with the surgery and the meds ..." She couldn't finish the thought. "All but one or two of the tests have come back negative, thank God."

"You shouldn't have gone through that alone," he admonished gently. "I should have been there with you, holding your hand if nothing else."

"I didn't want to worry you, Michael. You're still recovering."

MICHAEL ALLOWED her warmth to seep into him. Touching her was imperative; it gave him a sense of profound peace. As long as he could do that, anything was possible.

He prayed for the strength to be calm, caring, and supportive. If he had known about the baby, he would have done things differently, especially during that last mission. He wouldn't have tried to sneak into the camp on his own, his only thought being that his brothers had wives to get home to. That one uncharacteristically irrational act had almost cost his child a father.

But, as Taryn had pointed out, Maggie couldn't possibly have known such a thing was a possibility. She'd believed he was living at the pub, the biggest danger he faced being the short commute to and from the hospital. He could hardly berate her for withholding information when he had kept so much from her.

He wished there were something he could say, something he could do, to make her understand, to reassure her that no matter what, he was never leaving her side again. As it was, he would just have to spend the rest of his life convincing her.

He pulled her close and kissed the top of her head. Emotion swelled up inside him and filled his chest. "Ah, sweetheart. You went through all that on your own just so I wouldn't worry?"

She nodded against his chest. "I was going to tell you—I swear it. I just wanted to know what we were dealing with first. You were going through so much, and I didn't want to worry you unnecessarily."

God, he loved this woman even if she did make him crazy. The fact that she loved him that much made anything forgivable. But it couldn't happen again.

"Promise me you'll never keep anything like that from me again, Maggie."

She didn't answer immediately, and he knew she was thinking it over carefully. If Maggie made a promise, she would keep it. "Only if *you* promise not to get yourself killed, doing some incredibly brave, stupid thing."

He felt her fear—real, paralyzing fear, not just worry or concern—in the way her heart pounded so fiercely against his chest. In that moment, he realized just how much Maggie had been shouldering alone over the past few months. Suffering a near-fatal hemorrhage that had almost claimed her sight. Discovering she was pregnant from a man who had walked out on her. Flying halfway across the world after learning he had been near-mortally wounded and was not expected to live through the night. He silently swore, to himself and to God, that she would never have to face anything alone again.

"As long as I know you're waiting for me, I will always come back to you, Maggie," he vowed.

"You'd better." She warned, pulling herself atop him.

He groaned as she took him in her hand and guided him into her.

"You still haven't given me an answer, you know," he reminded her as she began to move, riding him slowly, taking him deeper with each stroke.

"Haven't I?" She hummed, her eyes half-closed as her nails curled into his biceps.

He gripped her hips with his strong hands and held her in place, keeping her from achieving the penetration she needed so desperately. "No, you haven't."

With one powerful stroke, he thrust upward, stretching and filling her until she cried out, "Yes, Michael! Oh God, yes!"

"Glad we got that settled then," he said roughly and spent the rest of the evening demonstrating what a good choice she had made.

CHAPTER TWENTY-FOUR

"S pencer!" Maggie exclaimed in stunned shock as she opened the back door.

She hadn't thought to check who it was when she'd heard the knock. Only close friends used the entrance off the kitchen. She'd been too busy daydreaming, replaying the morning's long, languorous lovemaking with Michael. Her body was still sensitive, still slightly swollen and deliciously heavy from his thorough possession.

"Hello, Maggie." Spencer Dumas offered her a pleasant smile. "It's been a while."

Not long enough, she wanted to say, but she refrained. Her grandmother had taught her better than that.

When Maggie showed no signs of inviting him in, he took the initiative. "May I come in?"

She didn't budge. "What do you want, Spencer?"

"I just want to talk to you, Maggie."

"About what exactly?"

Spencer grinned, showing off his perfect, white teeth. No doubt that smile had gotten him a lot of things. Unfortunately for him, Maggie was no longer affected by it. She'd learned her lesson well enough.

"Please, Maggie, for old times' sake. I won't take up much of your time, I promise."

Against her better judgment, Maggie stepped back and allowed him to enter. George came trotting in, tail wagging, expecting Michael or one of the others. As soon as he saw who it was, however, he turned tail and made a beeline for the living room, hiding behind the large recliner. Maggie found herself wishing she could do the same.

"Do I smell your cinnamon rolls?" Spencer asked.

Maggie fought the urge to roll her eyes. Ian was coming by later to pick her up—she still hadn't received medical clearance to drive—and she knew they were his favorite.

"Mmm. And fresh coffee?" he added.

She forced what she hoped passed as a polite smile. "Yes."

"It smells wonderful. You always were a fabulous baker."

Remember your manners, Maggie. She could almost hear her grandmother's voice whispering through the veil.

"If I offer you some, will it speed this along?"

Okay, so she wasn't exactly channeling Miss Manners, but she was trying to be civil. The most important thing was to get Spencer on his way before Ian showed up. If Ian found Spencer there, he'd go tattling to Michael and manure would hit the fan. Not that she felt she was doing anything wrong, but over the last few months, she'd come to recognize and appreciate the fierce protective instincts of the Callaghan men. Innocent as this visit might be, she couldn't envision Michael—or any of his brothers— seeing it that way. With everything they'd been through recently, they didn't need another reason to worry.

"You are an angel. I would love some, thank you."

Maggie fought to keep the neutrality in her expression. Spencer made himself at home and took a seat at the kitchen table, while Maggie poured coffee and put some still-warm rolls on a plate.

He was dressed impeccably, as always. Had he not followed in his father's footsteps, he could have been a male model. Spencer Dumas was an extremely attractive man with classic features and a lean, athletic build. But, as she'd found out so conclusively, looks weren't everything.

He occupied himself by looking around the kitchen. Maggie didn't miss the way his eyes lingered on the two coffee cups that sat in the drainer or Michael's heavy quilted flannel hanging by the back door.

"You look beautiful, Maggie," he said as she placed the plate and mug in front of him. "Much better than the last time I saw you. Radiant in fact. Like a woman in love. Or expecting. Or both."

She counted slowly to ten in her mind. She would not allow him to rile her this morning; she was too happy. She smiled sweetly and took a seat adjacent to him. "You're looking good yourself, Spencer. New blood in the secretarial pool?"

He chuckled. "You always did keep me on my toes. I miss the challenge. But I assure you, I am being completely sincere." He bit into the roll and closed his eyes. "Ah, perfection."

"I'm glad you like it."

She sipped her decaf and waited for him to get to the purpose of his visit. Spencer had a tendency to take his time, she knew. It was one of his little power games, intended to get people wondering, fidgeting.

She refused to play those games with him any longer. Maggie watched him patiently, her gaze unwavering, unwilling to be intimidated by the likes of Spencer Dumas.

"That's quite a lovely ring you've got there," Spencer said finally, appreciatively eyeing the white gold setting and brilliant diamond.

Maggie did not comment.

"I take it, you are engaged then?"

Pine Ridge was not an overly large community. Even if she was a fair distance from the town proper, news this juicy was bound to get around. She was sure she and Michael had provided much fodder for the local gossip mill.

"You didn't come all the way out here to look at my ring. Or to ask me questions you already know the answers to. What is it that you want?"

He looked hurt by her question. If she didn't know him so well, she might have fallen for it. But Spencer Dumas had the skill of a Hollywood leading man when it came to facial expressions and body language. He spent untold hours perfecting both. She'd even caught him practicing in front of the mirror once.

"We used to be very close, Maggie. I've been hearing things ..."

She offered him a smile that did not quite reach her eyes. "Have you now?" The soft Irish lilt colored her words unintentionally—an indication of the strength of the emotions running just below the surface.

"Yes." Spencer's expression shifted masterfully from "hurt" to "concerned." "Some of the things you are getting involved in ..."

"And what I do should matter to you why exactly?"

A quick flicker of hurt again, mixed with just a touch of confusion and ... longing perhaps? "I know things didn't work out between us, but that doesn't mean I don't still care about you."

Maggie's green eyes grew stormy as she fought to cap the rage building beneath. "Yes, Spencer, that's exactly what it means. Don't kid yourself. You never cared for me. The only thing you've ever cared about is my land."

"That's not true!" he insisted, losing some of his composure. For a few moments, it appeared that genuine emotion had broken through the carefully crafted, rehearsed presentation. "I care for you, Maggie. I admit, business might have been the initial impetus behind our relationship, but things changed as I got to know you."

"I caught you having sex with your assistant in your office the day after you proposed! And she was one of many!" Her voice grew louder. Even if she no longer cared for Spencer, the betrayal, the humiliation, still stung. "You don't do that to people you *care* for."

A reddish hue tinged his lightly bronzed skin, the tic in his jaw barely noticeable. "I am a man, Maggie. Perhaps if you'd been a little more attentive, things might have turned out differently. God knows I asked often enough."

"Don't you dare blame me for your indiscretions, Spencer. A real man takes responsibility for his actions."

Fire flew from her eyes as she shot to her feet, splashing her coffee across the table. He mimicked her actions, standing up and towering over her, all pretense evaporating.

"Damn it, Maggie! You left me no choice."

"You always had a choice, Spencer! Keep it in your pants or don't!"

"So superior, aren't you?" he said, his voice dripping sarcasm as the smirk danced about his lips. "Playing the virtuous little farm girl. Tell me, Maggie, are you just as virtuous with Michael Callaghan? Are you making *him* wait until you are married? Or are you just another Callaghan whore?"

Maggie's face flushed crimson as her temper flared. Before she could stop herself, her hand drew back and slapped him right across his face. *Hard.* The resounding crack split through the quaint kitchen like a shotgun blast. Spencer's smirk vanished instantly as the shock of the action seized him, his expression turning dark and stormy. Maggie took a step back, her eyes huge with disbelief at what she'd just done. She opened her mouth to say something, but the voice she heard was not her own.

"What the hell are you doing here, Dumas?" Ian's deep voice unexpectedly cut through the kitchen, startling them both. He strode across the room and angled himself protectively in front of Maggie.

"I don't see that it's any of your business, Callaghan," Spencer spat, bringing his hand up to the blossoming red stain across his cheek, as if he could wipe the sting away.

Spencer was tall and fit, but he was still several inches shorter and narrower than Ian.

Ian's eyes narrowed in warning. "Ah, now, that's where you're wrong." His voice was whisper soft, but there was no mistaking the threat it held. "Maggie is very much my business."

"Spencer just stopped by to see how I was," Maggie said, wishing her voice hadn't trembled.

Even overseas, she hadn't seen Ian like this. Gone were the roguish smile and laughing eyes, as was the ever-present air of fun and mischief she'd come to associate with him. Though his stance appeared relaxed, the tightly coiled tension was impossible to miss as he pinned his gaze on the other man, almost daring Spencer to refute him.

In those few moments, she saw Spencer's mind working furiously, the muscles clenching around his jaw and his hand fisting at his side.

Surely, he's not stupid enough to pit himself against Ian, Maggie thought.

Even she could see that he wouldn't stand a snowball's chance in hell. Despite her ire, Maggie didn't want to see it come to that.

Another quick glance at Ian suggested he was already considering various options for hiding Spencer's body after he was done with him. Maggie wasn't particularly fond of Spencer on a good day, and at that moment, he was pretty high on her shit list, but she had no desire to have his blood on her hands. Or in her kitchen.

"He was just leaving, weren't you, Spencer?" The plea in her voice was unmistakable.

Spencer's eyes flicked from Ian to Maggie and back again. Ian's eyes glowed, the hint of a smile inviting Spencer to contradict her. Probably hoping he would in fact.

Spencer nodded curtly, and Maggie discreetly released the breath she'd been holding.

"Excellent," Ian said. "I'll show you out."

"Make sure you know what you're getting yourself into, Maggie," Spencer warned, shrugging away from Ian's grasp.

"Don't worry, Spencer. You taught me that lesson well."

MINUTES LATER, Spencer's Mercedes drove around Ian's SUV and proceeded up the driveway under Ian's watchful eye.

Only once it disappeared from sight did Ian turn to Maggie. "You okay, Mags?"

She exhaled heavily, grabbed a rag from the counter, and began wiping a small puddle of coffee on the table. "I'm fine."

She didn't look fine. The flush was fading quickly, her hands trembling as the adrenaline surge drained away. Ian watched her closely, dialing down his aggression, but his protective instincts remained on full alert. It was more than a chivalrous reaction; he, like his brothers, had become quite fond of Maggie since their return from overseas. Any woman who would fly halfway across the world in the middle of the night for his brother's sorry ass was more than all right in his book. Had Maggie not done what she did, Ian was certain they would have brought Michael home in a body bag. She'd given Michael the incentive he needed to pull through. Not to mention, Lexi adored her.

Inclusion to the inner circle of the Callaghan clan, however, also meant that she was now under the watchful eyes of seven alpha males—eight, including the family's patriarch, Jack Callaghan—and Maggie was having trouble adjusting. As an only child, used to living alone and independently, she no doubt found the added attention overwhelming sometimes.

Her irritation was evident now. She made no attempt to hide it, stubbornly refusing to meet Ian's gaze as he studied her. Half of him wanted to give her a high five for standing up for herself; the other half wanted to give her a lecture on personal safety. He ended up doing both.

"Hell of a smackdown there, sweetheart. But don't you know better than to let a man into your home when you're here by yourself?"

MAGGIE CONTINUED to scrub at the table long after it was clean. Her heart was still thumping against the inner walls of her chest, but it was slowing. Another few deep breaths ought to do it.

"Funny how that rule doesn't seem to apply to you or your brothers," she said, crossing her arms. "I know I locked the front door after Michael left this morning. How did you get in?"

Ian shrugged, as if it were inconsequential. "I saw a strange car in your driveway."

"So, you picked the lock and let yourself in?"

For the first time, Ian seemed to realize that Maggie might have a problem with that. "I was worried about you. You're family now, Mags. And I've got a nephew to protect."

"What makes you so sure it's a boy?"

"Because Shane thinks it is, and he's never wrong." He grabbed a cinnamon roll and somehow managed to cram the entire thing in his mouth at once. Right before her eyes, the hard, lethal mask he had worn earlier transformed back into the delight of a roguish boy with gooey icing sticking to his lips.

She fought to keep the twitch of her lips from turning into a grin. The last thing he needed was encouragement even if deep down inside, she was thankful he'd arrived when he did.

Plus, it was hard to remain miffed with him when he said things like that, when he looked at her with so much affection. As if looking out for her was the most logical, natural thing in the world. Still, his total lack of repentance was irksome.

She released the pent-up breath she'd been holding inside. "I don't see how that gives you the right to break into my house."

Ian grinned and ruffled her hair. "That's because you're an only child. You clearly don't grasp the concept of big brothers."

The corners of her mouth twitched again despite

her best efforts to keep it contained. "I'm older than you are."

"True, but I am much bigger than you. Now, how about some of that coffee to go with these cinnamon rolls?"

"All right. But only if you teach me that awesome death stare you gave Spencer."

"Deal."

CHAPTER TWENTY-FIVE

"**D**umas was there?" Michael asked, accepting the draft Ian had poured for him. He'd refused initially but changed his mind after Ian convinced him it was a good idea. "Why didn't you call me earlier? Is she all right?" He kept his voice even but couldn't completely mask his displeasure.

"Relax, Mick. Maggie's fine. A little pissed off perhaps. From what I overheard, Dumas was trying to warn her off you."

Michael snorted. Maggie didn't do "a little pissed-off." Her fiery temperament didn't allow for such degrees. She was either angry or she wasn't, and he could guess which applied in this case. The thought of Dumas sniffing around Maggie created a blood-red haze that tainted *his* vision. It was probably a good thing that he'd had some business to take care of that morning. If it had been him walking into the kitchen instead of Ian, he might not have shown the same restraint despite the fact that on most days, he was the most levelheaded among them.

"Any idea why?"

Ian smirked. "Because he's an arrogant, self-centered prick who can't stand the fact that you, my brother, have succeeded in getting the one thing he can't have."

Michael grunted in response. He'd already wanted to kill the bastard for hurting Maggie over a year ago, though at the same time, he was immensely grateful that Dumas had been such a selfish prick. If he hadn't been, it would have made things more difficult.

If there was one thing Michael was absolutely certain of, it was that Maggie was meant to be his and his alone, and fate would have found some way to ensure that their paths crossed. Once he'd come in contact with her, he would have realized who and what she was to him. The fact that she was unmarried and uninvolved when he found her had made it easier, but the end result would have still been the same. When all was said and done, Maggie was his. That was the beauty of finding your *croie*.

"Maybe." He took a drink, letting the smooth brew roll around on his tongue before swallowing. "You were there. What did your gut tell you?"

Ian's eyes met his, and he had his answer. "He's up to something. I can feel it, and I don't like it, Mick."

Michael nodded. The Callaghan brothers had long since learned to trust their instincts, and his were telling him the same thing. When one of them had a feeling, it was nearly a sure thing. When more than one of them shared the same feeling, he could pretty much bet the bank on it.

"Feel up to doing some research then?"

Ian looked affronted. "Like you even have to ask. I've already kicked off a bunch of sniffers. Dumas isn't stupid though. He'll cover his tracks well. It might take a little time."

Michael nodded again. Ian was the best. If there was anything to find, he would, and then they would take care of it because that was what they did. They ferreted out and neutralized threats. What worried him more was the fact that Dumas had managed to get into Maggie's house so easily and that things had escalated enough for Maggie to hit him. Ian wasn't telling him everything—he was sure of it—but he also trusted Ian enough to know that if he needed to know something, Ian would tell him.

"Thanks, man. I'm glad you showed up when you did. What the hell was she thinking, letting him in like that?"

A slight frown creased Ian's boyish features. "I asked her the same thing. That got her back up though, and she said that *I* was the one who broke into her house."

Michael raised his eyebrows. "Did you?"

"Well, I didn't recognize the car and knew you'd already left," Ian explained.

"Perfectly reasonable."

"Yeah, that's what I thought too. But Maggie didn't quite see it that way. Go figure."

Michael's lips twitched. "That explains why you didn't call me right away."

"I didn't call right away because there was no need," Ian said firmly, suddenly finding a spot on the bar that needed attention. "Everything was under control."

"Meaning she offered to show you some creative storage space for some of her scarier kitchen implements if you tattled, all of which involved parts of your anatomy to which your wife is fondly attached?"

Ian's huge grin confirmed his suspicions.

Michael laughed. "Afraid of my little woman, are you?"

"No," Ian countered defensively. "But I'm not stupid enough to wave a red flag in front of a bull either."

WHEN MAGGIE CAME into the bar with Taryn an hour later, her face lit up at the sight of Michael. His heart swelled; he didn't think he would ever get used to the fact that she loved him so completely. Pulling her into his arms, he greeted her with a searing kiss, one that left absolutely no doubt to anyone within viewing distance exactly to whom she belonged. Let *that* get back to Spencer Dumas and his spies.

"Michael! I thought you had to work all day," she said breathlessly.

"I finished earlier than expected."

"Did you now?" Flames licked through her green eyes at the possibilities of exactly how they might spend the bonus time. That soft Irish lilt had him hardening painfully.

"Aye." It was the only way to answer when she spoke to him like that.

Ian cleared his throat, and their private world expanded to include everyone else again.

Maggie's eyes swiveled toward Ian accusingly. "You called him, didn't you?"

"Now, Maggie," Ian began.

"The question is," Michael said quietly, his deep voice commanding her full attention, "why didn't you?"

IAN ALMOST PATTED Michael on the back for his exemplary male behavior along with an encouraging remark or two but thought better of it as Maggie's eyes flashed, and he mentally prepared himself for her response. Amazingly though, the intensity of Maggie's fire dialed down to a low simmer as she dropped her eyes. It was one of the most impressive transformations he'd ever seen.

"It was nothing," she said unconvincingly. Her hand came up to Michael's chest, stroking in small, petting caresses meant to reassure.

Ian watched in fascination at the silent exchange

that followed. Michael wrapped himself around her protectively; Maggie snuggled in and calmed him. For a few minutes, they were oblivious to everything, except each other.

"So, tell me, do I have to kill him?" Michael finally said, making her chuckle.

"No. I think Ian scared him enough for one day."

"Thank God he was there, Maggie."

"I could have handled it."

Michael kissed the top of her forehead and said, "My fierce tigress. But I worry about you."

Maggie melted into him while Ian looked at Michael with something akin to hero worship. If it had been him, he would have reinforced how bad of an idea it was for Maggie to allow Dumas into the house in the first place. But Michael was a genius. He called her fierce and managed to convey his concern without pissing her off. He'd have to remember that one.

"I know," she sighed, but there was no trace of the irritation she'd harbored earlier. "I didn't check to see who it was before I opened the door; I assumed it was Ian coming to pick me up. I should have known Ian wouldn't have knocked; he would have just barged right in." From the protection of her husband-to-be's arms, she shot Ian a scathing glance, but the twinkle in her eye neutralized the effect. "Spencer said he wanted to talk to me about something."

"About what?"

Maggie frowned. "I'm not sure exactly. We didn't really get around to that."

"What did happen, Maggie?"

Maggie glanced at Ian, wondering how much he'd told Michael. Given Michael's relative calm, probably not *all* of the details. Ian earned back a couple of merit points for that.

"Spencer was just being Spencer. I shouldn't have let him get to me." Maggie guided Michael's hand to the soft swell of her belly, barely noticeable beneath the loose sweater she wore. "I'm going to blame it on hormones."

"All the more reason to be cautious, sweetheart. Promise me you'll be more careful. If he tries to contact you again, I want to know about it immediately."

"Okay, but I don't think he will."

She was pretty sure he wouldn't. She'd humiliated him twice; he wasn't going to give her a third opportunity. Once again, a feeling of unease took hold; it was the same one she'd been trying to shake ever since Spencer had arrived on her door earlier that morning.

Whatever the purpose of his visit had been, it was lost now. Maybe it had been as innocuous as a simple visit to see how she was doing, and things had just gotten out of hand. It wasn't totally impossible, however improbable. A more likely explanation was that Spencer was going to make another attempt at procuring her land before her marriage. Once she and Michael were wed, the property would become

Michael's as well, and Spencer had to know that as unlikely as it would be to convince Maggie to sell, it would be impossible to go up against the Callaghans.

She explained as much to Michael. He admitted it was possible, as did Ian, but neither seemed wholly convinced.

"He's jealous—that's all," Maggie concluded, hoping to convince herself as much as them. "He doesn't like to lose."

"YOU'RE PROBABLY RIGHT." Michael gently rubbed her back.

Looking over the top of her head, he caught Ian's gaze. Unspoken words passed between them. Ian nodded in understanding.

"Come on, sweetheart," Michael said, rising from the barstool but keeping his arm protectively around Maggie. "Spencer Dumas doesn't deserve any more of our attention. Let's go home. You can tell me all about what you and Taryn came up with today."

Maggie gave him a blank look. Warning bells started sounding in his head.

"Weren't you going to meet with the florist today after Lexi's?"

Maggie threw a desperate look at Taryn, whose face was suspiciously devoid of expression.

"Maggie." His tone was soft steel.

Maggie tried to take a step back, but his arms were

like iron bars, loosely caging her in. The most Maggie could do was wriggle a bit; escape was not an option.

Taryn was already slipping toward the door.

"And you"—Michael pinned his gaze on Taryn and spoke the command so sharply that she obeyed instantly—"stay right where you are."

Both women tried desperately to look innocent but failed miserably.

"Want to tell me what you ladies were up to today?" Michael's voice was forcibly calm.

"No, not really," Taryn said almost immediately, offering a quick smile.

Maggie shook her head in silent agreement. Both women suddenly seemed to find their shoes fascinating.

Who knew how long the game might have continued if Jake hadn't walked in at that moment, oblivious to the warning signs Taryn tried to flash him?

"So," Jake said, smiling, "how'd the tat come out?"

Ian coughed, probably in an attempt to stifle his laugh. Michael's normally implacable expression was frozen somewhere between shock and disbelief, his mouth hanging partially open. Taryn slipped behind her large husband, making sure he was in between her and Michael. Maggie was cornered, biting her lower lip, even while managing to suffuse her obvious anxiety with a touch of defiance.

"You got a *tattoo*?" he growled, abandoning any attempt to keep his voice calm.

Ian snorted and then looked away.

Maggie lifted her chin. "Yes."

"She was awesome," Taryn piped up. "She never even flinched, even when he—"

Michael's laser-like eyes swiveled in her direction. Jake quietly pushed Taryn behind him, managing to cover her mouth as he did so.

Michael turned back to Maggie. "Why, Maggie?"

Maggie straightened her shoulders and stood taller. That put her face-to-face with his collarbone, so she tilted her head upward to meet his gaze. "Because I am going to be your wife."

Michael searched her face, saw the resolve and pride beneath her fear of his disapproval.

"Taryn says that everyone in your family wears the crest," she continued. "That it's a symbol of the love and loyalty you have for one another. I wanted to be part of that too."

No one was laughing anymore. Maggie's eyes were bright with moisture.

"Show him, Maggie," Taryn spoke softly, a disembodied voice from behind Jake's massive frame.

Maggie carefully lifted her sweater above her head, leaving only the silky camisole beneath. She angled her body away from his, revealing the stark engraving behind her right shoulder. The Callaghan family crest, complete with Michael's custom caduceus. Beneath the medical symbol was a perfect rose—the traditional symbol of a Callaghan bride. The whole design was framed by intricate Celtic knots.

Michael reached out, his fingers lightly skimming

the edges of the cellophane bandage. Words failed him. It was ... *beautiful*. Somehow, the artist had managed to take the masculine crest and transform it into something inherently female. Feminine yet powerful.

Ian whistled as he leaned over the bar to get a closer look. "He outdid himself this time."

"Tiny?" Michael asked, his voice rough.

Tiny ran a tattoo and piercing shop over in Birch Falls; he had been handling the family ink for as long as they could remember.

"You think I'd trust her with anyone else?" Taryn scoffed.

"But she's *pregnant*."

"Yeah. Tiny didn't want to do it at first, but when he found out who Maggie was engaged to, he made an exception. He said not to worry. He triple-sterilized everything and took extra precautions."

Michael felt somewhat better after hearing that. Most reputable professionals wouldn't tattoo a pregnant woman because there was a risk the expectant mother could contract an infection. Tiny, however, was meticulous when it came to his art and his equipment. He was also a close personal friend and knew Michael well enough to know her aftercare would be assured.

"It's exquisite."

Taryn smiled. "I know, right? I liked it so much that I asked him to vamp up mine too." She smiled brightly, lifting her shirt to show off hers as well. "After all, we Callaghan women have to stick together."

A familiar hunger lit Jake's eyes when he saw Taryn's new ink. "Ian, watch the bar, man. Taryn and I have something to discuss." Without another word, Jake took her hand and led her from the room so quickly that Taryn was forced to jog to keep up with his long strides.

"Talking, my ass," Ian mumbled, but Maggie and Michael didn't hear him.

"Yeah," Michael said, helping Maggie put her sweater back on. "Maggie and I have some things to do too." Murmuring words of thanks to Ian, he led her out of the pub and into the Jag.

MAGGIE WASN'T QUITE sure what to think. Was he angry with her for getting the tattoo? She'd wanted it to be a surprise, a permanent expression of her love for him.

Michael remained unusually quiet for the ride home. He kept his eyes focused on the road, but every now and then, he'd glance her way, his expression unreadable. Maggie wanted to ask him what he was thinking but couldn't bring herself to do so. The only time she'd ever seen him like this was when something was bothering him or when he was angry. She remained quiet, trying to quell the nervous wriggling in her belly.

He parked the car. She followed him into the house. The second they were inside the door, he pinned her against the wall, his expression as fierce as she had ever seen it. His mouth came down on hers, hot and hungry yet incredibly tender.

"*Mine,*" he growled, and a bolt of pure heat shot through her.

Michael pulled away only long enough to relieve her of her clothes and then took her right there by the door.

CHAPTER TWENTY-SIX

Confirmation that Spencer Dumas was indeed up to something came a few days later when Lexi was called unexpectedly into a meeting with her longtime friend and business partner, Aidan Harrison. It was unusual for Aidan to summon her, especially when he knew she was busy with planning the evening's specialty menu.

Lexi did have a private office right next to Aidan's, but she was rarely in it, preferring to remain in the kitchen with the staff while Aidan oversaw the day-to-day business operations. Lexi was the "phantom" partner—the silent talent behind the unprecedented success of the menu, the one who regularly shunned publicity and whose loyal, devoted staff fiercely protected her privacy.

Several times throughout the day, Aidan tended to find his way down to her to discuss whatever needed to be discussed, to sample the day's creations, or to just check in with Lexi. He did everything he could to keep her away from the ugliness of the business, letting her focus on what she did best—namely, creating their unique culinary offerings and keeping Aidan grounded and in touch with the staff. They knew every one of their employees by their first names, as well as the names of their spouses and children, and treated them like family. For as elaborate and exclusive as the Celtic Goddess appeared from the outside, it was casual and informal within, a close-knit family that worked together remarkably well.

Lexi had therefore been quite surprised when she received the rather formal request at the hand of Aidan's personal assistant, an extremely efficient woman with sharp eyes and short hair and a heart of gold. Discarding her chef's coat, she smoothed down her cotton blouse, swapping her rubber-soled black Reeboks for a pair of slip-on gold sandals. With her faded blue jeans—standard attire for Lexi—and partially freed multihued golden hair, she looked more like a teenager than a world-renowned chef.

"Thanks for joining us, Lex," Aidan said when she entered the office.

He was, as always, impeccably dressed in a dark, tailored designer ensemble, though Lexi always told him he'd look just as good in Levi's and boots instead of his Dior slacks and Bruno Magli shoes. He stood and tried to bite back a smile as he discreetly wiped a smudge of flour from her cheek with his thumb.

"Lex, this is Spencer Dumas. Mr. Dumas, allow me

to introduce Alexis Kattapoulos, the heart and soul of the Celtic Goddess."

Lexi blinked questioningly at Aidan's deliberate use of her maiden name. She'd taken Ian's name upon their marriage, and she glowed whenever anyone referred to her as Mrs. Callaghan. Though his manner was outwardly pleasant, she'd known Aidan long enough to catch the subtle undercurrent of warning in his golden-brown eyes.

"It's a pleasure to meet you, Mr. Dumas," Lexi said politely. She'd heard the name often enough lately, though not in a complimentary way. Never having met him herself, she was curious.

He didn't look anything like she'd expected. Instead of the cutthroat, highbrow businessman she had envisioned, the man who stood before her looked like the boy next door. The boy next door in a two-thousand-dollar, custom-tailored suit.

"And you, Ms. Kattapoulos. I must say, you are nothing like I envisioned." His voice, too, was deceptive, as was the hint of a dimple that revealed itself with his disarming smile.

While Lexi was trying to decide whether he meant that as a compliment or an insult, he added smoothly, "You are even more beautiful than I imagined. Only now do I feel I have a better appreciation for the inspiration behind the Celtic Goddess."

In a gallant gesture, he took Lexi's hand and lightly kissed the back of it. "I am a great fan. Your skills are legendary."

"You are too kind, Mr. Dumas," Lexi said, blushing slightly.

Over the top of Spencer's bowed head, she looked questioningly at Aidan, who was watching the scene with genuine amusement. No doubt he was imagining what would happen to Spencer Dumas if Lexi's husband were witnessing this. Ian was very protective of what was his, and to Ian, Lexi was everything.

Outside of family, Aidan was probably the only other male on the planet permitted within her personal space, and even that was questionable at times. He was tolerated because, one, Aidan had saved Lexi's life on more than one occasion, and two, because Aidan was her best friend and Lexi would have it no other way.

"Mr. Dumas has brought some very interesting information to our attention, Lex," Aidan prompted.

"Ah, yes," said Spencer, releasing Lexi's hand somewhat reluctantly.

She didn't miss the way his eyes lingered upon her fingers, subtly checking for the presence of a ring. Lexi never wore her bands while cooking anymore, not since she'd accidentally lost one in several pounds of croissant dough that the staff spent the better part of an hour pulling apart. She guessed—correctly—that Spencer was adjusting his "presentation" based on her marital status.

"I know your time is precious, so I'll get right to the point. I understand the Celtic Goddess is interested in forming a business venture to procure locally grown organic produce."

Lexi flashed a look at Aidan and then back to Spencer. He could only be referring to the deal they were trying to put together with Maggie. Legal was still working out the details; nothing had been officially announced.

"I wasn't aware that was public knowledge, Mr. Dumas."

Spencer smiled, flashing several of his perfect white teeth. "I do not believe that it is, Ms. Kattapoulos."

"Mr. Dumas is well connected in the local business community," Aidan explained, pulling out a chair for her.

Lexi hoped she looked suitably impressed. "Do you hold such property, Mr. Dumas?"

He smiled confidently. "Not yet, Ms. Kattapoulos. And please, call me Spencer."

Lexi offered a demure and encouraging smile but made no such offer to him in return. She'd dealt with enough men like him to know that he would be disappointed if she didn't offer at least a slight challenge.

"The Flynn property is of particular interest to Dumas Industries," Aidan said casually, but Lexi knew him well enough to hear the warning in his voice. As handsome and smooth as Aidan was, Lexi always said no one ever saw the danger before it was too late.

"Ah, Mr. Dumas—Spencer—I do hope this does not mean we will be competing against one another."

His eyes glittered. "Not at all. What I propose is a collaboration, not a competition."

Lexi nodded, wondering where this could possibly be going. She sat back in her chair, taking her time in crossing one leg over the other. The flash of gold caught Spencer's eye for a moment. Lexi had forgotten she was wearing the gold and diamond anklet Ian had given her for Valentine's Day; it resembled something a belly dancer might wear. It was one of Ian's favorite pieces. Apparently, other men found it enticing as well.

"Please, continue," she coaxed.

Spencer's gaze snapped upward. "My sources tell me you are attempting to create an agreement with the current caretaker of the property, Magdalena Flynn, by which you contract for the fruits of the land but not the property itself."

"Your sources are quite well-informed."

He inclined his head in acknowledgment.

"But I fail to see of what interest this is to you." She allowed some of her Greek grandmother's accent into her words, intuitively playing the role Spencer expected to see.

"Beauty, talent, and intelligence," Spencer mused. "What a lethal combination. How do you stand it, Mr. Harrison?"

Aidan beamed beside her. "She brings out the best in me, Mr. Dumas," he answered sincerely. "Demands it of me repeatedly in fact." His lips quirked when she shot him an amused glance, as if they shared a private joke.

Spencer smiled knowingly at the inference, at the veiled warning. "Then, you are a lucky man indeed, Mr. Harrison." His manner lost some of its flirtatiousness then, though it didn't detract from his polished charm.

"To be quite honest, I would like to create a similar association between the Celtic Goddess and Dumas Industries."

"Forgive me, but I don't understand. You said you do not own the land, Mr. Dumas—Spencer."

"A temporary situation, I assure you. Let's just say that I am preparing the path for what will be."

Lexi arched a brow and looked questioningly at Aidan before turning her attention back to Dumas with a gentle smile. "I must admit, you have piqued my interest. Can you tell us more?"

Spencer's eyes sparkled; he was obviously pleased with Lexi's interest. "I'm sure you will understand that I cannot go into specifics just yet, Ms. Kattapoulos. Dumas Industries has not become the successful business it is by giving away all of its secrets prematurely."

Lexi had the grace to blush a little. "Of course. I'm afraid I don't have Aidan's aptitude for business." Lexi turned to Aidan, her face a mask of sultry innocence. She played her part well.

Spencer flashed her an indulgent smile. "For a comparable price, Dumas Industries could provide the same services without the start-up costs the Celtic Goddess would incur by dealing solely with Miss

Flynn. Would I be correct in assuming that might appeal to you?"

"It sounds wonderful, but surely, there must be more to it than that."

Spencer's indulgence turned to approval. "I wish all of my business associates were as straightforward as you, Ms. Kattapoulos. I assure you, Dumas Industries only requests a simple caveat. Something minimal really. Just a slight delay in the current proceedings to ensure that the underlying groundwork is laid appropriately. It will work to your advantage as well."

Lexi appeared to mull this over, letting her brows furrow ever so slightly. "Aidan? What do you think?"

He seemed to give it serious thought as well. "I think a slight delay is a reasonable expectation," he said slowly, "given the amount of research and analysis to be considered in our final decision. You know how difficult it can be to obtain the necessary information. I don't believe the county records are fully digitized, which means things have a tendency to be misplaced rather easily."

Lexi nodded. "It looks like you have your answer, Spencer."

With a satisfied smile, Spencer extended his hand to Aidan. "Excellent. We will be in contact."

"I look forward to it."

Spencer took Lexi's hand as well. "It has been a great pleasure meeting you, Ms. Kattapoulos. I now have a greater understanding of why Mr. Harrison keeps you shrouded in such mystery."

"And why is that?"

Instead of answering, Spencer kissed her hand again. "Until next time."

When he was gone, Lexi sank down into the chair, absently wiping the back of her hand on her jeans to remove any trace of Spencer's *adieu*.

Aidan chuckled. "What kind of bouquet would you like? That was one hell of a performance, Lex. You had Dumas ready to melt every time you spoke his name."

"I learned from the best." She grinned, but then her smile faded. "I'm worried. What is he up to, Aidan?"

"I don't know. Think Ian will work some of his magic and do some digging for us?"

"Absolutely. We've got to tell Maggie and Michael too."

"Agreed."

MAGGIE SIGHED against the warmth of Michael's solid chest, wondering how she'd ever managed without him. Her body was sated, but her mind refused to relax. Ever since Lexi had called and told her about Spencer's visit, she couldn't stop thinking about what Spencer might be up to.

"I must be slipping," Michael said softly against the top of her head. "Usually, I'd have you exhausted by now."

Maggie smiled lovingly into his face as he rolled

her over, positioning himself above her. She opened for him, cradling his hips as he lowered his head and kissed her.

"Don't you ever get tired?" she asked, amusement lacing her voice.

Michael had always been an attentive lover, but since she'd gotten the ink, he'd been insatiable. While she wasn't complaining, the pregnancy often forced her to take catnaps in between his attentions.

"Of making love to you? Not in this lifetime." He kissed along her jaw, his tongue swirling just beneath the bone.

They hadn't taken their vows officially yet, but she was his, in every sense of the word.

"You're worried," he murmured.

Of course she was worried! Dumas Industries hadn't become the mega-company it was by being nice and playing by the rules. Spencer was trying to sabotage her contract with the Goddess and get it for himself. Since that would involve taking her land away from her somehow—the only home she had ever known—she felt it was a reasonable cause for concern.

"Yes," she admitted.

Apparently, Dumas had been a busy boy; Ian was uncovering more every day, and none of it was good. Michael was doing his best to distract her. Thus far, his strategy consisted of keeping her occupied until she fell into an exhausted sleep. As plans went, it was simple but effective, but Dumas and his schemes were always there, lurking in the background.

Her hand roamed along his back, feeling the strength and corded muscle there, while the other tangled in his silky black hair. Maggie didn't think she would ever get used to the feel of touching him or the way it sent tiny electric impulses throughout her whole body.

"Don't be," he said soothingly. "Ian will work his magic, and we'll handle it from there. Dumas doesn't stand a chance against us."

He continued down her neck, across her collarbone, along the swell of her breasts. He ran his tongue around her nipple and blew softly, making her shiver beneath him. His teeth rasped the hardened tip and then nipped her as he slid himself into her, the slick fluids from his previous release easing his passage.

Michael began a slow, agonizing pace, withdrawing as he sucked her breast, penetrating as he nipped it. The result was a full body of sensations so intense that it began to push everything else from her mind.

"You're trying to distract me again," she said breathlessly.

"Mmhmm," he murmured against her breast. "Is it working?"

"Definitely."

CHAPTER TWENTY-SEVEN

Michael made lazy circles over Maggie's growing baby bump. Every day that his child grew inside her, he seemed even more fascinated by it.

"Mmm," she moaned softly. "Don't stop. That feels good."

Anytime Michael's hands were on her, it felt good, but she loved how the warmth of his hands seeped right down into her and their unborn. Suddenly, she stilled, placing her hands over his.

"What is it?" he asked.

"Did you feel that?"

"The baby moved?"

Maggie laughed in pure joy. "Yes! I felt it! Here, ..."

She repositioned his hands and held her breath. Michael detected the slight movement beneath his fingers.

"That was him? Are you sure?" His face held nothing but awe.

"Positive. There! He did it again. He knows your voice, Michael! Say something else."

"What did Dr. Foster say today?" Michael asked carefully as he waited for the next one.

"Why?" she asked. Whenever Michael used that cautious voice, she became concerned. "What's wrong?"

"Nothing's wrong," Michael assured her. "But that was a hell of a kick for this stage. Have the tests come back yet, specifically the one for gestational diabetes? What about the ultrasound results? They usually include measurements."

"No," she answered honestly. After all, it wasn't possible to get results from tests she'd never had. "But I think it's safe to say, he's going to be big and strong, just like his daddy."

Michael's eyes glowed with pride, but there was no mistaking his impatience. "What? There's no reason it should take that long to get results back, not when they have everything right there in front of them. You know what? I'm calling Bob Foster right now."

"Michael, please don't do that," Maggie begged. "It's late."

"He's an OB/GYN. He's used to getting calls at all hours of the day and night. Besides, he owes me. Where the hell is my cell? I've got his number on speed dial." Michael rolled out of bed, slinging on some loose pants with a drawstring and disappearing from the bedroom in search of his missing phone.

Maggie sank down into the pillows, waiting for the inevitable. *Wouldn't be long now ...*

"Maggie?" Michael said softly a few minutes later, leaning on the doorframe. "Is there something you want to tell me, sweetheart?"

He looked so hot, standing there, nothing but the low-slung sweats that clung to him deliciously. His love-tussled black hair and glowing blue eyes never failed to take her breath away.

"No, not really." It was an honest answer. She really didn't want to tell him that she hadn't kept a single follow-up visit with the obstetrician Michael had hand-selected. One had been more than enough.

"*Maggie.*"

"I don't like him."

Michael gave her a stern look, piercing her with those intense blue eyes until she squirmed.

"He's got bad breath and cold hands that he likes to put in places they have no business being."

MICHAEL PRAYED for patience and tried to remember Maggie's intense aversion to practically everyone in the medical profession. It had taken days of cajoling to get her to agree to go a month ago. Why he'd ever thought she would continue to go on her own was beside him. He should have known better. He should have insisted on driving her to each and every appointment personally.

"He's an OB, Maggie. That's his job."

Maggie pulled the sheet up, covering her breasts. "No, Michael. Touching me there is *your* job, not his. And I can't believe you actually want another man to be doing that sort of thing to your wife-to-be."

For a modern, independent woman, Maggie could be terribly old-fashioned.

"That 'sort of thing' is ensuring your health and that of our baby's. He's a *doctor*, Maggie."

"So are you. You can do it."

"I'm not an OB. I'm not qualified."

"You delivered Taryn's baby."

"That was different. There were extenuating circumstances."

"And you were there for Lexi."

"Now, *that* was a totally different situation."

"I don't care."

"*Maggie.*"

She crossed her arms and glared back at him, her green eyes just as fierce. "*Michael.*"

"Regular prenatal checkups are important."

"They're a waste of time—that's what they are. Taryn says all they do is weigh you, and believe me, I don't need anyone telling me how heavy I'm getting, thank you very much. And they measure your belly—again, not necessary—listen for a heartbeat, and feel you up. You're perfectly capable of doing those things, and it feels much better when you do it."

"Maggie—"

But Maggie was on a roll, gaining steam, and there was no stopping her. Her words came faster, spoken with the near desperation of impending panic. "I swear I will see Lexi's doctor at the very first sign of a problem. And because I love you so much, I *might* even agree to see Foster's assistant once in a while. I like her; plus, she's a woman who has a few kids of her own, and Taryn says she's not into unnecessary groping. Until then, I will continue to do what women have been doing quite naturally for centuries—without some pervert sticking his hands up my cooch for a freebie."

"*Maggie!*"

Her voice rose even higher, louder, until it became a full-fledged shriek. "Michael Patrick Callaghan, you put this baby into me, and you'd damn sure better be the one to get it out!"

Stunned silence filled the room for several moments, but then Michael couldn't help it. He laughed. And laughed. Then, Maggie started laughing, too, and neither of them was able to stop until tears came out of their eyes and their sides hurt.

Michael wrapped his arms around her and wiped away the tears streaming down her cheeks. "Ah, Maggie, love, I don't know what I'm going to do with you."

"Well, my suggestion is for you to make use of all those fancy letters after your name to take care of your woman and child."

And unfortunately, at that moment, Michael couldn't think of a good enough argument against it.

"Is she always like this?" Sean asked Michael as he took yet another roll from the plate Maggie had just placed on the table, slathering it with homemade preserves.

Maggie was already back at the oven, sliding in a fresh tray and rolling out more dough.

"Only when she's anxious," Michael answered, his watchful eyes following her every movement. It had been a mistake to tell her that his father and several of his brothers would be dropping by this morning with important news. She'd been up since the crack of dawn, baking. "It's how she handles stress."

He'd long since given up on trying to convince her to sit down and rest. After Maggie refilled everyone's coffee cups and murmured something about making more, he simply reached out with one of his long arms and snagged her, pulling her down onto his lap.

"Enough, woman. If you keep feeding them, they'll never leave," he said.

"Michael!"

Kieran laughed and winked at Maggie as he held up a roll. "No, he's right. But it's too late, Mick. We're already hooked. These things are addictive."

Michael groaned, but Maggie's eyes sparkled. She had confided to him that she loved their banter and teasing and was only too happy to indulge their massive appetites. She made a move to get up, but Michael held her to him easily.

"So," Ian said finally after everyone had had their fill and it was time to get down to it, "here's what it looks like."

Everyone quieted and turned their attention to him.

"Dumas is definitely trying to get his hands on Maggie's land."

"That's nothing new," Maggie muttered. "He's been trying to do that for years."

"True, but what *is* new is the fact that the Celtic Goddess is actively pursuing a contractual agreement with you for use of the land—as well as exclusive rights to the organic produce and secret family recipes."

"So?"

"So ... Dumas Industries is big but not big enough to take on the Goddess, and Dumas knows it. He's trying to cozy up while he can."

"Organics are huge right now, Mags. *Lucrative* doesn't begin to cover the deal you guys are cooking up," Kieran added.

Maggie shrugged. "I know you probably won't believe this, but that doesn't really matter to me. As long as I have enough to get by, I'm happy. Spencer knows that, though he never could understand it. And he knows I'd never sell out, especially to him or his company."

"I get that. But a seven-figure deal *does* matter to Dumas, which is why he had to get creative. You won't sell, so he's got to go around you and get your land another way."

"Sorry, Ian. I'm not following you. What other possible way is there?"

"Think about it. How does property change ownership? Through death and divorce mostly, right? But neither is applicable here. That leaves hostile reclamation, things like foreclosure or tax default auctions."

"But this property isn't mortgaged. And I pay the taxes in full and on time every year."

Ian turned his blue gaze to her, and she felt a sudden chill. "Do you?"

"Of course I do. I've got copies of my returns. I can get them for you."

"Not necessary," Ian said, waving his hand. "We've already been through them."

Maggie was glad at that moment that she'd never cheated on her taxes. "Then, you know I'm telling the truth."

"Relax, Mags. No one here is accusing you of cheating Uncle Sam."

"Then, what are you saying?" Michael asked impatiently.

Shane cleared his throat.

He was perhaps the quietest brother Maggie had

met so far with the exception of the eldest one, Kane. Though Shane didn't say much, Maggie had the impression he was soaking in everything around him. Michael had confided to her once that not only did Shane have a law degree, he was also the equivalent of a human computer; he had almost instant recall on everything he'd ever read or seen as well as an inherent gift for reading people.

When he spoke, it was with a soft, thoughtful voice that had an immediate soothing effect on her frazzled nerves, much like Michael's. She, like everyone else, turned her attention toward him.

"Okay," Shane began, "there are two things that are really important here: tax assessments and zoning. First, understand that the taxes you pay are based on the county's assessment of how much your property is worth. Valuation obviously changes over time, depending on a number of factors, such as location, development, the local economy, and job market—you get the idea. For this reason, reassessments occur periodically, like, say, when a house is bought or sold or when someone takes out a second mortgage."

Maggie nodded in understanding.

"But sometimes, a house or land can stay in the same family for generations, as in your case. The result is that the taxes you pay are based on a fraction of what this place is currently worth. For this reason, some counties, like ours, schedule periodic reassessments to keep the tax base equitable."

"My taxes have remained pretty much the same

since before my grandparents passed," Maggie pointed out. "I know, because I did their taxes for years."

"Exactly. And that's where the zoning comes in. Your two hundred acres is zoned as prime agricultural, which means exactly what you think it does. The land you hold is ideal for farming, which is probably why your family was so successful at it over the years. Since you assumed ownership, however, you have not claimed any agriculturally based profit or loss."

"No," she agreed, drawing the word out. "There hasn't been much in the way of active farming here for quite a while. My grandfather had his little roadside stand, and my grandma had her remedies, but they weren't dependent on the income at that point."

With her natural talent for organization and figures, Maggie had set them up with comfortable retirement accounts. It hadn't been much, but it had been enough for them to be able to enjoy their golden years.

"It's pretty hard to operate a farm single-handedly," Michael pointed out.

"Not to mention, Maggie has held employment outside of the family farm. She's been paying taxes on every penny she's earned, just like the rest of us," Kieran said in her defense.

Maggie's heart warmed with the way they rallied around her. She'd never had that as an only child, but as Ian was constantly telling her, she'd get used to it eventually.

"True. But ... properties designated as prime agricultural are given special consideration. The county, you see, receives federal subsidies for land that is actively farmed, as opposed to land that is sold for things like subdivisions or to businesses. It's a way to keep the land green and discourage overdevelopment. The county passes a percentage of these boons to the landowners. Some of these perks include a lower tax rate than residential or commercial properties as well as an exclusion from the mandatory reassessments."

"Wait," Maggie said, beginning to catch on. "You said 'actively farmed.' "

Shane nodded approvingly. "I did. Because you have not claimed the farm as either a source of income or loss, there are those who are vying to rescind your special tax status."

"So, Maggie's taxes will go up," Kieran said, shrugging. "So what?"

"That is a gross understatement, I'm afraid. Unless Maggie uses at least part of the land for agricultural purposes, the entire property will be rezoned and reassessed."

"I still don't see what the problem is. Won't the agreement with the Goddess take care of all that?" Sean asked.

"It would, if Maggie could retain ownership long enough to see that come to fruition."

A shiver ran the length of Maggie's spine. "Shane, what is it you aren't saying?"

Shane blew out a breath. He looked so apologetic that Maggie felt a stab of sympathy for him. "There's a motion before the county board to not only reassess and rezone your property, but to also make the changes retroactive, back to when Maggie assumed ownership ten years ago. To make matters worse, they are planning on charging Maggie with tax evasion and fraud, saying she knew what she was doing all along and has deliberately been abusing the privileges of her special status."

"That's insane!" Michael said vehemently.

Several of them voiced similar opinions.

"Those charges will tie the property rights up in red tape indefinitely," Shane continued. "Any tentative agreement with the Goddess effectively becomes meaningless. Then, between the fines, penalties, back taxes, and interest ... Maggie, we're talking about an ungodly sum of money."

The color drained from her face. "Can they really do that?"

"Don't worry, sweetheart. We're not going to let that happen," Michael assured her, tightening his hold on her.

"Hell no," Ian agreed heartily.

The next hour was spent discussing options and ideas. Maggie remained silent throughout most of it. It was hard for her to believe that Spencer would go to such lengths to destroy her, even with the amount of money involved. How could she have underestimated him so?

"Shane?" Maggie asked quietly, laying her hand on his forearm as he walked out into the hallway. She'd been waiting for a chance to speak with him out of earshot from the others. "When we marry, will Michael then become liable as well?"

Shane shifted his weight from one leg to the other.

Clearly, he didn't want to answer the question, but Maggie persisted. "Please, Shane. I have to know."

Shane exhaled. "Yes. According to Pennsylvania state law, assets and liabilities are shared jointly between spouses unless special arrangements, like a prenup, are made." He paused, as though unsure of whether or not to continue. "But I have to tell you, Maggie, getting something like that done at this point would not be advisable. Not to mention, Mick would blow a gasket."

Maggie nodded. It was as she'd suspected. "And Aidan and Lexi? If I sign those papers, then they'll be in limbo until this gets resolved, right?"

"Yeah, pretty much. But they're not going to back out on you, no matter what. None of us will."

"Thanks, Shane." She patted his arm and turned to go.

"Maggie? You okay?"

"Yeah," she said quietly. "Thanks."

WHEN SHANE REENTERED the kitchen a few minutes later, he was instantly and violently pinned up against the wall. Ian had his left side, Kieran his right.

"What did you say to her?" Ian demanded.

"What are you talking about? I just went to take a pi—"

"You left the room. Maggie followed you out. Two minutes later, she ripped the Goddess agreement in half and told Michael the wedding was off. What the fuck did you do?"

The color drained from Shane's face as he realized what Maggie had just done. "Fuck. Where is she?"

"Upstairs. Michael's trying to talk some sense into her."

It was obvious a short time later by Michael's expression that he hadn't been successful, but Ian decided to ask anyway, "Any luck?"

"No," Michael answered in a low growl. From the set of his jaw and the way he kept running his hand through his hair, his frustration came through clearly. "She says she's not going to take us down with her."

"That's bullshit!" Sean exclaimed.

"Well, of course it is," Jack Callaghan scoffed. "But Maggie's a good woman. She's going to protect the ones she loves."

"Unfortunately, Dad's right," Michael exhaled. "You don't know Maggie. She's stubborn as hell, and I don't think she's going to budge on this."

Shane stood and said with determination, "Then, I guess it's up to us to make sure this gets cleared up quickly."

CHAPTER TWENTY-EIGHT

"I don't care that he's busy. I'll wait." Maggie took a seat outside of Spencer's office, refusing to budge until he saw her.

The personal assistant—not the same one from a year and a half ago, she noted—frowned. It had been no easy feat to slip out from beneath the watchful eyes of her self-appointed big brothers, and she was not leaving without speaking to him.

"Is there a problem, Janice?" Spencer asked, stepping out of his office.

"This woman insists on speaking with you," Janice said. Disapproval dripped from her perfectly coiffed form, evident by the distinct downturn of her scarlet lips and scathing glances from her artfully smudged, lined eyes. "She refuses to leave. I was just about to call security."

"No need," Spencer said smoothly when he saw Maggie. "Maggie is an old friend."

Janice looked like she wanted to argue, but her lips, thinned in irritation, softened when Spencer smiled at her. Maggie fought the urge to roll her eyes. Apparently, Spencer's female fan club was still going strong. She wondered vaguely how many "bonuses" this one earned and then realized she didn't care.

Spencer led Maggie into his plush office. Not much had changed since the last time she had been there, though this time, she was able to appreciate the quality decor since her eyes weren't drawn to the sight of Spencer having sex with his secretary bent over his desk.

"Please, sit down, Maggie. Would you care for some tea? You were quite fond of jasmine, if I recall."

"I would love some, thank you." Maggie sat down carefully in an expensive leather chair.

He was clearly surprised by her easy agreement, as his eyebrows rose slightly, but he recovered quickly. Pressing a button, he made the request.

Spencer stepped in front of his desk and then leaned back against it, facing her in a classic power pose. The bespoke navy suit screamed wealth and privilege. The blue-and-gray striped tie was a bit conservative for him. Maybe he was finally growing up.

"You look beautiful, Maggie," he said. "Radiant in fact. Pregnancy agrees with you. But then I always knew it would."

Maggie wasn't quite sure how to respond to that. There was no use in denying it at this point, she supposed. Everyone in Pine Ridge probably knew.

"Thank you," she managed.

"Michael Callaghan is a lucky man, Maggie. I hope he has more sense than me."

It was a good thing she was already sitting down since his unexpected words would have knocked her on her behind. Not so much because of the words themselves—Spencer could charm the scales off of a snake if there was a profit involved—but because he sounded sincere.

How exactly was she supposed to respond to that? Thankfully, she was saved from having to by a soft knock on the door, announcing the arrival of the refreshments. Spencer thanked Janice, who glared daggers at Maggie behind his back, and then he proceeded to pour a cup of tea for Maggie and coffee for himself. Rather than sit behind his massive desk, he took the matching leather chair adjacent to hers.

"So, tell me, Maggie, to what do I owe the pleasure of your visit today?"

The tea smelled wonderful, but Maggie's stomach was doing flip-flops. "I think you know why I'm here, Spencer."

He raised one eyebrow and sipped his coffee. "Maggie, every time I thought I knew what you were thinking, you proved me wrong. I wouldn't dare to suggest I have even the slightest clue this time."

Despite the gravity of the situation, the corner of her mouth quirked. She had forgotten how charming Spencer could be when he wasn't laying it on thickly.

"Ah," he said. "You see? A smile is the last thing I

would expect to receive from you, yet you have surprised me once again. I must tell you, I prefer it to your hand across my cheek."

Maggie had the good sense to look abashed. "I am sorry for that, Spencer. I shouldn't have lost my temper."

Spencer inclined his head. "Apology accepted, but I daresay I deserved it." He lifted the mug to his lips again. "But you didn't come by today simply to apologize, did you?"

"No. I came to ask you to call off your hounds. I will gladly have the property reassessed, and I will pay the back taxes. But you know that what you are proposing will ruin me."

"Don't be melodramatic," he chastised with a dismissive wave of his hand. Charming Spencer was gone; ruthless Spencer was back in control. "It is simply business, nothing personal. And you will be quite well taken care of, I'm sure. You are marrying into a very wealthy family." He smiled at her look of confusion. "Oh, they don't flaunt it much, but the Callaghans are the real deal, Maggie. You did well for yourself."

Her features hardened. The hand holding her teacup began to shake; she put it down a little too hard, causing tea to slosh over the side. "You of all people should know that money is not that important to me, Spencer. Other things, like doing right by the people you care for and making sure they don't suffer for your mistakes, *that's* what is important."

The steel she tried to instill into her words, the

fierce, stubborn pride, was interwoven with under-tones of hurt, shock, and betrayal. She'd spoken similar words after she discovered his infidelity, when he tried to dissuade her from ending their engagement by telling her that he would lavish her with any gift she desired in penance for his transgression. She had refused, saying that no amount of money was worth betraying someone for.

It still wasn't.

His smug smile faded; his brow creased. "Maggie, what did you do?"

She took a deep breath, steadying her voice before answering. She hadn't shown weakness before Spencer Dumas last time; she would not do it now. "I've called off the wedding."

"Why on earth would you do such a thing?" For the first time, Spencer seemed shaken. He stood up and paced back and forth. "Do you have an obsession with breaking off engagements or something?"

She flashed him a withering glance. "Do what you want to me. But I will not let you hurt them too."

"Jesus, Maggie. What the hell were you thinking?"

"I was thinking that it is my home, and it was my responsibility to know what was required of my land. It was foolish on my part not to. And I refuse to take good, decent people down with me because of it."

"But, Maggie—"

"But *Maggie* nothing. You know I'm an honest woman, and I'll make amends. Every cent, without complaint. But even you must understand that if you tie up my land with trumped-up charges and make it impossible for me to farm it, I have no hope of earning enough in this lifetime to do so." She sat forward on her seat. "Please, Spencer. All I ask is that you drop the charges and free my land. It's been in my family for generations. I'll work it myself if I have to."

Spencer looked at her with pity. "Even if I wanted to, there is no way I could contact everyone in time. The county board meeting is in less than four hours. It's too late. It's out of my hands."

"Surely, there is something you can do."

"I'm sorry, Maggie."

Maggie's eyes filled with unshed tears, but she refused to let them fall. She stood to leave.

Spencer put his hand on her arm. "Go back to Michael. Let him take care of you."

She looked at him in disbelief. "You really don't understand, do you? I don't want anyone to take care of me like I'm some helpless child. If you believe I could do that, Spencer, then you never knew me at all."

Maggie wrenched away from his hand, refusing to listen. The only thing she wanted to do was get as far away from Spencer Dumas as she could before she did something she would really regret.

SPENCER'S DAY, it seemed, was not about to improve. He arrived at the county board meeting late because of the throng of people that had shown up. Every folded chair was occupied; people stood two and three deep in the limited available space. The crowd even spilled out the door.

Spencer's feeling of dread worsened when he saw the first two rows before the head table were comprised entirely of Callaghans and their ilk. A closer look showed him that Maggie was noticeably absent.

Some of the board members shot him irritated glances when they spotted him. Spencer's acute self-preservation instinct had him deciding to stay in the back, near the doors, and observe from there.

The chairman called the meeting to order. Introductions were made along with a brief welcome. The secretary then rose. The first order of business, as always, was to approve the minutes from the previous meeting. When that was taken care of, the room grew silent once again.

"It is encouraging to see so many concerned citizens here this evening," one of the board members said with a twinkle in his eye.

Dirk Bailey was one of the few local politicians who couldn't care less about Spencer Dumas or his company. His warnings to the others about leaving sleeping dogs lie had gone unheeded, and as he gazed out on those gathered, he looked as if he was going to enjoy the results of that. Deep laugh lines were etched in his weather-beaten skin—a result of many hard years of farming his own acreage before his sons took over. With his bolo tie and cowboy hat, he looked more like he hailed from Texas than northeastern Pennsylvania.

Another member of the board, Lance Williams, cleared his throat. He was a large man, dressed in casual slacks and a designer sweater, no doubt purchased for him by his wife on one of her Fifth Avenue shopping sprees. Unlike Bailey, Williams's hands were smooth and manicured—a result of his VP position at a Dumas subsidiary. It paid to marry into the Dumas family.

"Yes. Especially when this particular meeting was not on the public schedule." Williams muttered the words, clearly forgetting that his microphone was turned on.

"The only item on the agenda for this evening is to vote on the motion to rezone certain sections of the county and allow our tax board to reassess affected properties as soon as possible."

"How many properties are affected?" a disembodied voice asked from the back of the room.

"For those of you not familiar with the protocol for these meetings, questions or comments must be first recognized by the board," the secretary said icily, shooting another irritated glance toward the back.

At least two dozen hands shot into the air. The chairman ignored all of them.

It was Shane who stood up. "I wish to speak on the matter."

"And you are?"

"Shane Callaghan."

The chairman's lips grew into an even thinner line. "Proceed."

"As I understand it, you are looking to rezone the Flynn property because it has not been used for agricultural purposes. Is that correct?"

"It is not our intent to target a single property, Mr. Callaghan," Williams said with a forced smile that did not reach his eyes. "We seek to make the tax base more equitable for everyone. The zoning ordinance is very clear on this." He looked out into the audience, hoping to see some agreeable nods, finding none.

"Yes, it is," Shane said in his calm, quiet tone. Shane didn't have to raise his voice or use a microphone to be heard. When he spoke, people couldn't help but listen. "The ordinance clearly states that the land be used for agricultural purposes. Nowhere does it state that such purposes must be for profit."

On the raised dais, a few members of the board shifted on their seats.

"Excuse me?"

"Maggie Flynn *has* been using the land for agricultural purposes. She cultivates organic herbs for home remedies, which she provides to several members of the community on a regular basis, free of charge. She allows the local elementary schools to make use of her land for educational purposes, hosting field trips every fall. She opens the orchards up to the locals of Pine Ridge so that they might pick from them—again, without charge. She donates untold bushels of produce to local shelters and charitable organizations throughout the year."

Williams shuffled a few papers. "None of that appears in our documentation, Mr. Callaghan."

"Obviously. That is why there are over one hundred constituents present here this evening, willing to provide testimony."

The board members exchanged glances.

"How many of you wish to speak on this issue?" the speaker asked.

Nearly every person in the audience raised their hand.

Far in the back, Spencer slipped away, smiling to himself.

CHAPTER TWENTY-NINE

Maggie unplugged the landline and turned off her cell phone; she couldn't stand the incessant ringing any longer. Her answering machine was full, the voice mail on her cell maxed out. She closed the curtains and locked the doors. If it were dark, she would turn out the lights, but the brilliant summer sunshine prevented her from hiding in the shadows.

She sat at the kitchen table, staring at the scarred top, running her fingers over the wood, worn smooth as glass over the years, relishing the feel of each nick and gouge. How much of this would she lose? She would probably end up selling everything just to try to make a dent in the balloon payment she knew was forthcoming. It would only be a matter of time now.

The county board had met last night; she hadn't been able to bring herself to attend. Instead, she'd huddled beneath her grandmother's quilt with a cup of hot cocoa and George snuggled by her side. Michael had insisted on going and encouraged her to go, too, but said he understood why she didn't want to.

Tears filled her eyes again. Telling him she couldn't marry him had nearly destroyed her. After his initial resistance, he'd just held her with that implacable calm, promising her that everything would work out. She wished she shared his faith.

At least she still had her dignity. If she'd attended the meeting, there was little chance she'd be able to say that. She knew she wouldn't have been able to hold her tongue when the politicians started waggling theirs, preaching about fairness and honesty, accusing her of deliberately trying to cheat the system. Especially when most of them were probably involved in much worse—not to mention the fact that they were most likely snugly aligned in Spencer's pocket.

No, sometimes, it was better to stand up and take what was coming with as much self-respect and dignity as she could muster. She knew she hadn't done anything illegal. She knew she was an honest person. Just as she knew, deep in her heart, that legally distancing herself from Michael and Lexi was the best thing she could do for them, no matter how much it hurt.

The knock on the door didn't surprise her; what was surprising was that it had taken this long. She took a deep breath, exhaling slowly. Maybe it was the sheriff, serving her papers. Maybe it was Spencer, coming to gloat. Or maybe it was a compassionate soul who had come to offer support. In any case, she wanted just a few more minutes of peace and solitude to brace herself for what lay ahead.

"Aren't you going to answer that?" Ian asked from behind her, startling her so much that she cleared her seat by several inches. He strode across the kitchen and took everything in. Every available surface was filled with pastries, cookies, pies, and breads. That was what happened when Maggie was stressed out and unable to sleep a wink.

"Christ, Maggie. Forget farming. You should open a bakery, you know that?"

"You really need to stop breaking into my house." With a pang of sorrow, she realized she wouldn't be able to say that much longer.

After agonizing over the available choices, Ian finally decided on a bear claw. His eyes rolled back in his head as he took a big bite.

The heavy knock sounded again.

"She's not going to answer it," he called out cheerfully. "You might as well just come in the front. I left it open."

Maggie looked at him in disbelief. He smiled unapologetically. Before she knew it, Sean was striding into the kitchen, followed by his twin.

"You could have just opened the door, asshole," Sean griped at Ian.

Ian grinned, unrepentant. "Not my house."

Taryn and Jake came in next with their daughter, Riley, in tow. Taryn went right over to Maggie and gave her a big hug. Riley put her pudgy little hands on Maggie's cheeks and gave her a slobbery, wet kiss.

Lexi followed with Jack holding Patrick. Aidan and Kieran brought up the rear. Soon, her kitchen was filled, looking remarkably smaller than it had only a few minutes earlier.

Maggie tried hard to summon a smile. "Did you come to help me pack?"

"Why? Are we going somewhere?" Michael's deep voice resounded through the kitchen. He strode over and kissed Maggie, as if nothing were wrong.

"Last I heard, I was," she said, looking in puzzlement at the crowd in her kitchen, most of which was made up of large men eating.

It certainly didn't look anything like the pity party she'd been expecting. As a matter of fact, they all seemed strangely ... happy.

"Not anymore, sweetheart," Michael said. "The county board has had a change of heart."

Maggie stared around in disbelief at their smiling faces. "What did you do?"

"*We* did nothing," Ian said around the pastry he'd stuffed into his mouth. "But apparently, *you* have done a lot. At least a hundred people spoke on your behalf last night, Mags." He laughed. "The meeting went until well after midnight."

"I don't understand," Maggie said, shaking her head. "I don't even know a hundred people."

"Ah, but they know you," Michael said, gently guiding her to a chair.

"It's true," Jack explained. "All the field trips, food donations, and natural remedies you've been giving people over the years—they were qualified, legitimate agricultural uses regardless of whether or not you charged for them."

Maggie blinked and looked over toward Shane, knowing instinctively he had been the one to find a way out of this. He looked almost embarrassed.

"I get to keep my land? My house?"

"All of it," Shane confirmed.

Tears formed in her eyes.

"Ah, don't cry, Mags," Ian said, even as Michael knelt beside her chair and pulled her against him.

"It's okay, sweetheart," Michael said soothingly. "I've got you."

It took a few minutes, but Maggie was finally able to pull herself away and wipe at her eyes. No matter what they said, she knew they were responsible for this. For all of it. "I don't know how to thank you."

"Well, I do," said Jake, his eyes twinkling, his deep, booming voice resonating throughout the kitchen. He didn't talk much, but when he did, you couldn't help but pay attention. "The first thing you can do is tell our sorry-ass brother that the wedding is back on. We're tired of him moping around the pub. It's bad for business."

Maggie framed Michael's face with both of her hands and looked into his eyes. "I can do that," she said softly.

"And the second thing," Aidan added, "is to sign

this contract with the Celtic Goddess so that we can move forward with our new organic menu." He slid a stack of papers across the table and handed her a gold pen.

"I've already been through them," Shane said around a strawberry-and-cheese danish. "And I can tell you the Goddess is being extremely generous. The land, the house—it all remains yours. The Goddess will provide the equipment and the labor."

"It also names you as a member of the Celtic Goddess board," Lexi said excitedly. "Director of the new Organics Division."

Maggie was at a loss. "I don't know what to say ..."

"Don't say anything. Just sign it," Taryn coaxed.

With trembling fingers, Maggie did just that.

"Oh, and one more thing," Ian added mischievously. "You've got to promise never to stop making these bear claws."

Michael and Maggie's wedding was held a week later. Rather than a big to-do, they opted for an intimate evening candlelight service for close family and friends only, followed by a low-key dinner at the Goddess. After everything that had happened, they were thankful for the quiet affair.

"Maggie." Spencer Dumas stepped from the shadows while Maggie waited for Michael to bring the car around. "You look absolutely beautiful."

"Spencer?" she asked with a note of fear in her voice.

Spencer smiled. "Relax, Maggie. I just wanted to wish you the best."

"Oh. Well, thank you."

"I'm glad everything worked out for you. I really am." With one last smile, Spencer turned and walked away, back into the shadows.

"Are you okay, love?" Michael asked as he opened up the passenger door of the black Jag for her and saw her looking off to where Spencer had disappeared only seconds earlier. The man always did have an impeccable sense of timing.

Maggie turned to her new husband, snaking her hands up around his neck. "Everything is perfect. Absolutely perfect."

Seeking Vengeance (Sean's story) is the next book in the Callaghan Brothers series. Read on for a preview ...

READY FOR SEAN?

Check out this excerpt from *Seeking Vengeance*, book 4 in the **Callaghan Brothers** series

"Hold on there, sweetheart. I'm not finished with you yet."

So, this is Nick's boss, the infamous Sean Callaghan, Nicki thought. Her brother Nick had talked enough about him, but nothing could have prepared her for meeting him in the flesh. The guy screamed intensity and power and radiated a raw sexuality that called to her most primitive instincts.

Without conscious effort, she memorized every nuance of his facial and bone structure. It was a skill she'd developed over the years, ensuring that should she encounter him again, she would recognize him without fail even if he attempted to change his appearance. Not that she would be able to forget him easily. His very presence commanded her absolute and undivided attention, which automatically raised her hackles. Nicki, like her brother, had a natural resistance to authority figures.

It was a hell of a presence for a simple mechanic. Even as the thought entered her mind, she dismissed it.

Sean Callaghan was no more a garden-variety garage owner than she was a Sunday school teacher. His countenance, the way he held himself, the silent arrogance—they reeked of special forces training. Marines. Navy SEALs. Black ops maybe. It all added up to the same thing—*danger*.

His dark hair, cerulean-blue eyes, and strong, masculine features reminded her a lot of the guy who owned BodyWorks, the local fitness center. The resemblance was uncanny.

Brothers most likely, she thought to herself.

The BodyWorks guy was younger and broader but didn't have the breath-stealing, bad-ass intensity of this guy.

All of this passed through her mind in a second, maybe two. The bottom line: the sleepy little town of Pine Ridge had its share of secrets. It was intriguing, but unless it had a direct correlation to her purpose, none of it mattered. The best thing she could do was just stay the fuck out of his way.

And if he knew what was good for him, he'd stay the fuck out of hers.

"But I am finished with you, *baby*," she purred. To further illustrate her point, her hand reached out and covered his crotch. *Oh yeah, this guy was made for hot, sweaty sex.* One side of her mouth curved upward with a knowing smile as her hand ran the length of him, firmly cupping his balls through his jeans.

"Nicki!" Nick said in a low, warning voice.

Her eyes flickered toward her brother. She'd momentarily forgotten he was there. Her hand dropped away, and the smile was gone in an instant. She stepped back, all playfulness replaced by a mask of cold indifference.

"My debt's paid. I'm outta here."

"Nicki, wait."

"Sorry, sweetie. Can't be late, or the natives get restless." She tossed one more smoky glance Sean's way. "Nice package, by the way."

She began to walk away but didn't get more than a step or two before Sean's hand reached out and clamped around her wrist like a vise, stopping her in her tracks.

One corner of her mouth tilted up slightly, though her eyes flashed silvery fire. "Ooh, I bet you like it rough, don't you?" She smirked, her voice a husky growl.

"Sean. Mr. Callaghan. Please, let her go." Nick's voice, laced with an edge of panic, cut through the tense silence. "*Please.*"

Nick's boss narrowed his eyes but released the grip on her wrist.

She reclaimed her hand and smiled, showing perfect white teeth. "Later, hard-ass."

Nicki Milligan walked—no, *strutted*—out of Callaghan Auto like she owned the place. She paused just outside, letting the cool air drift over her bare shoulders. Then, she took a few steps to the left, out of the reach of the spotlights and into the shadows. There, she promptly collapsed against the side of the building, hands gripping her trembling knees while she gasped for breath and fought the urge to cry.

She was used to dealing with dangerous, brutal men. Her whole life had been an in-depth study. Sean Callaghan was no ordinary man. It had taken every ounce of courage she had not to run from the sheer intensity of those blue eyes. But she'd learned a long time ago never to show fear; attitude was survival, and she planned on being around for a while yet. With shaking legs, she mounted her cycle and kicked it into high gear, racing down the street as fast as her machine would take her.

CONNECT WITH ABBIE

Sign up for Abbie's newsletter today! You'll not only get advance notice of new releases, sales, giveaways, contests, fun facts, and other great things each month, you'll also get a free book just for signing up, access to exclusive bonus content not available anywhere else, *and* be automatically entered for a chance to win a gift card every month, simply for reading it!

Go to
https://abbiezandersromance.com
and click on SUBSCRIBE to sign up!

Connect with Abbie on social media and your favorite book-centric sites:

Facebook
Zanders Clan Reader Group
Instagram
Goodreads
BookBub

Callaghan World Timeline Reading Order

Can't get enough of those Callaghan boys? They appear in more than just their own series, you know. Here's a complete list of books in which they appear by the Callaghan world timeline. Sometimes it's just a cameo; other times, they play a pretty major role.

1. Celina (Connelly Cousins, Book 1)
2. Jamie (Connelly Cousins, Book 1.5)
3. Johnny (Connelly Cousins, Book 2)
4. Dangerous Secrets (Callaghan Brothers, Book 1)
5. Michael (Connelly Cousins, Book 3)
6. First & Only (Callaghan Brothers, Book 2)
7. House Calls (Callaghan Brothers, Book 3)
8. Seeking Vengeance (Callaghan Brothers, Book 4)
9. Guardian Angel (Callaghan Brothers, Book 5)
10. Beyond Affection (Callaghan Brothers, Book 6)
11. Having Faith (Callaghan Brothers, Book 7)
12. Bottom Line (Callaghan Brothers, Book 8)
13. Forever Mine (Callaghan Brothers, Book 9)
14. Two of a Kind (Callaghan Brothers, Book 10)
15. Spencer and Kayla's Wedding (short / subscriber bonus)

16. Protecting Sam (Sanctuary, Book 1)
17. Not Quite Broken (Callaghan Brothers, Book 11)
18. Danny's Happy Trails Ranch (short / subscriber bonus)
19. SEAL Out of Water (Silver SEALs)
20. Best Laid Plans (Sanctuary, Book 2)
21. Callaghans in Quarantine (short / subscriber bonus)
22. Shadow of Doubt (Sanctuary, Book 3)
23. Nick UnCaged (Sanctuary, Book 4)
24. The Proposal Plan (Sanctuary short / subscriber bonus)
25. Organically Yours (Sanctuary, Book 5)
26. Callaghans Down the Shore (short / subscriber bonus)
27. Finding Home (Long Road Home, Book 3)
28. Prodigal Son (Sanctuary, Book 6)
29. Cast in Shadow (Shadow SEALs)
30. Home Base (Long Road Home, Book 8)
31. Too Close to Home (The Long Road Home, Book 13)

ALSO BY ABBIE ZANDERS

<u>Abbie Zanders Starter Set</u>

For those who like a little bit of everything, this is a great intro to some of Abbie's series. Includes the first in series for the Cerasino Family Novellas, Callaghan Brothers, Mythic, Sanctuary, and a Timeless Love

Abbie Zanders First in Series Collection

<u>Contemporary Romance – Callaghan Brothers</u>

Plan your visit to Pine Ridge, Pennsylvania and fall in love with the Callaghans

Dangerous Secrets

First and Only

House Calls

Seeking Vengeance

Guardian Angel

Beyond Affection

Having Faith

Bottom Line

Forever Mine

Two of a Kind

Not Quite Broken

Callaghan Brothers Collection #1 (books 1-3)

Callaghan Brothers Collection #2 (books 4-6)

Callaghan Brothers Collection #3 (books 7-9)

Contemporary Romance – Connelly Cousins

Drive across the river to Birch Falls and spend some time with the Connelly Cousins

Celina

Jamie (novella)

Johnny

Michael

Connelly Cousins Complete Series

Home Base (Connelly Cousins / The Long Road Home crossover)

Contemporary Romance – Covendale Series

If you like humor and snark in your romance, add a stop in Covendale

Five Minute Man

All Night Woman

Seizing Mack

Contemporary Romance – Sanctuary

More small town romance with former military heroes you can't help but love

Protecting Sam

Best Laid Plans

Shadow of Doubt

Nick UnCaged

Organically Yours

Finding Home (Sanctuary / The Long Road Home crossover)

Prodigal Son

Sanctuary Collection 1 (Books 1-3)

Sanctuary Collection 2 (Books 4-6)

Cerasino Family Novellas

Short, sweet feel-good romance that'll leave you smiling

Just For Me

Just For Him

Just For Her

Just For Us

Cerasino Family Novellas Collection #1 (books 1-3)

More Contemporary Romance

Standalone & crossover titles

The Realist

Celestial Desire

Letting Go

SEAL Out of Water (Callaghan Brothers / Silver SEALs crossover)

Rockstar Romeo (Cocky Hero Club)

Finding Home (Sanctuary / The Long Road Home crossover)

Cast in Shadow (Shadow SEALs / Callaghan / Sanctuary crossover)

Home Base (Connelly Cousins / The Long Road Home crossover)

Time Travel Romance

Travel between present day NYC and 15th century Scotland in these stand-alone but related titles

Maiden in Manhattan

Raising Hell in the Highlands

A Timeless Love Box Set

Paranormal Romance – Mythic Series

Welcome to Mythic, an idyllic community all kinds of Extraordinaries call home.

Faerie Godmother

Fallen Angel

The Oracle at Mythic

Wolf Out of Water

Paranormal Romance – Beary Christmas Series

Sweet holiday romance with an ursine twist

A Very Beary Christmas

Going Polar

Bearly Festive

More Paranormal Romance

Standalone, complete stories

Vampire, Unaware

Black Wolfe's Mate (written as Avelyn McCrae)

Going Nowhere

The Jewel

Close Encounters of the Sexy Kind

Rock Hard

Immortal Dreams

Rehabbing the Beast (written as Avelyn McCrae)

More Than Mortal

Falling for the Werewolf

Historical/Medieval Romance

A Warrior's Heart (written as Avelyn McCrae)

ABOUT THE AUTHOR

Abbie Zanders is a USA Today Bestselling Author with more than 60 published romance novels to date. Her stories range from contemporary to paranormal and everything in between. She promises her readers two things: happily ever afters, always, and no cliffhangers, ever.

Born and raised in the mountains of Northeastern Pennsylvania, where she sets most of her stories, she's known for small town romance featuring golden-hearted alpha heroes and strong, relatable heroines. Besides being an avid reader and writer, she loves animals (especially big dogs), American muscle cars, and 80's hair bands.